The Crooked Sea

The Crooked Sea

TREVOR RAISTRICK

First published in the United Kingdom in 2009 by
Bank House Books
PO Box 3
NEW ROMNEY
TN29 9WJ UK
www.bankhousebooks.com

British Library Cataloguing in Publication Data
A catalogue record for this book is available from the British
Library

ISBN 978-1904408-475

Cover artwork by Colin Beats

Typesetting and origination by Bank House Books
Printed by Lightning Source

This book is dedicated to the memory of my aunt Mary Ward, without whom it could not have been written

The rivers Leven and Kent ran in separate channels until perhaps they joined the River Lune and formed the great estuary which Ptolemy names Morecambe . . . This Morecambe, the 'crooked sea' or 'bending shore', agrees not only with the nature of the place and the observation of Ptolemy, but also with the name of the mountains which form the bay on one side.

The Antiquities of Furness by Thomas West, 1799

One never gets tired of looking out across the Bay with its ever changing light. Nothing could ever compensate me for my memories of the past . . . my constant challenge with quicksands, fast racing tides, swirling currents, deep tidal channels and the most stunning but notorious landscape. My second home – the sands of Morecambe Bay.

Between the Tides by Cedric Robinson MBE (the Queen's Guide to the Sands), 2007

Acknowledgements

Many thanks to:

My sister-in-law Susan Raistrick and Bradford Public Library for help with many invaluable sources for research into Victorian Bradford;

Ann Grainger, Jacki Jackson, Margaret Baddeley, Sandra Whitehurst and many friends for their comments and support in the writing of my first novel;

Mr Colin Beats for the cover design;

Mr Cedric Robinson MBE for his advice about Morecambe Bay;

My wife Pauline for her forbearance and encouragement throughout the time of writing and editing;

My son Matthew for his work in setting up the website www.thecrookedsea.com.

Chapter One

Walter Adams Clough's 'death' was as public as he dared make it. He strode out into the bay, first across the pebbles that clattered embarrassingly under his shoes, warning the few families scattered around the beach of what he was doing. His head stayed down and his shoulders were hunched, as if weighed down by the guilt of his actions. He was uncomfortably near to the few brave souls who had ventured out to Morecambe's sparse eastern shore, yet just far enough away for them to do little about it. Had he been dressed as a fisherman or workman no one might have paid him the slightest attention, but, smartly dressed in a dark suit and homburg hat, he must have cut a strange figure marching out on that expansive shore. His brain was racing. Had he brought everything he might need? Had he chosen the right route? Had the storms and tides of the past week changed the treacherous landscape, as they often did? Had they made fresh dangers of which he was unaware?

The shingle under Walter's feet quickly changed to the ribbed brown sand that was so typical of that coast. He recalled all the memories it held in its coarse dark silt from his own past, especially from the previous year, that glorious summer of 1898, when he had watched and played with his own dear children.

* * *

1

'Oh, Daddy, my tower's fallen down,' Rosie cried, as the sandcastle was undermined by the tide as it seeped into the moat that she and Thomas had just dug.

'Never mind,' Walter replied, 'we'll build an even bigger one tomorrow. Perhaps Hannah will come and help us.'

Perhaps his elder daughter would put away her sketchbook and not pretend to be so grown up. But at heart, like her father, she was still a child, digging, paddling and messing around in the sand; unlike him, though, she still found it hard to admit it. It wasn't as if she minded the telling off from her mother.

'Just look at you!' Annie protested. 'You're none of you fit to be let back in our lodgings, and that includes you, Walter!'

* * *

Despite the sands' waterlogged and dangerous character, the lone walker knew instinctively that most stretches were firm enough to support him. They could even bear the weight of horses and carts, which were driven out by the locals to collect the precious cockles. Indeed, in the height of summer between the tides some parts were baked as hard as concrete and became painful to walk on. Walter had learnt all this during the few months that he and his family had spent on the edge of that beautiful bay. He understood how to read the changes that each tide brought and to avoid the gullets dredged out by the voracious sea. He knew how to test with a stick those indeterminate stretches that could be the most hazardous of all.

'Watch out for the man on the horse,' he said to himself, but he knew he would be unlucky to come across the guide to the sands at that time of day, when he would be looking after the Ulverston crossing or supervising cocklers out on Cartmel Wharf. Perhaps he was even having a drink at Dalton or over at Flookborough, well out of the way.

Walter's first mile towards Hest Bank was safely accomplished; the first part of his daring and hazardous plan. He turned to look back. Morecambe stretched away to the south, its new tower rising above the silhouettes of the guesthouses, shops and theatres like a malevolent skeleton. The previous summer he and Hannah had taken a ride to the top. Annie had objected but her daughter had been defiant: aged ten, she already had her father's stubborn streak, coupled with his indomitable taste for adventure. It was what Enos would have called 'one of your bloody daft ideas'; but it was more than that. It mixed a thirst for knowledge and new experience with imagination and a hint of recklessness, and he rejoiced that he had passed it on to his eldest daughter, even though it annoyed his wife so much.

Hannah was tall for her age, thin and a little ungainly: she would never be described as graceful. Her angular face was not pretty yet, but her intense eyes hinted at a stubborn intellect and unfettered imagination that schooling and convention would never quell. Her pale face was framed by a mass of dark blonde curls that fell on to narrow, bony shoulders. For a second the background of sands and sky faded as he held her image in his mind, watching her skipping along that pier from plank to plank avoiding the cracks, followed by Rosie and Thomas in admiring imitation. He smiled at his memory of her silly little joke.

'Why is it called a pier, Daddy?'

'I don't know.'

'Because you can peer down at the sea.'

Walter laughed, but a lump came to his throat and a tear appeared in the corner of his staring eye. He knew he would never see her or joke with her again. Returning his gaze to the minarets and dome of the Pavilion Theatre, the Taj Mahal as it was known to the locals, to the red-brick curves of the Winter Gardens and on again to the crowds along the stone jetty, his eyes finally stopped on the long low outline of Morecambe's railway station, which was partly hidden by the Midland Hotel. It had been his last port of call before his walk out to the sands.

It had been crowded in the station's central hall, many travellers preferring to stand under the light and airy glass roof rather than sit in the gloomy tile and brick waiting rooms. Walter had stopped there for some twenty-five minutes to observe the throng of holidaymakers, businessmen and casual travellers. Whether this was deliberate, so people would register his presence, or last-minute doubt, he could not decide.

No, it was not the latter. He knew what he had to do. He wandered over to the left luggage office. It was rather busy so he decided to hang back; he knew that he wouldn't be noticed in a crowd.

Walter recalled every detail and word of his conversation with the man at the ticket office. The faded blue uniform strained around the buttonholes. His ruddy face was framed by mutton chop whiskers, and his eyes smiled through a pair of round wire spectacles.

'Can I help you, sir?' he enquired.

Walter was a good actor, and not just for the local theatricals. In life he could play whatever the occasion demanded, be it confident salesman, bluff Yorkshireman or charming companion. Today it was someone not at ease with himself, distraught, even a little unbalanced.

'Want to deposit this for a . . . a . . . a few hours,' he stuttered. He looked down, then sideways, unwilling to meet the railway employee's gaze.

'Certainly, sir. Fine case you've got there, sir.'

It certainly was. Walter was never to be seen on his travels with anything battered, brown or cardboard as many other salesmen might carry. The small black leather case that held his samples had fine hand-stitching and bright brass fittings. It always made the right impression, just like its owner. His tall, slim frame carried the stylish three-piece suit well. His homburg (never an ordinary bowler) was set at a slightly rakish angle. Walter always impressed his customers and their female assistants. But here, in the hands of a stuttering ninny, the smart black case seemed out of place.

'Yes, yes!' Walter squeaked. 'Paid a lot for that, a lot for that.'

The clerk tried not to show his puzzlement. He met all sorts, but here was a queer one indeed. 'That'll be threepence then, sir.'

Walter fumbled in his pockets, pulling out a silver coin. He dropped it, scrabbled around on the stone floor for it, then embarrassedly placed it back on the counter. The perplexed railway employee handed Walter a ticket, which he clumsily inserted in his waistcoat pocket.

'You all right, sir?' the clerk enquired.

Walter nodded nervously and moved away, walking head down to the station exit. When he reached it he turned to see if the bespectacled eyes were still following him, but the left luggage office was busy again and the clerk was continuing his cheerful banter with his next customer. It was important, Walter thought, that his last conversation should be recalled. The clerk should remember it, wonder about it, be concerned – but not be alarmed enough to do anything. Walter judged that his little charade had left the right impression both with the railway employee and with anyone else who had noticed it. If enquiries were made his pantomime would be brought to mind. And if the case were opened it would give no hint of his motives. No need to leave a note; that was too obvious. You had to keep everyone guessing. Besides which, what was the loss of half a month's wages compared with the sacrifices he was going to make – of his comfortable existence, his adoring family and the certainty of life?

Walter turned and strode further into the wilderness, occasionally following the tracks of the cockle-pickers for safety, sometimes veering away if he was getting too close to a group. He could see them all around him, like small clumps of tiny bent sticks, insular folk despised by the townsfolk of the bay and permanently stooped by their back-breaking labour. They kept themselves to themselves, which suited the lonely walker.

He stopped on the edge of a pebbly skear. It was getting warm; time to dispose of his hat and jacket. He took his jacket off first, as it was the larger and more easily seen item and might be carried back into Morecambe on the next tide. He would discard the hat a little further on, where it might reach Hest Bank or the marshes. If one was not picked up then the other would be, but if they were both found and recognised, people would wonder why they were so far apart. That was the trick: you had to keep everyone guessing. He looked a ridiculous figure marching along in a waistcoat and hat, but who was there to notice him? As if to answer his unspoken question a faint call reached his ear.

'Hey! What thee doing out here?'

Walter turned sharply to see where the shout had come from. Two or three hundred yards away a distant figure was converging on his path. It looked like a fisherman, probably one who had been out on the ebbing tide to set his stake nets. Walter turned and waved enthusiastically, hoping he could allay any concerns the stranger might have and thereby avoid any contact or recognition. He then gradually but deliberately changed direction to take him away from the stranger's path. His whole venture would collapse if it were betrayed through this unlucky meeting, just as his early hopes had been betrayed by a chance discovery all those years ago.

Chapter Two

Walter was just eleven, an ordinary boy living in the village of Bowling on the edge of the great city of Bradford. It was on an unremarkable Saturday morning that his mother caught the horse bus to go shopping down the hill in the busy city.

'I won't be long, Walter,' Harriet called out on her way out. 'I'll bring you sweets from the market, those special humbugs you can't get in the village.'

That was typical of her. She always thought of her only child, even doted on him, but he didn't mind. He knew that despite life's disappointments and upsets he was special in her eyes. Walter gave his mother a final wave from the bedroom window.

Enos, his father, was busy below with customers in the draper's shop; Walter had been left to his own devices. He played card games for a while but was bored. No friends called and grey drizzle fell on the flagstones outside.

He wandered out on to the landing and drifted almost without thinking through the half-open door into his parents' bedroom. His mother must have been in a hurry that morning for she had left the wardrobe door open. And there at the bottom lay the black tin box in which he knew all the important documents were kept. But something was different today: the key had been left in the lock. No doubt his mother had been in a

7

real hurry to catch the bus, at the last minute rifling through the papers for a bank book or document she needed in town.

Walter stared at the box for a full minute. Although outwardly an obedient child, there was always a daring, curious, even adventurous streak about him. He knew it was wrong. Although he didn't fear punishment from his father any more, he didn't want to hurt his mother. Eventually his curiosity got the better of him and, lifting the heavy box up on to the bed, he paused to listen. All he could hear was his heart pounding in his chest. Carefully he turned the key. With a loud click the lid jumped up a couple of inches, as if it were relieved from the effort of holding down the tightly packed contents. Walter took hold of the lid, then paused again, straining to catch the slightest sound. Apart from the mumble of conversation below there was nothing, no creak, no wheezing or breathing on the stairs. Slowly he eased it back.

On top were some things he recognised, insurance books with the words 'Prudential' and 'Bradford Mutual' printed on the covers. He knew what they were and what the amounts written in the columns signified. He thought of the shabby-suited men with black bowler hats who called to collect their pennies and tuppences each week. Once Walter had asked why they handed over these sums, but as usual Enos had no time for him.

'Thee'll never learn t'value of brass. Why does thee want to know?' he sneered.

Below the insurance books and others marked 'Yorkshire Bank' lay a pile of typed papers headed 'Halliwell and Hutton: Solicitors'. Walter was about to lift them out when he thought he heard something on the stairs. He waited, breathless. 'No it's nothing,' he whispered to himself, 'but I must be careful.'

This was Walter to the letter: at times daring and unconventional, yet always ready to think ahead and minimise the risk. He was a thinker and a planner, different from most of his childhood friends, yet they did not despise him for it, as they welcomed his ideas and followed his plans. It was his cousin Albert who was the really reckless one, brave and bold without any thought for the consequences. When they followed *his* lead . . . well, it usually meant trouble.

Walter placed the documents in small piles, noting the

order in which they came out of the secret box, so he could put them back quickly and correctly in case he was disturbed. Many of them included long words and sentences that were beyond his comprehension, even though he was the brightest pupil in his class. Near the bottom he came to a small collection of sheets on thicker parchment-type paper, bearing the titles 'General Register Office' and 'Registration Office of Bradford'. Names, places and occupations were written in a variety of careful hands. Some names, such as Enos and Harriet, he quickly recognised; others he did not. He was brought up with a jolt when he read his own name, or rather part of it, staring up at him in a neat copperplate script. 'Walter Adams' it read; 'Boy'. What surprised him was the next column, which was headed 'Name and Address of Father': it was blank save for a short, precise, horizontal dash. His mother was there as Harriet Adams, but the next column showing his father's occupation was again blank, except for the perfunctory dash. The place of birth was strange too, not Bowling as he had expected but the village of Idle, north of the city.

Walter remembered Enos's joke about a workman who had done a small job at the shop. 'I knew he was bloody useless when he told me he was an Idle man.'

It had made him laugh at the time, but staring at the yellow paper Walter was too worried even to show the faintest smile. It took a minute or so for the enormity of his discovery to strike him. He lay back on his parents' bed and cried softly. It was not just the secret he now held, a secret that, if the other children at school found out, would make his life a misery. He knew the word, the 'B' word. When a girl whose mother was the target of gossip in the village had come to their school a year ago he had joined in the chant of 'Betty Bastard! Betty Bastard!' She had left in tears, never to return.

What was worse was that he now knew he didn't have a real father. The man to whom he gave that name, and who was always critical and hostile, had nothing to do with him at all.

'You idle little devil!' Enos would shout. 'Always day-dreamin' or yer 'ead stuck in a book. What use will that be when you want a job?'

Now it seemed as if his mother had betrayed him. Walter cried because he knew he had been deceived by the one person he loved. Harriet had always defended him against Enos's excesses, had wiped away his tears, had been the rock to which he could cling. Now that rock had dissolved before his eyes. He had a secret that would follow him his life through. He had never felt so alone.

Voices from the shop brought him back to his senses. He was about to put back the neat piles when another dreadful thought struck him. Were there other secrets in the tin box? This might be his only opportunity to find out the truth. He looked through the faded certificates again, more closely this time. It was true. The marriage certificate for Enos and Harriet confirmed his discovery, showing a date three years after his birth. It revealed other secrets too, or rather confirmed shadowy, hidden stories that had lain at the back of his mind. The eighth column was headed 'Father's Name and Surname', the next 'Rank or Profession'. Enos's father was listed as 'Aaron Clough (deceased)' and 'Former Wool Winder'. It didn't say how he'd died, though, falling down a coal shaft in his usual hopeless state of drunkenness. Walter had overheard that during conversations in the parlour, when grown-ups thought he wasn't around or was too young to understand. He had heard the official Clough history, of course, many times from Enos's own lips: how the business started with the bequest of a sewing machine to Enos's mother; how she had sewn together Sunday best clothes for her own impoverished family; then made up and sold additional garments to the neighbours, buying more materials to start a profitable sideline. The 'sad accident' to Enos's 'dear father' had forced her to become sole breadwinner, and she had done enough to drag her family out of grinding poverty. Walter was told how Enos, as the eldest son, had to push a handcart around the villages of south Bradford to sell the clothes she made.

'Plain, simple, well-made clothes they were,' Enos would drone on, 'just reyt for poor working folk. Not this fancy rubbish you see in t'shops nowadays.'

The legend continued: how Mary Clough, before her untimely death, had purchased the small shop on Bowling Old Lane close to the new mills and the numerous back-to-back houses that were springing up. It always ended with the same moral: how thrift and hard work had turned the wretchedly poor family of mill workers into 'respectable businessfolk'.

Of his mother's side Walter had heard nothing, yet he could just remember in the far and distant past a large and airy drawing room, with a wonderful plant called an aspidistra flowing from a large bowl. A large figurine of the 'Whistling Boy' rose from a sideboard beyond his reach, and above it was that tranquil landscape in a gold frame that his mother now cherished and dusted with a devout attention. Everything in his memory of that wonderful room seemed large but warm and welcoming, even the kind, bespectacled old lady in a smart black dress, whose grey hair was tied back in a tight bun. Was it something he had dreamt or was it real?

Walter turned his attention back to the box. Beneath some more papers lay another brown certificate, entitled 'Certified Copy of an Entry of Death'. It was dated a few months after Harriet's marriage and referred to a woman called Hannah Adams, who died at a house in Idle in the parish of Calverley. She was the widow of Seth Adams, an ironmonger, the same name he had seen on his mother's wedding certificate. What he could not understand was a word in the sixth column headed 'Cause of Death'.

'Walter, what's thee up to?' came a voice from below.

Quickly but carefully he repacked the papers, pushed down the lid, turned the key and returned the box to the bottom of the wardrobe. Tiptoeing through the gap in the door, he was back in his room and on his bed, a book loose in his hand and an innocent, sleepy expression on his face before Enos was halfway up the narrow stairs.

'What do you think you're up to, you idle monkey?' came a voice from the landing. 'Reading and sleeping, that's all you're good for. Get downstairs at once. There's some boxes to shift, and I want you to run a message.'

Half an hour later Walter still remembered the words. They were most unusual: '*pthisis pulmonalis*'.

* * *

Now, decades later, the lone walker understood them: they signified the dreaded consumption. Walter had seen them again on Enos's death certificate eighteen months before. Unlike his sorrow long ago for his kindly but little-known grandmother, Walter had shed no tears for the old tyrant of the draper's shop, whose sharp tongue never showed any kindness or sympathy to his stepson, and who by a single and vindictive stroke had denied him a chance to better himself. Enos was a short-sighted man in every sense. He had always been so. Even at his end he had tried to persuade Walter to leave his job and take on the shop.

But Walter the romancer, the lifelong adventurer, whose imagination and sense of wonder had always been encouraged by his mother, was aware of the changes that were taking place as Bradford and the rest of Britain neared the end of the century, while the ill-educated, narrow-minded shopkeeper could not see beyond his own front door. He had tried to reason with his stepfather.

'People won't shop for their clothes in a small village draper's. The new electric trams are coming. From Bowling it costs a penny, and it'll take less than fifteen minutes right to the centre of Bradford. They've got bigger shops there with choice, modern styles and prices you can't match.'

'Rubbish!' Enos shouted. 'Modern rubbish! You always had yer head stuck in t'clouds, and this gallivanting about from place to place has made it worse.'

'But Father,' Walter persisted, 'there's a lot more money about now, and Bowling folk want choice and style. Brown and Muff are planning a new department store, like those in Leeds or London. They'll have four floors of everything you can think of in tailoring and haberdashery.'

'Brown and Muff!' roared the old man. 'Staffed by a load of young trollops and managed by a lot of nancy boys! Bowling folk want plain clothes, not to be tarted up like shilling wimmen.'

He ranted on, his head firmly stuck in the sands of time past. By now the effort of arguing sent him into a fit of violent coughing. It was a rattling, dry cough that rendered him incapable for a few minutes, and in the next two months would render him dead. A cursory glance at the books had satisfied Walter that the draper's business was barely making a profit; indeed, it had shown a steady decline over the last three years since Enos, in a fit of temper, had sacked the one person who could keep his shop in the black. Walter's predictions of the rise of the brash new city centre shops were true. But the draper's shop was on a prime site in Bowling Old Lane, and he knew that Jabez Hall, the ironmonger, or the Holmes brothers, who ran the greengrocers, might pay a tidy sum to move into a shop that was so well situated. After all, nobody lugged coal irons, buckets or potatoes all the way from Bradford.

Enos Clough's funeral was quite a lavish affair for a modest draper. He had been a lifelong member of the Oddfellows Society in Bowling, a collection of shopkeepers, clerks and minor professionals who on a Thursday night once a month conducted their secret rites and business behind the closed doors of the Mechanics Institute. Walter had once seen Enos in his regalia. Finding it hard to suppress his laughter, he had vowed he would never undergo with a straight face the strange rituals beloved by his stepfather. Practical benefits resulted, however, as Enos often pointed out.

'We always look after our own. No Oddfellow – you mark my words, young Walter, you who thinks he knows everything and knows nowt – no Oddfellow will ever die a pauper's death!'

And for once he was right. Two black Belgian horses pulled a finely carved hearse. Flowers and black plumes abounded. Two mourners' wagons followed, for the draper had a large family spread around the district. But that was not the end of the organisation's beneficence. It also provided a modest pension for Harriet and ensured she was comfortably housed in what was known as a tradesman's home. Small but well-appointed dwellings were springing up around Bradford and other cities to meet the retirement needs of friendly society members and their families who were in reduced circumstances. Harriet had achieved her heart's desire. She could move from the dingy home behind the shop, which she had hated for so long, into something smart and modern. It was as if the death of her husband had released a burden from her shoulders. With Walter's help she attended to the funeral arrangements and the sale of the shop, and her mourning for Enos was observed in the proper manner – but, as her son wryly noted, her grief was a good deal shorter in duration. His mother was a smart and handsome woman for someone approaching her sixtieth year. Her greying hair still held hints of its former striking raven crown, while her eyes were a kindly brown, her face regular and her mouth always holding the trace of a smile. There was a confidence in her manner that thirty years of marriage had not quelled.

This confidence led her, to the surprise of Walter and the rest of the family, to rent a stall in Kirkgate Market. The sign above proudly read 'Clough's Book Stall and Magazine Emporium', and it was no surprise that the venture thrived. When Maud Hobson asked why it had not been Clough's Drapery Stall, Harriet gave her a withering look that needed no explanation. A year or more later it was not the only thing that was beginning to thrive. The neighbouring stall, Hargreaves Glass and China Fancies, was run by a kindly widower. Charlie Hargreaves had helped Harriet in those first weeks; indeed, no sooner had she stepped into the market than he had offered a hand.

'Let me help you carry those boxes in, love,' were his first words. 'You don't want to hurt yourself before you even open the stall.'

In Walter's eyes he was everything Enos had never been: considerate, pleasant, even jolly, with a wide knowledge and sensible understanding of the world around him, despite the lack of much formal education. He made a fuss of Hannah when she turned up on Saturdays to help on her grandmother's stall and he was a kind and indulgent grandfather to his own, who regularly delighted in visiting him at work.

* * *

Walter stopped on the endless expanse of sand and smiled. No doubt it was perverse, but widowhood seemed to have given his mother a new lease of life. For the first time in many years he was not worried about her. He knew she would be devastated by his present actions, but she had the comfort and consolation of her grandchildren and her new blossoming friendship – which obviated some of the guilt he felt for the course he had to take. He thrust his hands into his waistcoat pockets and fumbled, distracted by something he could feel lodged deep in the lining.

With difficulty he pulled it out and found himself staring at a small, black-edged card, one he'd had printed for Enos's funeral. It brought it all back to mind, but this time with a broad smile. He remembered his mother's extravagant mourning dress of finest Parametta silk and Hannah's attempt to emulate her by demanding a mourning dress for herself. He could see the long cortège walking behind the hearse and recalled the conversation in the privacy of the first wagon . . .

'It's nice so many people have come to pay their respects,' Annie had observed.

'And no doubt they'll pay good respect to the funeral tea at the Mechanics afterwards,' Walter had replied to his wife.

Hannah suppressed a giggle: she had caught the twinkle in his eye. Even Harriet smiled. He had paid due reverence, after all, in the guise of a dutiful and inconsolable son, if only for his mother's sake. At the interment and funeral tea the social niceties of the occasion had followed their appointed dreary course: so much was said and so little meant. Still, in the end Walter had the final laugh. He had chosen the most inappropriate verse he could find for the mean old tyrant, and no-one had got his little joke. The lone walker looked down and read the card in his hand:

In Affectionate Remembrance of Enos
Beloved Husband of Harriet Clough of Bowling

Lay not up for yourselves treasures upon earth,
where moth and rust doth corrupt
and where thieves break through and steal,
but lay up for yourselves treasures in heaven.

He laughed out loud to the vast emptiness around him, tore the card into tiny pieces and threw them into the wind.

Chapter Three

Far away from the lonely traveller a train chugged along the margins of sand and salt marsh, belching out quantities of steam and smoke as it went. It was not one of the sleek expresses that glided along that brief stretch of flat landscape on Morecambe Bay, its only glimpse of sea between London and Glasgow, but a local train that clung to the edge of the bay on its way to Barrow, sharing with its passengers every wonderful seascape it could find. It would edge the marshes at Carnforth, where the lucky traveller might see flocks of geese, terns or shelduck feeding on the mud between the coarse grasses, and rising *en masse* in terror as the clanking, hissing monster passed. It would chug across the Arnside and Leven viaducts, with their view of the wide sands and, on a clear day, the magnificence of the Lakeland fells.

* * *

Walter was fascinated by trains and had been so from his earliest days in Bowling, when he could hear them from his tiny bedroom window as they slowed down for the station, or with a piercing whistle, plunged into the tunnel under the brickworks. He listened to them late into the night and tried to imagine the wonderful places they were going to. Bowling might have been a typical mill village but to Walter's young mind it was a treasure chest of sights and sounds and, above all, characters.

His favourite place was the blacksmith's, which was full of clattering sounds and smoky aromas, humming with activity. The young boy often stood in the doorway with his mother, fascinated, watching a horse being shod by Joe Haggas. The animal blinked indolently, as if it were oblivious of all going on around it, dreaming of a patch of rich green pasture. Joe's confident hands picked up the red hot shoe, laid it on the hoof, changed its profile with a few deft blows of the hammer, refitted it and nailed it to the hoof in but a few seconds.

'Well, Missus, I suppose you want *him* shoed now?' Joe would shout.

He stretched out his hand to grab the little boy, but he was gone. It became a running joke between the three of them.

Young Walter was popular with most tradesmen of the village. His polite and inquisitive manner set him apart from many of the unfettered urchins in the area, and they welcomed his conversation and answered his questions. Peter Illingworth, the shuttle and bobbin maker, once made him a toy, a small round clown figure that would always spring upright no matter how often you knocked it over.

'How does it work?' Walter asked him.

'Won't tell you that now, lad,' the kindly young man replied. 'You take it home and play with it. When you come by again tell me what you think makes it bounce back.'

But he never did. When Walter passed the next time he found the workshop empty. Illingworth's had moved to a larger workshop with steam-driven lathes on Canal Street, the other side of Bradford, where he employed half a dozen men to make bobbins and shuttles to feed the insatiable appetite of Bradford's ever-expanding factories. And it wouldn't have mattered anyway. A week or two later Walter had shown the clown to his cousin Albert. And Albert, naturally, had broken it.

Albert Dowgill was trouble. His friendship always was, from the first time they met aged five until his flight to Liverpool some eighteen years later.

* * *

But here out in the wind-blown wilderness, Walter saw him again. The family of cocklers were out on their own, working near Priest Skear. Walter wanted to skirt round them but the sands to the left and right were dotted with pits and gulleys. Reuben had once warned him that 'Them dips mean trouble. Tides left soft sand round 'em. Keep away.'

He went on and would have ignored the cocklers but for the skinny lad shouting, 'Hey mister! What are you doing out here?'

Walter looked up, waved and said nothing. The youth and a younger girl were working a patch ahead of the rest of the family, the boy rhythmically pounding the surface, the ragged girl almost bent double by her load and raking the cockles into her basket. As he approached the boy looked up and gave a cheeky grin. Then Walter saw the half-innocent face, the blond tousled mop, that he remembered from all those years before . . .

* * *

'Now, Walter, say hello to your cousin Albert,' Harriet began, when the company had sat down. 'They've lived in Shipley for a few years but now they're back in Bowling. You'll like Albert: he's a nice boy, like you.'

His aunt winced. Walter looked into the face of a little angel. But, like most boys, he could easily see that Albert was one of Satan's fallen ones. Aunt Leah looked uneasy. She reminded Walter of a female version of his father: a plain, flat face, square jawed with pale eyes, topped by a mop of straight mousey brown hair tied in a bun.

'Go and show your cousin round the house,' went on his mother, 'and don't forget to share your toys.'

And so began a friendship that lasted many years, eventually much to the annoyance of his mother and the loathing of his wife, for although Albert had a quick brain and sense of adventure Walter found he also had a reckless propensity for mischief and danger, and a natural inclination to shift blame, especially on to his cousin.

The piano incident happened not long after their first meeting. Enos was out at the pub and Harriet had decided to slip down the street to a neighbour, leaving the two boys alone in the house. Walter brought out his lead soldiers and the two of them commanded their armies over a battlefield of cushions, the fender, armchairs and a forest of chair and table legs.

'My soldiers have climbed t'cliff,' triumphed his cousin, proceeding to lay them along the edge of the piano.

'No, Albert. We're not allowed on the piano in case we scratch it.' Albert opened the lid and marched his soldiers up and down the keys. 'Hey, no!' shouted Walter. 'We can't do that!'

'They won't scratch t'keys,' replied Albert, 'and this is my army's marching song.' He proceeded to thump the piano with his soldiers in a regular rhythm. Eventually Walter was persuaded to join his cousin for a duet, which grew louder and louder and eventually became a competition as to who could make the loudest noise – which Albert won by banging the notes with his boot. This lasted for a few seconds until some of the keys flew off on to the rug. A sudden silence pervaded the room as the two boys realised the enormity of what they had done.

'We'll get leathered for this,' squealed Albert in panic. 'We've got to stop them looking in t'piano.' After a while he came up with a plan. 'I know. If thy mother or father can't get t'lid up, they'll think it's stuck and send for t'piano man. He'll think they broke t'keys trying to open it. What's thee got that'll keep t'lid down?'

Walter thought for a minute. 'Dad's got some cow glue,' he suggested, 'but you have to heat it up. He's got a hammer and nails in the cellar and some screws.'

'That'll do!' declared Albert triumphantly. 'Thee can go and fetch t'hammer and t'nails cos thee knows where they are.'

Walter hurried to the cellar and emerged with the equipment. Kneeling on the piano stool, Albert tried to nail through the lid to the ledge below. Not knowing about such things as veneer and hardwood, he could not envisage the mess that would ensue. The splits, cracks and bent nails were all too clearly visible, and Harriet's sudden return prevented attempts to cover it up.

'It were Walt's idea,' Albert explained. 'He knew where thee kept t'nails.'

This ensured that Walter took all of the blame. Despite his protestations he was sent to bed to await his father's return, whereupon he was strapped. The pain lasted a few days, the shame and hostility weeks. Harriet remained suspicious of Albert's share of the crime, but Enos insisted that the bad blood was not in his family. Walter learnt the hard way that friendship with his cousin could be fun but had painful consequences.

The vision faded and became the cocklers' children once again . . .

* * *

They were a hardy breed, wrapped up against the winds that constantly blew across the muddy wastes even in the height of summer. They were as poor and wretched a group of folk as Walter had ever seen, even in the worst slums of Bradford: the boys in their coarse woollen jumpers and the girls in their thick ragged coats, every garment stained by the cloying mud. For them there would be little chance of schooling, unlike even the poorest children in Bradford, who at least had the opportunity to grasp the fundamentals of literacy and arithmetic.

* * *

Walter's lot had certainly been more fortunate. As luck would have it, as he came to school age a new building was erected by the Education Board on Bowling Old Lane. Bradford was in the forefront of the education movement and provided its children with as good an education as any industrial city in the land.

The new school was a place of some enlightenment thanks to the appointment of a far-sighted young headmaster. Donald McIntosh was a lowland Scot who had settled in Bradford after marrying a local girl. Though strict, demanding the best of all who worked with him and under him, he was never unfair and was always ready to encourage and innovate for the benefit of his pupils. His influence spread to his teachers, pupil teachers and scholars. It was a well-ordered school and a happy one. Tosh (as he was secretly known) was a respected member of the village: a Methodist who abhorred drink and idleness and had become a well-known local preacher in the chapels of Bradford. His tall frame, black hair and mutton-chop whiskers cut an imposing figure, but the eyes were kind eyes. He encouraged those who strived by their own efforts to better themselves, had a reassuring word for the distressed child, and was fair in his administration of justice – as quick to recognise the innocent as to punish the guilty.

Walter recalled with amusement his initial encounter with the headmaster, on his first day at school. Tosh visited the class to introduce himself to the new pupils.

'Do any of you know who I am?' he enquired in a kindly voice.

Some children not yet used to the customs and discipline of school life called out answers but Walter, having been carefully prepared by his mother for its rules and conventions, and being naturally a polite boy, raised his hand and beamed at the tall gentleman, who smiled back.

'Yes, young man, you know how to answer but do you know the answer?'

'You're the headmaster,' replied Walter. 'You're in charge of the school.'

'Well done. And do any of you know my name?'

Walter was ready to answer again, but felt his cousin tugging his arm back down. Not to be outdone, Albert shot his hand up in front of the headmaster's face, following Walter's example.

'Yes, young man?'

'You're called Tosh!' the boy blurted out.

There was silence in the room, and Miss Lloyd, the teacher, blushed to a deep beetroot red. It was followed by a moment of suppressed laughter before the face above them clouded and the thunder rolled down. 'No, boy! My name is Mr McIntosh, and that is what it will always be to you!'

School was not just for learning, though. It had introduced Walter to a much wider circle of friends, many of whom would remain so throughout their school lives and into manhood. They formed a gang, eager for adventure and not averse to mischief, as all boys are and always have been. Bowling may have been their only world, but it was a world to explore. Beyond Old Lane and the back-to-back houses growing up around it was a landscape of fields, paths, lanes and woods intermingled with wasteland, ponds and small factories. As they grew older, new and exciting places opened up as their playground: the stream winding south from Bowling through Burnett Fields, the coal pits and quarry workings that dotted the country round about, and, best of all, the railway. There was nothing better for a group of boys on a summer's day than to sit on the bank, level with the top of the engines, and wave to the drivers and firemen, who waited until they were level with them and sounded their whistles at full blast, evoking a hysteria of waving and shrieking. Sometimes they stood above the tunnel entrance, and laughed as they emerged grimy from the clouds of steam and smoke. On other days the gang played on the Roughs, a hilly patch of woodland ideal for soldiers or pirates, or ventured further to the grounds of Bowling Hall, dodging from bush to bush or creeping through long grass, seeing who could get nearest to the house without being spotted. Albert was nearly always the winner, being bolder and nimbler than the rest.

Life was not without its dangers. Venturing further one day, the boys got as far as the hamlet of Roley. After climbing a dry stone wall they crossed a field, only to be confronted by a farmer. Worse still, on leashes were two fierce dogs of indeterminate breed. Walter felt afraid from his first glance at the man, whose heavy eyebrows, sharp nose and dark pointed beard reminded him of a picture of the devil he had once seen in a book.

'What's thee ruffians doin' on my land?' growled Lucifer. 'Up to no good, I'll be bound!'

'Nay, mister, we're only goin' to have a look at t'old iron pits,' explained Joseph Lumb, a podgy boy who was a year older than the others.

'Oh no you're not! You can go right back the way you came,' was the uncompromising reply. 'Ah knows you and your kind. If you're not larking about you're causing damage. Get off me land or I'll set t'dogs on you!' Resentfully the group turned away and wandered back across the field. 'And mind you be careful with my walls,' they heard him shout as they clambered over into the lane.

'Thee's just a narky old bugger,' yelled Albert, 'and here's what thee can do with thee bloody walls.'

He picked up a stone and threw it into the field. One or two others did the same and the whole gang took up the chorus of 'Narky, narky, old bugger!'

With one swift movement Satan unleashed his hounds of

hell. The dogs were halfway across the field before the boys knew what was happening. They took to their heels as if one body, running for their lives. Albert was the quickest, and first to cross the lane, jump the stream and reach the muddy path. Walter was not far behind, his long legs pounding, his heart thumping and his mind full of the terror of what might happen if he were caught. Fortune dictated that halfway down the lane a tall gate barred their way, but this was no obstacle to the young escapees. With the agility of circus acrobats each one was up the bars and over the top safely; except for Joseph Lumb. He had his feet on the third bar when the leading dog jumped and sank its teeth into his leg. Joseph's howl of pain was followed by an involuntary leap right over the gate and a flat landing on the other side. The dogs stopped at the gate, glorying in their triumph, their blood lust satisfied.

On the other side the gang raced on. When a quick look behind told them the chase was at an end, they cautiously crept back across the field to the gate, concerned at their prostrate comrade but still fearful of their own safety. Poor Joseph lay still, but as they gathered round the stricken figure he slowly raised himself and started to moan. He was no longer winded but he was wounded. Harriet always ensured that Walter had a clean handkerchief each morning, one advantage of owning a draper's shop. He immediately put this to good use, tightly binding the bleeding wound. The impromptu bandage quickly turned red, but despite his moaning the others were able to lift Joseph to his feet. Supporting his weight on each side, the sorry party wound their way home across the fields and through Woodroyd's brickyard. Here they were stopped by the foreman, who called to them on seeing the state of the stretcher party.

'Hey, lads,' he shouted, 'what's up with t'poor little blighter? Bring him into t'shed and let's have a look at him.' Used to the frequent accidents that occurred at the brickyard, he was able to expertly clean and bandage the wound, which had finally stopped bleeding. 'Who bound this hanky on?' he asked the group.

'I did,' volunteered Walter nervously.

'Well done, lad. You made a right good job there. You probably saved his leg going septic and certainly saved him losing a lot of blood. Now let's see if there's a cart going into t'housing sites in Bradford. No more walking today for this young man.'

Walter felt proud, and for a time became the hero of the gang. He wondered, too, if he might become the hero of Emily Lumb. Now that was a prize worth winning. It was amazing to Walter that the fat and ugly Joseph Lumb had such a pretty sister. She was a slim girl, as tall as Walter, and though dressed in dowdy hand-me-downs like most girls of her age, she wore them with a certain style. Although she wore a shawl, she never covered her hair with it. Why should she when she had such jet-black hair and deep brown eyes to match? Walter felt that her dark and striking complexion gave her the look of a gypsy girl, which added to her mystery and to his secret admiration.

It was even obvious to the milkman's horse that she was the prettiest girl in Bowling. Mind you, he was a special horse. What Ben didn't tell anyone was that Harlequin had been a circus horse before being passed on to him for his milk round. Every morning Ben travelled slowly from house to house, ladling out the milk from his budget into battered jugs or filling those left on the doorstep, carefully refitting their lids to keep out dust and flies. Sometimes he had time to stop and chat, and often an audience formed in the hope that Ben would let Harlequin perform his tricks.

'Harlequin, how many pints has Mrs Binns had today?' he would ask. The horse would nod three times. The children were amazed, for somehow he always got the answer right.

Harlequin was also a shrewd judge of character. If asked, 'Who is the cleverest boy in class?' he would look at each, then bow to Walter. Jeers and shouts of 'clever clogs' always followed his decision.

Still better was the question, 'Who is the stupidest scholar in school?' The horse inevitably moved towards Horace Sowden, pulled off his cap and trotted on down the road. When Horace ran after the horse to retrieve it, the audience fell about laughing.

Once, and only once, Ben asked the amazing Harlequin, 'Now, my clever fellow, who is the prettiest girl in Bowling Village?' The animal pondered, moving from one girl to the next, then finally bowed his head in front of Emily. The boys went wild, whistling and cheering, and Emily Lumb stood there, self-assured, milking the adulation. Walter was silent, not wanting to join in with the rest. He had thought he was her only admirer, and it was a shock to find that almost every lad shared his secret passion. It was even more galling to know that Albert was one of them: with his natural confidence, his bravado and good looks, he stood a better chance of gaining her attention.

The acorn incident confirmed this. One day the two boys were cradled in the boughs of a tree that grew over the lane next to the chapel. It was bent low enough to provide access to the bottom branches, offering a safe seat and an excellent viewing point for the whole of Old Lane, right up to St Stephen's Church. Albert had climbed out on an overhanging branch when they spied a group of girls coming up the lane. The group skipped, giggled and buzzed around the queen bee, Emily, who made stately and majestic progress, like the calm eye in the middle of a bustling storm. Suddenly acorns showered down and the girls scattered in all directions as they tried to find cover. Emily Lumb imperiously stood still, disregarding the chaos even when a few acorns bounced off her head and shoulders. A faint smile crossed her lips and the dark eyes glanced upwards at her grinning assailant.

'Come on, girls,' she called, 'let Albert Dowgill and his friend have their bit o' fun. They won't hurt thee.'

* * *

Walter could still see her as she strode off without so much as a backward glance, and there was still a niggling worm of envy in his thoughts. It had never gone away. The ground beneath his feet had become softer as he approached a small dyke: it was as if the sand's unsure spongy tread were reminding him of his own uncertainties and inadequacies. Approaching the stream, he realised the flowing water had dug a deeper and faster-flowing gullet. With a slow, deliberate step he took it in his stride. It was too small to deflect him from his path.

Chapter Four

The lonely figure plodded on. Here the Warton Sands became flat and featureless, uninterrupted by streams or stony outcrops. The treacherous boundaries of mudflats and salt marsh were far to his right. He watched the oystercatchers, the 'sea-a-pies' as the locals called them, intently feeding in small flocks on the edge of the channel. Shrimps, cockles, mussels, lugworms: all the bay's creatures were a harvest for them.

The trek had become predictable, rather like the comfortable, secure routine of his childhood. But of course there were the special days that lived long in his memory. Sometimes they came without warning; others he knew of in advance, and the excitement built up for days, perhaps even weeks. He remembered how Harriet had promised him one such day, shortly after his ninth birthday . . .

* * *

'Holmes's have opened a new department store,' she announced. 'It's one of the biggest in Yorkshire. There'll be a chance for you to come with me and spend some of your birthday money and those pennies you got for doing jobs. The shops and markets will have a lot more than Bowling's.'

Walter's eyes shone brightly. 'Ooh yes please, Mother,' he

26

replied. He rushed upstairs to count his money and carefully plan his campaign.

On Saturday morning he was up early, washed and dressed in record time and downstairs eager and ready. There was, however, a frown on Harriet's face. 'I'm not taking you to Bradford like that,' she complained. 'Your hair's down to your collar. We'll have to call at the barber's first thing. If there's not many in you can get it cut. I don't want to be seen in the best shops with a scruffy urchin. They'll think you've sneaked in off the street.'

Walter silently groaned: he had been trapped. His mother had outwitted him. He had slyly ignored her promptings for a few weeks now, dodging any opportunities she might have taken by going out to play or visiting friends' houses. Most boys tried to avoid the barber as a matter of principle, but Jack Bairstow was the one whom they all shunned without exception. He hated little boys and they hated him, a fact he was well aware of and even seemed to delight in.

As luck would have it the barber's was almost empty: just one old man had been in for a shave and he was leaving. Jack chewed on a slice of bread and dripping, his skeletal face showing no smile or welcome as he uttered the order, 'Next!' He stared suspiciously down at Walter, contemplating the prospect of a small, wriggling enemy, who would take twice as long to cut and only commanded half the usual fee.

'I'd like his hair cut, Mr Bairstow, if you don't mind,' Harriet informed him.

Jack nodded, then turned to face his victim. 'Now, young un,' he barked, 'don't thee move about or thee'll get hair down thy neck hole, or worse still I'll nick thee with me scithers.'

His lack of front teeth hindered his pronunciation as well as preventing him eating the crusts from his breakfast, which lay on a narrow counter under the mirror. He banged down a rough board, which fitted into two grooves cut halfway down the inside edge of the brown chair's arms, then bade the boy to climb up and sit on it. Walter grudgingly obliged. It was no use. No matter how still he sat, hair would fall down between his neck and the dirty cloth wrapped around it, causing him to itch and wriggle. The barber managed to nick him a couple of times, Walter suspected on purpose. After ten minutes of unmitigated torture Jack put the scissors down and took the tuppence Harriet offered, without an apology for the pain he had inflicted.

They walked out on to the lane, through the half-empty streets and past the countless terraces, shops and chapels of Bowling. They turned by Ripley's Mill and reached the Manchester Road. From here it was an easy walk down the hill to catch a horse bus, which took them the rest of the way into the centre of Bradford.

On their arrival Walter was amazed. As they walked past the towering columns of the Civic Hall and into the main shopping streets, surrounded by the most magnificent buildings clad in golden sandstone, the contrast between the mean exterior of Clough's drapery and these wonderful shop windows could not have been more striking. Annoyingly for his mother, Walter recited the name of each shop they passed: 'John Foster, Henry Lingard, Brown Muff, Milligan and Forbes, Ellis and Grimshaw, Aber . . . Aber . . .' He got stuck on Abercrombie.

Walter was even more impressed when they swept in through wide doors under a sign that read 'John Holmes – Draper, Clothier, Milliner and Household Goods'. The windows were expertly dressed and attractive, even to young Walter. Inside was even more wonderful. An array of counters faced them, staffed by smart young men in dark suits or pretty young ladies immaculately turned out in black dresses and starched white blouses. Rows of labelled drawers and shelves stocked with perfectly folded items of clothing enticed the eye.

While his mother made her purchases, Walter looked round the large shop. He caught sight of a plaster mannequin smartly attired in a dark three-piece suit and sporting a walking cane. He wandered over and, standing next to it, struck up the same elegant and dandyish pose, much to the annoyance of a salesman who was dashing round the gents' clothing department in an overtly foppish manner, adjusting a tie here and flicking off a speck of dust there. This is how I'll dress when I'm grown up, Walter thought: no more of Father's tatty clothes.

Harriet finished her shopping and took her son up a steep street to the indoor market. His senses were assailed by a range of wonderful smells the moment they passed through the doors: cheese and baking bread, flowers, perfumes and lotions, and spices and confectionery. The noise was deafening: people were talking loudly, stallholders were shouting their wares, and from the numerous tea stalls and cafés round the perimeter of the giant building came the clatter of crockery and the hissing of giant tea urns.

Normally Walter's first inclination would have been to rush around, to see every stall as quickly as possible, but much to his mother's surprise he wandered slowly down the aisles, his eyes searching in all directions. Despite this being his first visit, he knew what he was looking for: he'd had plenty of time to think about what he wanted to buy. With singular determination he led his mother to the far corner of the crowded market. There, beneath a sign boasting 'An Excellent Choice of Books for Boys', he was engrossed for a full twenty minutes as he thumbed through a wide array of stories and adventures. Some he had heard of; other tales of explorers, soldiers and heroes were new to him.

One book in particular, entitled *The Boy Who Sailed With Blake*, caught his eye. It was better bound and thicker than most around it, and the first page promised adventure, battles, foreign places, pirates, Spaniards, storms, treasure and incredible heroes. What worried Walter was the price. It cost a shilling, a full tuppence more than he had in his pocket. He reluctantly put it down and chose a thinner book about soldiers.

His mother intervened. 'Are you sure this is the book you want, Walter?'

He nodded his head, but it was a slow and reluctant nod.

'Really? I think you'd like that one there.' Walter remained silent. 'Well, you've been a good boy, very patient in all the shops and polite to everyone. I think it's the one you deserve.' She took out the extra tuppence and handed it to him. Walter did not know whether to laugh or cry. He squeezed her hand tightly.

The day went from strength to strength. A hot cup of tea and a sugary bun were a perfect end to their expedition. Walter almost floated out of the market and down Darley Street to pick up the omnibus. As they reached the bottom of the hill his mother had another surprise in store for him.

'I suppose, as you like watching trains so much, you'd like a quick visit to the station. It's not far.'

Walter was too excited to say anything. Sure enough, round the corner was the forecourt to Bradford Exchange Station. Black hansom cabs waited in a line for customers, and people hurried to and fro, some clutching items of luggage. Beyond was the crowded concourse and the noise of hissing steam, whistles and clattering doors. He was more excited when he saw the destination board, promising journeys to Halifax, Manchester and even London. Even more amazing were Blackpool and Morecambe – seaside towns where you could play on the sands, go out on boats and walk along the promenades by the sea. For a moment Walter was lost in wonder, then he pointed up at the board.

'I'd love a journey to Morecambe,' he sighed, 'especially if we were going there on holiday!'

His mother smiled. 'Well, perhaps one day, when I can persuade your father . . . '

For a few minutes Walter stood silently, looking at the board, the trains, the guards, the porters and the passengers. 'I'd like to be a stationmaster,' he announced.

Harriet smiled, and looked at the large black and white clock. 'That's enough for today. Now let's get back and see if there's an omnibus waiting.'

Later that evening Walter was engrossed in his wonderful new book.

'He's quiet,' muttered Enos. 'Perhaps if they books can do that to him, all this education and learnin' has some use after all.'

The approaching winter, though a season of discomfort and hardship for older folk, was a time of excitement for Walter and his friends. A wet December morning became one of those unexpectedly wonderful and special days. Clearing skies and a sharp afternoon frost turned the whole of Bowling into an ice rink, and all the boys were soon out to enjoy the mayhem. Albert came up with a new idea. 'Let's make a giant slide,' he suggested.

By evening the gang had made the gentle slope of Round Street into a perfect slide that finished with a flourish at the junction of Old Lane. If you gathered enough speed you could make it across the lane and into the hedge at the far side. Walter tried it, warily at first, then more boldly as he gained his balance, until he was able to shoot right into the lane and pull up just before the far side.

Abraham Harvey, or 'Arby' as he was known, took the next turn but lost his balance halfway down and slid the rest of his way on his back, scattering a group of younger children who stood round to watch. They roared with laughter, but the thin, spiky-haired lad took it in good heart.

Herbert Craven was never very good at this sort of thing and came to grief very quickly. His talent was making them laugh, by clowning around and mimicking teachers, shopkeepers, prissy girls – all fodder for his talent.

Tom Pickersgill showed them how. His tall thin frame held its balance all the way down to the mouth of the street before falling, but he got back to his feet triumphant. The challenge was set. The gauntlet had been thrown down.

Albert made his run perfectly. With the balance and power of an ice skater he roared down the track, only to be met near the end by two women emerging gingerly from the side street. Albert narrowly missed them, and they berated him while he vehemently protested his innocence. After they had gone it became clear that Albert's timing was not so innocent: he had noticed them coming down the street before he started his slide. Thereafter this became the object of the fun, the last boy down standing at the corner and signalling to the slider when to start, so as to cause the most panic to passers-by. Three girls coming home from the Band of Hope were the first target, followed by the unfortunate Horace Sowden carrying a bag of potatoes, many of which ended up scattered across the lane.

Then Joseph Lumb prepared for his run. Albert signalled that a potential target was coming along the lane and the tubby boy launched himself down the slide. As soon as Joseph had reached the point of no return the others were off, running in all directions for all they were worth. The huge and unmistakable figure of Constable Zachariah Booth hoved into view, resplendent in his blue uniform and cape and sporting his tall blue helmet, embellished with the bright silver badge of the Bradford Police Force. He carefully crossed the corner of Round Street, right into the path of the unstoppable force that was Joseph Lumb. Joseph screamed, and the policeman turned in horror to view the projectile that was hurtling towards him.

'Stop, stop, you stupid lad!' he bellowed.

Constable Booth made a last-minute attempt to get out of the way but his feet only slipped and slid on the icy surface, and he remained firmly in the line of the approaching missile. With a look of horror from both participants, an awesome crash ensued and two bulky forms careered across the ice-bound lane, ending up in the hedge. Over them, in a graceful parabola, sailed the fine blue helmet, ending its journey with a crack on the frozen pond beyond. Fortunately their landings were well cushioned by their ample frames, which ensured no serious damage. Joseph's experience with the fierce dogs had given him confidence in his ability to move quickly when the situation demanded, and he was on his feet and legging it up Old Lane as fast as the treacherous surface would allow, while Constable Booth lay winded on the road.

'Stop! Stop in the name of the law!' the policeman roared. But he was too late.

* * *

The traveller laughed as he brought the scene to mind. The gang's friendship had been one that lasted. Despite sad losses and a few additions, it had stood the test of time, from the days when they were roguish boys until they were eager young men setting out on the adventure of life. Some of those friendships had lasted to the present, but they too had to be sacrificed now.

* * *

Christmases were a fairly quiet affair for the Clough family. With no brothers or sisters on Harriet's side, the few visitors were neighbours or from Enos's family. Enos complained, as he did every Christmas, that trade suffered because he had to shut up shop. What he failed to mention was that scarves, socks, gloves and handkerchiefs sold well when the weather was cold, and more than made up the deficit.

Harriet ensured that the house was cheerful and welcoming. One afternoon she and Walter were decorating the Christmas tree when there was a knock at the door. It was Albert, Tom and Arby, who wanted Walter to go out with them.

'I'll tell you what you can do,' his mother suggested. 'You can collect some holly. Only those branches with berries on, mind you.'

At Tom's suggestion, the boys sneaked into the grounds of Bowling Hall, where there was an abundance of holly hedges.

'Why don't we all get some?' said Albert. 'We can sell it in Bowling. I bet we'll make a fair bit for extra presents.'

They collected as much holly as they could carry. On the way back Walter, always the most knowledgeable, pointed out some mistletoe growing round the branches of a large tree. With great dexterity, Albert scrambled up and cut a couple of bunches, hiding a sprig under his jacket when he reached the ground. Walter sensed his chance to get one up on his cousin. 'Why have you put that bit under your coat, Albert? Are you going to sell it or are you going to use it for yourself?'

Others followed his cue, joining the teasing to suggest some possible recipients. 'I know,' said Arby, 'it's for Grace Naylor.'

'No!' interrupted Walter, twisting the knife, 'it's for Madge Leadbeater.'

The mention of the smelliest girl in the class brought a chorus of groans and retching. 'Fancy kissin' 'er!' roared Tom, 'you'd be sick fer a week.'

Albert took it all in good heart, and then delivered the counter-punch that he knew would hurt Walter. 'Lads, you're all wrong,' he replied eyeing his cousin. 'It's all for Lumpy's sister.'

This was met with a chorus of approval from Arby and Tom and silence from Walter – who went home with his holly when they reached Old Lane, not joining their sales venture. He later learned that this had been a failure. On seeing the boys' enterprise, shopkeepers had chased them off, threatening to call Constable Booth. One mention of his name and they had scattered, dumping their wares in the beck.

When Walter awoke that special Christmas morning it was still dark. The room was cold but he didn't care. He shuffled down his bed and found the stocking tied to the frame. He untied it, pulled it under the bedclothes and began to investigate it, as much by touch and feel as by what he could see. The apple and orange were easily located, as were the bags of sweets and nuts. When he came to the soldiers he opened the curtains and stood the figures along the window-sill, so that the emerging rays would catch their red tunics. Further down he came to the square corners of a book. To his delight he made out in the half-light that it was the book of soldiers that he had almost bought in the market. He jiggled the stocking. There was definitely still something in the bottom, something quite heavy and substantial stuck between the toe and heel. It was wrapped as well, so it was difficult to make out precisely what it was. A surprise, he thought. Mother's so good at them. What can it be? Walter carefully manoeuvred the package to the top, and with trembling hands pulled the paper off. In the dim light he saw the outline of a beautiful small boat. With it were a mast, which had to be inserted in a hole in the deck, and a sail, to be attached by rings to the mast. He spent a few minutes putting it together, then gazed in admiration at the most perfect sailing boat he had ever seen.

The rest of Christmas couldn't pass quickly enough for Walter: the service with its lovely carols, the delicious Christmas dinner and the visits from carol singers and relatives all dragged by, as he waited for the moment when he could sail his new boat. Even Albert was impressed by it. 'Eee, Walter, it's a right bobby-dazzler!' he exclaimed in awe.

It was weeks, though, before the opportunity presented itself: it was a cold winter and the ponds were frozen for a full two months. Walter contented himself in the meantime with keeping the boat in a small box and sailing it across the parlour floor. An upturned stool served as an enemy Spanish galleon, a formidable foe for Captain Blake's small but nimble English man o' war.

When the thaw came and Walter ventured out to sail his boat, his mother warned him to be careful near the ponds. 'Bring yourself back in one piece,' she said, 'and don't sail it too often. You never know – some day you might get the chance to sail it on much more exciting waters.' Walter was puzzled. Only later did he understand what she meant. It was a special surprise indeed!

* * *

The solitary rambler had picked up a small piece of driftwood, and as he came to a small stream he bent down and set it free on the trickling waters. He watched it float away for a few yards until it came to rest on a small sandbank. No matter: in a few hours the inrushing tide would set it free. Would he also be released from his present burdens? Would his long journey bring a different and more satisfying life? He knew it should. Would his past stay behind him? He hoped it would.

Chapter Five

Silas Chipping was not unlike the crabs that occasionally scuttled across Walter's sandy track. He was, Walter recalled, round, short and squat, and had no neck to speak of. Two small, dark, piggy eyes stared out at the world, partially hidden among jowls and dark whiskers. His movements around school were most uncrablike, though, being slow and accompanied by a slight wheezing sound, which acted as an alarm for any miscreant. Mr Chipping had been Walter's teacher throughout the boy's tenth year, and although he was generally neither cruel nor ironic, his humourless demeanour and almost total obsession with neatness meant that his class was rather staid and boring. Being a year younger than most of the other pupils, Walter did not have the maturity and fine hand control of some of his fellows. Besides, being enthusiastic and excitable, he was keen to get his ideas on to paper or work out arithmetical problems in his head, without the need for elaborate setting down. His teacher seemed to berate him constantly. 'Handwriting is the key to good education and a good job. What do you think you're going to be with your fancy stories, Clough, another Charles Dickens?'

Walter found the mastery of pen and ink most difficult. It was the time he most dreaded, when the ink monitors came round with their pots and each pupil was given a wooden pen with an attached metal nib. Mr Chipping presented the class with a blackboard full of immaculate copperplate handwriting and they endeavoured to copy it into their best books. For the first few months in the class Walter found it difficult to gauge the correct amount of ink to keep on the pen. Being the youngest he was often given the worst pen by the older monitor. Sometimes it had a bent, twisted or wobbly nib, which made neat writing nearly impossible. Walter's efforts usually consisted of a series of blotches and scratches intermingled with a few letters.

The teacher was scathing of his efforts and any attempt to point out his faulty implement ended inevitably with the comment that 'A bad worker, Clough, always blames his tools.'

Walter's innocence was a source of amusement to his older classmates, and on one occasion a cause of Mr Chipping's embarrassment. During a Bible lesson the class was reading aloud the story of Joseph and his brothers. Each child read five verses, accomplishing the task with varying degrees of success. Chipping had evidently forgotten that the story involved Joseph and Potiphar's wife, and as the reading progressed he realised to his horror that the verses he would have censored were upon them.

Walter was a confident and eager reader, and before he could be called upon to stop he had started the seventh verse: 'And it came to pass after these things that his master's wife cast her eyes upon Joseph; and she said lie with me but he refused.' Walter stopped, lifted his head and asked his teacher in an innocent voice, 'What does it mean, Mr Chipping, when she says "lie with me"? I don't understand.'

There was a long silence. Their teacher's face turned a deeper and deeper red. Half the class began to laugh, while the other half silently read on to discover what other forbidden secrets these verses of Genesis might reveal. Mr Chipping stuttered and stumbled for a few moments. 'I . . . I . . . I . . . suppose it means she was tired . . . and thought he was tired too with all the work he did as a slave.' By now the whole class was in uproar. 'That's enough Bible study for today,' he concluded. 'Hand your Bibles to the monitor and get your pencils out.'

'But Sir,' interrupted Isaac Buttershaw, the class comedian, 'it seems a very interesting story. Can't we read it to the end?' He *had* read on, and was determined to prolong the mischief.

'No you can't!' shouted the panicking teacher. 'Pencils out –

we have some sums to do!' With that he retreated to the blackboard and started writing furiously. Behind him the commotion subsided, but not before several of the brighter children had finished the episode before reluctantly giving up their Bibles to the monitor.

For some weeks Chipping regarded Walter with suspicion and resentment: he found it difficult to believe that the boy's question was totally innocent. His attitude eventually softened, partly because Walter's handwriting and presentation improved, and partly because of a significant event later that term. Neither Walter nor his fellows were to know it, but Walter saved Silas Chipping's bacon.

It was the time of the annual inspection. In a system known as Payment by Results, the inspector's report influenced the school's funding for the coming year. It was a nervous time for teachers and pupils alike. The inspector observed teaching, and asked the pupils questions to judge their progress in arithmetic, English and other subjects. However, Silas's obsessive insistence on neatness and presentation meant that lessons involving history, geography and science were few and far between.

The inspector visited Walter's class much to Silas Chipping's discomfort. A tall man with a pair of spectacles balanced precariously on the end of his nose, the inspector observed the class and looked through the children's books before addressing the pupils.

'Now, children, I will ask you various questions regarding the knowledge you have gained in Mr Chipping's class during this year.' Their teacher's face became a mask of gloom and worry. 'When I ask a question do not call out or even raise your hand to volunteer the answer. I will choose who will answer it. Is that understood?'

The class nodded assent. In truth the session did not go too badly. The testing of their mental arithmetic went well, and by sheer luck the inspector alighted on some of the brighter and better-informed pupils for most of the other questions. Then he turned to the squirming and unctuous teacher.

'I assume, Mr Chipping, that you have covered some of the important dates in British history?'

'Most definitely, Mr Atkinson,' he lied.

'As time is short, I'll only need to ask a few questions.' Unfortunately these few questions, which involved the Battle of Hastings and Magna Carta, were met in stony silence. Chipping shifted in his chair. The inspector frowned. 'What was the date of the Spanish Armada? You answer, boy.'

He pointed at Walter – whose young chest burst with pride. He not only knew the date but who the main participants were, indeed every detail, for he had frequently enacted the encounter on the parlour floor, with his boat as Howard's flagship and the stool as Medina Sidonia's magnificent galleon. 'It was in 1588 in the English Channel.'

The inspector smiled. Silas Chipping heaved a sigh of utter relief, and the sweat poured from his brow. His face paled two shades of red to a dark pink. 'That's a nice, confident, correct answer, young man,' concluded the inspector. 'Now, Mr Chipping, if you'll allow this boy to show me the way to the senior class I'll be on my way. Quite satisfactory, but you must ensure a bit more work is done revising and retaining historical knowledge. That is all for now.'

Walter politely held the door for the visitor, who gave him yet another smile. He boldly guided him down the corridor to his next port of call, and returned to find his teacher and Ben the caretaker deep in conversation outside the classroom door. For once Chipping let his guard slip. 'The only part of inspectors I ever want to see again is the tails on their coats!' Walter could swear he even saw his teacher give him the faintest of smiles.

After the inspection Walter's stock in the class grew. Their teacher even tried to introduce a little elementary history, geography and science, which made the days less boring. Isaac Buttershaw, being a bright boy, recognised in Walter a kindred spirit and occasionally invited him to play with his older classmates. That kindred spirit matured over the years into a deep friendship and trust. But he couldn't confide now, even in Isaac. Although Isaac was understanding and perceptive, the solution was in Walter's own hands. Not even the brilliant and ebullient Isaac, who made light of his own terrible disfigurement and tragedy, could square the circle. His friendship would be gone, but Walter's memory of him would not. He thought with a shudder of that terrible day a few months after the inspection.

They had started a game of tip cat on a piece of waste ground. The equipment needed was very basic: a striker, a substantial piece of wood about two feet in length, and a chattie, a smaller piece sharpened at each end. The game had several variations but all involved one boy hitting the chattie on one of its ends to propel it some distance, so the striker could make a run and return to the circle drawn on the dirt before the missile was recovered and thrown back. Isaac took up position just outside a striking circle and the chattie was struck by one of the older boys. Instead of flying into the air it rebounded on a low trajectory, the pointed end hitting the unfortunate Isaac full in the eye. He let out a piercing scream, which Walter could still remember with horror twenty-five years later. His friend fell to the ground, his face covered in a mask of blood.

Walter heard later that Isaac was admitted to Bradford's new Eye and Ear Hospital, but there was no chance to save the eye. It was some weeks later that he returned to school, the empty socket covered with a patch. But such was Isaac's spirit that he made light of this terrible misfortune, indeed would take great pleasure in removing the patch to scare girls and younger children with the unpleasant sight. Some time later he was away from school for a couple of days, returning with the patch gone and sporting a glass eye.

Amid the fun and amusement that Isaac often led, Herbert Craven related the story of a man from Horton Lane who had lost his eye as a soldier and also sported a glass eye. 'I tell you it's true,' began Herbert in dramatic style, using a marble as a convenient prop. 'He takes his eye out in t'morning before he goes off to work, puts it on t'mantelpiece and tells his childer he'll be watching them, and if they're naughty they'll get a right belting when he gets home at night. His missus swears they're t'best behaved kids in Bradford.'

'My mum doesn't need owt like that to know what I'm doing,' boasted Albert. 'She found out as I'd sold her old shawl to t'shoddy man, the one she never uses and were hidden in t'cupboard for years. God knows how she did! She must 'ave spies on every street in Bowling.'

In reality, it transpired that the shoddy man was not averse to selling on decent stuff, rather than taking it back to the mills in Batley for reconstituting into rough blankets. He had sold the

shawl to someone in a nearby street, and it was seen by Leah
Dowgill the next day. Albert's reward of balloons and marbles
was heavily paid for. He seemed, however, to regard punishment
as the unimportant outcome of his actions, not something that
would deflect him from creating the maximum amount of
mischief for his own amusement and that of his friends. But
occasionally, just occasionally, he came across someone who
taught him that his actions had real consequences.

Young lads of Albert and Walter's age were always running
errands to the shops in Bowling, fetching bread from the bakers,
potatoes from the greengrocers or any number of goods from one
of Walter's favourite shops, Murgatroyds the grocer. They had
two shops in the area: the management of the larger West
Bowling shop fell on the shoulders of Hilda, while her husband
Jabez watched over the East Bowling shop on Wakefield Road.
Hilda was helped by her eldest son, a miserable sallow-faced
youth who did the carting and door-to-door deliveries. She was a
pleasant, accommodating soul, hard-working and capable though
inclined to gossip; but without doubt she was the driving force
behind the business. Jabez was an Oddfellow like Enos, and his
drinking partner, but Hilda held the purse strings and kept the
business on an even keel. Walter's family patronised the
Murgatroyds' establishment as did many Oddfellows, as Enos
and his fellow tradesmen had little time for the Co-operative
movement that was developing in Bradford. He and Jabez
protested against the starting up of such a shop down the
Manchester Road. 'Bowling Pioneers!' Enos shouted on his
return from the Oddfellows Meeting and the pub. 'They're
t'work of Satan; ne'er-do-wells and political agitators, undoing
the work of honest businessfolk.'

The Murgatroyds' West Bowling shop was crammed from
floor to ceiling with every conceivable kind of produce. The
main counter was narrow and dominated by a pair of large black
scales. On the floor behind it were sacks, barrels and large tins
containing sugar, tea, rice, flour, tapioca, dried peas and lentils,
which were weighed out into bags of every hue. To the side
stood a small counter covered by a cold and shiny stone slab. On
this rested blocks of butter, fats and cheeses, ready to be cut to
the customer's requirements and weighed out on a smaller pair of
shiny scales. It was the custom of some lads to scoop up crumbs

of cheese when they thought Hilda's back was turned. She was well aware of this, as she could see their reflection in a large glass-fronted cupboard, but for the most part she ignored these minor thefts. Albert, however, was bolder than most, and was not averse to taking the occasional separate small lump or picking at the cheese to dislodge a tasty piece. One day when he went in with Walter, who was on an errand, Hilda had seen them coming and was well prepared. Albert's eyes darted to the cheese counter, where a creamy yellow wedge of cheddar was proudly standing on the slab; from it had fallen a plump morsel the size of a small matchbox, just enough to fit into his mouth. Hanging back by the door, he awaited his chance. Hilda turned to fetch something from the shelf, and in a flash Albert darted forward and popped the dainty morsel into his mouth.

'And how are you today, young Albert?' Hilda asked. He took a quick bite to demolish the morsel so he could reply. A look of horror shot across his face as he realised he had chewed into a piece of soap. 'Well, then, aren't you going to answer? Has the cat got your tongue?' Hilda continued nonchalantly, as if unaware of his predicament.

Albert took the bull by the horns and swallowed. His face turned a shade paler. 'Very well, Mrs Murgatroyd, thank you,' he mumbled.

'And how's your mother? I haven't seen her this week. I hope she hasn't caught a winter cold,' the torturer calmly went on. Albert could taste the disgusting soapy foam in his mouth and down his throat. He tried to speak but no words came out. The shopkeeper's pleasant manner had turned into an icy stare, which transfixed him. But from the stern and cruel face there came a sweet and pleasant voice. 'Now come on and finish what you're eating. I'm sure your mother and father didn't teach you to speak with your mouth full. I know they always insist on you showing good manners.'

It was no use: Albert was trapped. It could not have been worse if she had pinned him to the wall and beaten him with one of the large brooms that leaned against the side of the counter. Too late he realised that the formidable Hilda had been well aware of all his tricks and was exacting a cruel revenge. He took his life into his hands and swallowed the remaining piece of soap, then stuttered, 'Sh . . . she's well, Mrs Murgatroyd, thank you, very well.' He turned to make his escape, but not before the torturer turned the screw for the last excruciating time.

'Remember me to her. Tell her I look forward to seeing her in the shop sometime and that we've got some nice cheddar in this week! I know your family likes a nice bit of cheese.'

Albert spent the rest of the afternoon painfully emptying the contents of his stomach.

A day later Leah Dowgill remarked with a crafty smile, 'You know, Albert, you haven't looked right well this week. Mrs Murgatroyd said as much when I was in the shop this morning. She said you looked off colour when you called in with Walter on Wednesday. Do you want summat for it, cod liver oil or stomach medicine, perhaps?'

Albert kept his counsel. He was chastened by his punishment, and for once didn't harbour thoughts of revenge. He had met his match, and he was wise enough to admit it – but that didn't stop him from continuing in his wild and reckless ways. No punishment or sanction could do that, even if it meant paying the ultimate price.

* * *

The thought of danger and death suddenly loomed large in Walter's mind. He had come to the River Keer, which ran out from the Carnforth marshes. Normally narrow and benign, it could also be one of the most treacherous, unforgiving waters that poured out into the bay. Narrower than the Kent, its sands could rapidly change after a rainstorm, and the beguilingly innocent surface could be deceptive and deadly. Today, after a couple of fine warm days, it was at its most peaceful again. Walter waded in, confident that it held no dangers for the present. The sun was out and only tiny flecks of wispy white cloud dotted the horizon. It was a similar day when he and Reuben had laughed at Hannah's antics near here, some two years before.

Chapter Six

It had been twenty-five years earlier that Walter had first seen the wide expanse of sky and horizon that now arched above him, when he was an impressionable ten-year-old boy.

The summer holidays had begun and one evening, as they were sitting in the parlour, his mother casually remarked, 'Walter, have you saved up your pocket money for the Tide Fair this August?'

'Ooh, yes,' he replied, 'I can't wait for Wakes Week to come.'

'Well, we won't be going to the Tide Fair.' Walter's face dropped, not realising that she was teasing him. 'I've persuaded your father to let us take a holiday. We're going to Morecambe. You'll be able to sail that boat of yours for real.'

Walter had never felt such excitement. He was too overcome to say anything, and rushed over to give her the biggest hug she had ever received from him. Then, much to Enos's embarrassment, he rushed over and hugged him too.

'Now mind you keep it a secret for the moment,' his mother advised him. 'Don't go boasting to your friends. Most poor folk in Bowling are happy enough to have two or three days off from the drudgery of the mill, never mind a week's holiday. A few coppers to spend at the fair is the only joy they get.'

Walter promised solemnly.

The weeks dragged by. He had never spent so little time with his friends during the summer. Instead he was busy shovelling coal, swilling front steps, running errands, doing anything that neighbours would pay a ha'penny for. When asked why he was so busy he had his answer ready.

'My cousin from Thornbury has told us the fair is bigger than ever, with lots of new rides and shows, so I'm getting some brass for when it comes here.'

Walter was still tired at first light when his mother woke him. He had hardly slept, imagining what the seaside would be like, dreaming of giant sandcastles, fun fairs and sailing his boat across Morecambe Bay. For once Harriet did not need to hurry him to wash, dress and eat his breakfast. The grocer's cart took them and their luggage through the awakening streets of Bradford, and then they made their way into the station and on to the platform.

Walter had never seen a railway engine so close up before and it was even more magnificent than he had imagined, standing proudly at the platform in its bright green livery, with hissing clouds of steam shooting from its black underbelly and shiny pistons. He stood staring at the engine driver, who smiled down and obliged him with a pull on the whistle.

Enos promptly found an empty carriage and they all climbed in. They did not have the compartment to themselves for long, but the elderly lady and her husband who joined them were pleasant company. They were dressed in their Sunday best, the gentleman sporting a silk top hat and the largest pocket watch the young boy had ever seen, while the lady wore a wide, feathered, pink hat, which she managed with difficulty through the carriage door. They had hardly sat down and exchanged pleasantries than there was a lurch, a clattering of couplings and chains, and the train moved off. The old gentleman took a particular shine to the inquisitive lad and Walter was soon engaged in conversation with him.

'Will we see any giant ships at Morecambe?' he asked.

'No, young man, I doubt that, but you might get a trip on a small steamer or fishing boat round the bay if you're lucky.'

The train rumbled on. Mills and canals were replaced by farms, fields, cows, villages and distant churches. Beyond Skipton the country changed and mountains and hills came into view.

The old gentleman's knowledge was encyclopaedic, and he pointed out to his eager pupil the mountains of Pen-y-Ghent and Whernside and the flat-topped loaf that was Ingleborough. The journey seemed to fly by, and after a snack of boiled eggs, bread and a bun, washed down with lemonade, the scenery changed again as they reached the wide valley of the River Lune. Almost imperceptibly the train slowed to cross the river, and they steamed into Lancaster for a short stop. Walter could see stone quays, sailing barques, warehouses with cranes and pulleys, quaint old stone houses and above them all, high on a hill, a magnificent castle, just like the ones he had seen in his history books. The train moved off again, the wide river swung away to the south and they crossed a patchwork of fields and marshes.

'Won't be long now before we reach Morecambe, and then your wonderful holiday can begin,' said the old man.

'Oh but sir, it already has,' gasped the excited young boy.

As the train slowed Walter's heart beat faster and faster. When it finally stopped the passengers disgorged on to the platform, to be welcomed by lads with handcarts crowding round, offering to transport the mountains of luggage to the boarding houses. After an argument Enos agreed a fee, and they emerged from the crowded station into the open air.

Even before they reached the station exit Morecambe *smelt* different: no smoke or chemicals but a salty, tangy, fresh smell. There was a murmuring whoosh of water and the sharp cry of giant white birds that wheeled above their heads. And the sky! It seemed to go on for ever, from way across to the left, into the distance then far away to the right, with no buildings or hills breaking it up: just bright sky and a line of grey-green sea that broke into thin lines of white surf. For a small boy who had never seen the coast before it was a wonder. Walter stood for a moment rooted to the spot, his mouth open in awe of the scene before him. Boats with dark triangular sails were dotted around the grey-green sea or tied to landing stages. People strolled along the promenade dressed in their best. Carriages waited at the side, their patient horses oblivious to the throng around them, and to the left and right were small stalls and kiosks advertising a variety of gifts and strange foods. Far to the right was the strangest bridge he had ever seen, spanning sand and water far out in the bay. It was all so different and utterly wonderful.

Walter had scarcely had time to take in the scene when a shout from Enos brought him back to reality. Their cart turned away from the sea and down a street lined with tall houses displaying signs for bed and board. After negotiating two streets they found their destination and knocked on the door.

A large and lantern-jawed woman appeared at the door, wearing a brown dress overpinned with a stained white apron. She addressed them abruptly and looked at Walter in a disapproving manner. He expected to see a sign that said 'Little Boys Not Welcome Here' among the myriad notices announcing meal times, payments, locking-up times and as many 'Rules of the Establishment' as anyone could imagine. After depositing the luggage in their room, Walter and Enos went to the sitting room, which looked out on to the street. Harriet had gone to buy food for the evening meal and for the following day, the landlady, whose job it was to cook the meals, having told her which shops and stalls she should buy from.

Walter was bored after the excitement of the journey and their arrival. He contented himself with a book he had brought, then counted the spending money in his pocket over and over again. Enos also seemed miserable, and looked wistfully through the window in the direction of a pub they had passed, the Fisherman's Arms. By the time Harriet returned rain had set in, and the family were confined indoors for the rest of the afternoon.

After the evening meal, which Walter noted was rather tasteless compared with his mother's offerings, the skies cleared, and he was excited when Harriet announced they could take a short evening walk.

The shops were closed now, so they made their way to the jetty. Here Walter was interested by the fishermen who had brought their haul on to the slipways, and with their families were shelling and preparing their catches of shellfish and shrimps for market. As they turned to walk back the setting sun was sneaking over and beneath a line of thin ragged clouds far out in the west. It bathed the whole scene in a kind of mottled orange glow, and it seemed to Walter that the sea was on fire. Even Enos was amazed at the scene's beauty and remarked, 'Eee, you don't see owt as good as that in Bradford of a night.' As they strolled back along the promenade he added, 'I tell you what, you two can go back to t'digs. I'll pop in for a last pint at that pub there.'

Mindful of the rules of the house and its formidable landlady, he arrived back in good time and still sober. His first words on his return were, 'You'll never guess who I've met in t'pub: Henry Slingsby, the bootmaker from Heaton Moor. He's an Oddfellow, you know. Him and 'is missus is on holiday too. Isn't that a coincidence?'

Harriet thought it was too much of a coincidence, but said nothing.

Walter slept so soundly that his mother had to wake him. But he was quickly up and ready for the adventures on the first full day of his holiday. As it was a Sunday they attended morning church, and the afternoon was spent walking around in the warm August sunshine.

They got as far as the strange, bridge-like structure Walter had noticed on his arrival: Morecambe Central Pier. As it was considered a suitable entertainment for visitors on a Sunday, it was crowded with people taking advantage of the fine weather. All were dressed in their Sunday best: the men in three-piece suits adorned with heavy gold watch-chains, while the women wore white blouses or ornate dresses with billowing sleeves and voluminous bustles. Individual touches such as flowered hats, straw boaters, pretty parasols and striped blazers changed the dull uniformity into a gentle pattern of colour and style. At the end of the pier the sudden breezes ensured that people held on tightly to their hats, but Walter was amused to see that some unwary promenaders had lost them to the vagaries of Morecambe's winds and tide.

Harriet suggested they should pay a weekly ticket of sixpence each. 'As children are allowed free, it makes good sense.'

Enos reluctantly agreed. His wife was determined to get as much out of this holiday for herself and her son as she could, and to restrict the amount of money that would end up in brewers' pockets. A walk on the pier each evening might also restrict the time available for the Fisherman's Arms, The Boat and any other hostelry that took her husband's fancy.

Walter stood on the pier with the water all around him. He could have been in the middle of the ocean on the bridge of a giant ship. It was the first day of the best week of his life.

It was a week that passed all too quickly. A beautiful sunny Monday encouraged a host of people on to the sands. Harriet had bought her son a small spade, and Walter set to work building a harbour for his boat and a channel to welcome the incoming tide. But the sands of Morecambe proved its downfall, and it filled with water and collapsed too quickly for him to rebuild it. Eventually his mother let him paddle in the sea. He found it cold at first, but the shallow water warmed gradually and he ventured back to her, sitting on the edge of the promenade, to collect his boat, the envy of other children who admired its sleek hull and colourful blue sail. He spent the rest of the afternoon sailing it in the shallows of the incoming tide.

For Walter the rest of the week was just as exciting. There was so much to see and do. Besides paddling, sailing, digging and skimming pebbles across the water, he found rocky outcrops where small pools held crabs and other sea creatures. Harriet enjoyed the holiday as much as her son, but mainly through his excitement of a new-found world. Only once did she let slip that she would have liked to participate more actively, when Walter asked about the horse vans standing on the beach.

'They're bathing vans. I'd love to try one,' she murmured wistfully. 'They say that sea bathing's so good for you.'

'I'm not letting you show yourself in such a manner!' Enos stormed, with a look of horror. 'It's not decent for the wife of a respectable businessman like me.'

Harriet might have argued the point but she thought better of it. You would never change the prejudices of a narrow-minded bigot.

The week had its upsets as well as successes. When Walter tried to sail his boat on the outgoing tide it decided suddenly to veer seawards. In his effort to catch it he lost his balance and fell in the sea. Harriet took him back to the lodgings so he could change into other clothes, but for the next two days paddling was forbidden. The landlady viewed his dripping state with disgust, and for the rest of the week passed curt comments on children and the mess they created.

Around the town were a variety of street sellers and entertainers unlike any in Bradford. There was the gypsy entertainer, sporting a large earring and a blue velvet waistcoat, who played a concertina. A monkey, attached to him by a long

chain, perched on his shoulder and danced to the tunes. Walter
was so entranced by the little show that he put a ha'penny in the
man's hat. To his surprise the kindly man offered him the
monkey to stroke but he, wary of being bitten or scratched, held
back.

'Nay, lad,' Enos scoffed. 'Summat as small as that'll not
hurt thee.' He made a sudden move forward to stroke the small
animal. Frightened, the monkey bit him on the end of the finger,
much to the amusement of the small crowd. Enos yelled out and
the monkey curled up under the arm of his master. 'I'll have thee
for that! Yon beast is dangerous – ought not to be let out! I'll tell
t'council and t'police.'

'Your fault,' retorted the impassive musician. 'You shouldn't
make a sudden movement towards any animal. He thought you
was attacking him.'

Enos was in too much pain to argue. Harriet quickly took
him back to the lodgings. Walter followed behind with a smug
look of 'I told you so' etched across his face, but his father was
too preoccupied with the pain to notice. Harriet bandaged the
finger while Enos grumbled, but took no notice of his empty
threats.

On the Thursday they wandered along the jetty, and Walter
was thrilled to see a large steamer moored at the end. It was a
magnificent machine some seventy feet long, its two massive
paddle wheels as big as Ripley's mill wheels and its long black
funnel belching smoke and steam. Walter begged to go on it, but
before Enos could deny him Harriet firmly quashed the idea.

'We can't,' she explained. 'It goes across the sea to the Isle
of Man and it doesn't come back until late.' Walter was
disappointed but his mother seemed firm.

All too soon they came to the last day of that wonderful
holiday. Walter awoke early on Friday morning eager to find out
what they would be doing.

'You've still got some pocket money left,' his mother said at
breakfast. 'Do you want to have a look round the stalls and
shops?'

'Please can we go on the sands for one last time?'

'I don't think so. I was thinking we might have a boat trip.
Not as far as the Isle of Man: just round the bay will have to do.'

Walter was overjoyed but Enos seemed less enthusiastic, as

if he had planned some other activity. He revealed his hand halfway through the morning, when Walter had just spent the last of his pocket money on a large bag of humbugs. 'I were goin' to say goodbye to Henry Slingsby and his missus. You know, you haven't been right sociable to them and they've invited us over to t'Midland Hotel by the jetty for a drink or two. T'lad can sit outside and I'll buy him some ginger beer.'

Harriet was angry, and for once she let her husband have the full force of her tongue. 'If you think I'm letting my son sit on his own outside any pub for a few hours while you get yourself drunk on the last day of our holiday then you've another think coming, Enos Clough! Go to your pub and your friends, but I'll be at that landing stage at two o'clock for me and Walter to take a boat trip. It's up to you if you want to join us!'

Enos stood open-mouthed at the barrage from his usually quiet and compliant wife. People passing turned to look at them. Men smiled, children stared in blank surprise and women looked at him with disdain. Never had she spoken with such fierce, determined rage. In full public view there was no opportunity to argue back. He slunk off in the direction of the hotel, leaving the two of them to finish their shopping.

When two o'clock came he appeared, a little unsteady but in a false convivial humour. Both parents hesitantly followed the eager child along the narrow wooden slipway. Enos paid the large red-faced fisherman who helped them down into the small boat.

It had been cleaned and freshly painted, but still had a lingering odour of fish. The vessel was no more than twenty feet in length and clinker-built with overlapping boards, which were well caulked on the inside. Although not big enough for the open sea, it was sturdy enough to serve mussel-gatherers in the shallow waters. Walter settled himself in the bow, and when ten more would-be sailors had been persuaded to part with their money the two jolly brothers, both owners and crew, pushed the boat away from the jetty. The older of the two spoke.

'Welcome aboard the *Lancashire Lass,* ladies 'n' gentlemen. Please keep well inside the boat 'n' don't lean over the side. Watch out for the wooden boom 'ere, 'cos we swing it over when she changes direction. We'll be half an hour out to Heysham Head and just over half an hour on the way back. We have to be back afore tea 'cos me missus is a landlady in the town, and if

51

I'm late or any of her guests are late for tea, she don't half give me a tellin' off.'

The passengers laughed, and the heavy canvas sail bulged out as they made their slow and stately progress out to sea in a slight southerly breeze. For Walter this was definitely the highlight of his wonderful week. He watched the shore slip further and further away until the crowds on the promenade were dots and the houses were like matchboxes. He imagined he was sailing under a fearless captain like Drake or Raleigh or Blake and let the fine spray rush against his face, imagining he was facing the Roaring Forties or a tropical hurricane.

Enos, in the back of the boat, was not enjoying the trip as much as his wife and son. The gentle pitching of the craft was uncomfortable and his face was gradually turning paler. He was learning that seawater and beer do not mix too well, something he would have to endure with a brave face for what might be the longest hour of his life. Walter was oblivious. All he could think of was the wonderful scene around him. Seagulls wheeled around the small mast, thinking that a small fishing smack pulling out to sea would mean an eventual bounty for them, while the hills on the far side of the bay came into sharp focus. Beneath them he was sure he could pick out villages, churches and jetties.

They passed a few larger boats, which sported a foresail as well as a rear spanker. The seagulls that had followed them out joined others screaming and circling round the fishing boats.

The captain bent down out of the breeze to speak to Walter. 'Them are shrimpers, young feller,' he shouted. 'Bit bigger than us and they can fish all year round. You've tried our shrimps from the Bay?'

'No,' said Walter, shaking his head to make sure he had been understood. He had seen the shrimp stalls on the front, and although many people seemed to enjoy them, one look at the little black eyes staring up from the pans had put him off the celebrated delicacy.

The younger fisherman in the stern turned the rudder and the small vessel caught the breeze side on. The boat gave a slight roll. There was a shriek from one or two passengers caught out by the sudden movement and a roar of laughter from the brothers. In the back Enos turned even paler. At that moment Walter caught sight of a magnificent sailing ship, far on the horizon. It was long and elegant and its three masts were covered with white sails, which were catching the afternoon sunshine. He gave a sudden 'ooh', which the older fisherman heard.

'Aye, lad. 'Tis a fine ship indeed. It's a barquentine bound for Liverpool coming close in to Sund'land Point to follow the coast down.'

'It's the most beautiful ship I've ever seen.'

'Nay,' the sailor replied. 'If you was to see them schooners or clippers then there's a feast for your eyes. Four masts or more some of them have. But they're not as common as they were. These new-fangled steamships are taking over. Very reliable they are but not as pretty.' He suddenly bent down and reached into a sack at the bottom of the boat, pulling out a piece of wood. Walter could see at once it was being carved into a fine ship. 'See that? Going to make it into a two-masted brig like the one they're building at Glasson Dock. Her will sail too, and right well.'

Walter told him that he had a model boat and had sailed it in the sea. For the rest of the journey the fisherman and the boy engaged in a lively conversation, but all too soon the boat turned to make its last run to the shore. As they approached the landing stage the breeze grew stronger and the fishing boat wallowed a little in the breaking waves.

'Well, ladies and gentlemen, I promised you we'd be back in time for tea, didn't I?' boasted their jolly host.

The mention of tea was too much for Enos, who made a quick movement to the side of the boat and spent the last minutes of their voyage emptying his beer and lunch into Morecambe Bay. He had no evening meal, which was as good a plate of fish and chips as Walter had ever tasted. The landlady was complimented by his mother and for once she warmed to them, her stern face breaking into a smile.

'Well, my love, if we Morecambe folk couldn't cook a good fish supper it would be a pity, wouldn't it? But thank you very much, anyway.'

She quickly reverted to character by reminding them to be out on the morrow by ten o'clock, as she had new lodgers coming in after lunch and needed time to prepare the rooms. Enos was nursing his stomach and wouldn't venture out, so Harriet and Walter took a walk to the front and along the pier. Enos's absence suited them both.

'Do you know,' Walter said, looking up at his mother with a smile, 'I'll remember this week for the rest of my life.'

* * *

And he did, right up to that moment on his long trek across the sands. Now, though, he knew there could be danger as well as beauty in that glorious seascape; that men risked their lives at times on the treacherous bay, in their search for its bounty. He had heard how a cockler had perished out on Cartmel Wharf, right in the middle of the bay, when stranded by the incoming tide. As a man who had experienced tragedy and sorrow, Walter was not naïve about the precarious balance between life and death out in that dangerous expanse – but this did not detract from its ever-changing beauty.

Chapter Seven

Bitterness and loathing for Enos had stayed with Walter all his life, welling up within him whenever he recalled his obstinate and vengeful stepfather. It was a cancer that would always be with him. Even now it was difficult to believe that those few months, twenty-five years before, had changed his whole life.

* * *

After their return from that eventful holiday in Morecambe, Enos had been strangely quiet as if biding his time. The young lad had noticed nothing but Harriet seemed nervous, as if she feared the calm before a coming storm. In his innocence Walter did not realise the tensions that had started to build up between his protective mother and the jealous head of the household, who had begun to realise that he would never father his own offspring – and would pass on his business to someone he regarded as his in name only. For Walter the few quiet days seemed a relief, as he was free from his father's criticism, but his mother knew better. She sensed that Enos had been affronted and even humiliated by her stand against him, and she had learned that he was not a man to take such a thing lying down.

Walter's main preoccupation, however, was his return to school and his early promotion to the senior class, which was taken by Mr McIntosh, the headmaster. He ignored the frightening stories he heard of constant canings and lines if pupils came in late or got their sums wrong, recognising them for what they were: lies to frighten the younger children. Walter had always got along well with Tosh, answering questions in assembly, smiling when he met him around the school and beaming with delight when was praised for his work. The headmaster's class held no fears for him because he trusted Tosh as his mentor and guide, and was determined to do his best for him at all times and in all subjects.

On the very first morning there was an opportunity for Walter to show his prowess at the activity he enjoyed most of all, writing an essay. The start of the term was always a busy time for the headmaster, and so he could attend to administration and business he announced that during the first lesson they would be writing an essay entitled 'My Holiday'. Many in the class groaned inwardly, but Walter eagerly accepted the exercise. No title could have suited him better and he set to with a will to recount the wonder and beauty of his week in Morecambe, remembering every detail of the scenery, the people he'd met and the amusing incidents that had occurred. He determined to pick his words and phrases carefully to make his account as effective as possible.

He remembered the couple of occasions on which Tosh had taken his class for essay writing and recalled his advice. 'Don't forget you're writing for an audience. It may be me or another teacher but try to pretend you're writing a book or for a newspaper or magazine. Make your audience share what you see.' Walter took this to heart. He pretended he was writing it for the *Bradford Argus* and was determined that its readers would enjoy his account. When the bell was rung for the lunchtime break he was still writing and oblivious to what was happening around him. On discovering the classroom empty he rushed home, gobbled his dinner (much to his mother's annoyance) and was back well before the start of the afternoon to continue his work.

A little later Mr McIntosh found him in an otherwise empty classroom. 'Well, young man, I see you haven't finished your essay yet. All the others handed them in long ago.'

'I'm sorry, sir, but there were so many wonderful things that happened on my holiday that I haven't had time to put them all down.'

'You'll have to hand it in now, young Clough, because I'll be marking them later.'

'But please, sir,' Walter protested, 'you've always told us that we must write our best for our audience. I'm sure my audience won't want to read something that's half finished.'

Tosh was startled at having his own words thrown back at him. Many a teacher would have been angry at the impertinence, but he was wiser than most. He recognised the logic of his pupil's argument, and besides he had already taken a peek at the piece and was impressed by Walter's imagination and style. To stifle such ability would be a crime indeed. 'All right, young man. You may stay behind after school if you wish to complete your essay. But if you want to present it as a finished piece of work don't rush the ending. The conclusion is as important as any other part. Don't forget that.'

'Oh thank you, sir,' said Walter. The bell had rung and the other pupils were already streaming back into the classroom.

He was glad when the afternoon session came to an end, even though it was an enjoyable science lesson energetically delivered by Mr McIntosh. Walter liked Tosh's lessons. He ran his class with a calm but firm hand and had no time for the silly or lazy pupil. What surprised the boy was that he did not rail against the one or two older children who dozed or fell asleep in afternoon classes. They were the few part-time scholars who had spent the morning, since before eight o'clock, working in the mills, quarries or brickyards. Tosh gently woke them up after a short doze and bade them continue their work.

Walter resumed his essay as the others filed out and took great pains to finish it carefully as his teacher had suggested. He took it to the headmaster's study and gave him a smile as he handed it over. Tosh read it through quickly, with a smile of satisfaction on his face, before consigning it to the pile in front of him.

'I notice there are one or two careless mistakes, which we can put down to your enthusiasm. If you want to be serious about your writing I'll have to teach you about drafting and reviewing. A good writer or journalist knows how to condense his piece when necessary, picking out the important ideas, re-ordering it and eliminating mistakes. But never mind, young Clough, such things will come with time and experience. At first glance it looks well written and very interesting.'

The boy's chest swelled with pride. Tears of joy welled in his eyes, and to avoid being seen he turned and with a mumbled 'thank you' and 'goodbye' was off down the corridor. He ran through the streets with a skip in his step, twirling round lampposts and jumping puddles with gay abandon. He arrived at the front door of the shop to be met by a worried Harriet and a very angry Enos.

'What the hell has thee been up to at yon school?' growled his father. 'No good, I'll be bound. Albert told us thee'd been kept in by t'headmaster at dinner time and long after school an' all. Thee must have been in right trouble on t'first day to get that. And I'll give thee a right good belting to go with it!'

'But I haven't been in trouble!' protested the frightened lad. 'Honest! I wanted to stay in to finish the essay we were given and Tosh let me. It's the best one I've ever written. It's about what happened on our holiday and it's pages and pages long.'

One mention of the word 'holiday' was enough to stir Enos into further anger. His face turned a deeper red and the veins stood out on his neck and temples at the thought that his wife's progeny had spilled the beans on the humiliating events that had taken place at Morecambe.

'I'll give thee holiday, thee evil little cuckoo,' he raged. 'Thee's lying through thy teeth. That's always been thee, a liar and a dreamer and a cheat. God knows where thee's got that from.' He turned to look at his wife. 'It's not from a good God-fearing family like ours!' With that he struck Walter hard on the side of the head: the cuff sent him spinning to the floor. He looked up, terrified of the enraged figure above him. Harriet, too, was trembling in fear of the uncontrollable anger of the man she had married in hope but was now beginning to hate.

Walter rose, bloodied, frightened but unbowed, and, with a courage that came from where he knew not, looked his enraged tormentor in the face. 'He's still down at school marking those essays,' he said calmly. 'If you go down now you'll see if I'm lying or not.' He turned to his mother. 'Tell him, Mother. Go to the school and see Tosh. He'll tell you who's telling the truth.'

Before Enos could speak or move, Harriet had placed herself between him and her son. One look at Walter had been enough for her to see the truth. If her husband wanted to harm her son he would have to knock her down as well. 'He's right.

We've got to go to school and find out the truth. You can't accuse him just on the say-so of your vile little nephew. He'd not think twice about getting Walter into trouble.'

'Aye, we'll go down to see that headmaster at t'school,' Enos shouted, 'and when I find what trouble thee's been in I'll strap thee even 'arder for it.' With that he was off down the lane with Harriet at his heels.

Dazed and frightened, Walter could not believe what had happened. He flung himself down on the bed and wept bitterly.

Donald McIntosh did not lack personal courage when facing parents; nor was he insensitive to their thoughts and feelings. On many occasions he had been able to sympathise with them when they had presented him with genuine problems that affected their children. These normally concerned the abject poverty that some families were suffering, and if he could help with a small action or a word in the right ear he was not afraid to do so. But when he was confronted with an obnoxious and unreasoning individual he stood firm for what he believed was right against those who deliberately deprived their offspring of the right to learn, or those who thought they could intimidate him when he had rightly and reasonably administered punishment.

Everyone in the village knew how he had even put down the formidable Amos Leadbeater when he had stormed into the school. His poor children had been taken home after arriving at school in a filthy and stinking condition. He had tried to explain to the sad figure of their mother about health and social acceptability, but was faced the next day by the giant frame of Amos, as repellent as his unfortunate offspring.

'Thee don't bloody smell 'em! Thee bloody learn 'em!' he had bawled.

Tosh raised himself to his full height and faced out the mountainous stench with a few home truths. The stern threat of the constable or council health inspectors made Amos back down.

But today was a puzzle indeed, when he saw a deeply worried Harriet and an enraged Enos Clough outside his room. 'Whatever he's been up to, thee 'as my support to cane him hard,' were the father's first words, 'and I'll give him a thrashing to back it up.'

59

'I beg your pardon, Mr Clough. I'm afraid you're rather wide of the mark.'

Harriet intervened before her husband could speak further. 'We would like to know, Mr McIntosh, why Walter was kept in after school and for part of the dinner break.'

'He's not been in *any* trouble, Mrs Clough, in fact the very opposite. He's written an excellent essay, one of the best it's been my privilege to read from such a young child. It was he who wanted to complete it in a full and proper manner, and although it was an unusual request I felt I had to encourage such talent and effort because his work was so good. It was an essay about his holiday, and the effort he put in was commendable.'

The mention of 'holiday' again roused Enos's anger. 'Aye, and why's thee letting him write down all what's said and done in a family, I'd like to know. That's us own business, not thine.'

'What your son described, Mr Clough,' the headmaster replied firmly, 'was the journey, the town, the seaside and his trip on a boat, *not* family details. He is a sensible and sensitive boy, of that you can be sure.'

The wind was taken out of Enos's sails. He had little answer to the perceptive and educated man in front of him. He tried his last ploy. 'What thee wants to teach him is to write bills, to add up and see how a business is run, not all this fancy learnin'. Ah wants 'im to work in my shop and be a right good draper's assistant with his feet on t'ground, not 'ave 'is 'ead stuffed with all this rubbish that'll never do t'likes of him any good.'

Donald McIntosh stiffened. 'Since you're bringing up the subject of your son's future, I think you should listen to my advice and views on the matter. Your son, Mr Clough,' Enos winced visibly, 'is a very able pupil and a very enthusiastic scholar. I feel he would benefit enormously from being allowed to sit the exam for a grammar school scholarship. I'm in no doubt that he would be successful. I have every confidence that with the right encouragement and support he would be able to take full advantage of a grammar school education and its wide range of subjects. Naturally it would require some sacrifice on your part: the provision of uniform, travel, equipment and other requisites is not cheap . . .'

'Too right thee is, and too much sacrifice it'd be for poor folk like us,' interrupted Enos. 'That's road to t'workhouse for us who've pulled ourselves up by our own bootlaces to be respectable businessfolk. It would be clogs to clogs in three generations. You and your fancy ideas! No wonder he's got his head in t'clouds all day. It's thee and thy like who make him what he is.'

'There are,' insisted the headmaster, 'grants and funds that you could apply for, to help with the financial burden. Bradford is one of the most forward-looking councils in the country with regard to opportunities in education.'

'Charity!' raged Enos. 'I'll not take charity from anyone, least of all t'council.' He stormed out of the room, and Harriet followed him in tears. Tosh maintained a calm, stoical exterior, but deep down he could have wept for the intelligent prodigy who had the ill luck to have such an ignorant and short-sighted parent.

If Walter had been unhappy before his parents' visit to school, he reached depths of utter wretchedness on their return, when Enos announced the conclusion of their meeting with his headmaster and triumphed in his selfish, vindictive decision. The thought of continuing his education at one of Bradford's fine new grammar schools filled Walter with pure delight. To have this dream dashed by his father in such a manner reduced him to utter despair, and he spent the night crying inconsolably into his pillow. He could not have slept anyway, for the evening was filled with his parents' raised voices.

Walter could not catch many words at all, but at the height of the row he heard his father shout, 'If thee wants him to go, thee pays for him. He's not having my money for that. He's not o' my loins. Why should I waste me brass on the likes of him?' These words troubled him. He did not understand them, but deep down they gave him a sense of unease. It only became clearer a few months later when he made that momentous discovery among the secrets in the tin box, from which time his sadness was tinged with hate and loathing for a man who was not his father and who had exacted his revenge on a boy who would never be his son.

Walter's mother came into his room later that night and tried to comfort him, but he was inconsolable. She sat there for several hours, his head on her lap, before she went downstairs again to a silent house.

For weeks afterwards the atmosphere was cold and bitter. Enos was at the pub most nights, and while Harriet did her best to encourage her son there was a sadness that had come over him which he couldn't escape.

* * *

The next few minutes of Walter's tramp across the bay were filled with 'might-have-beens' as he dreamed of an education in Bradford's foremost school, of the doors it might have opened and the opportunities it might have given him. He remembered watching the grammar school boys, with their white stiff collars and bundles of books, going eagerly to school, happily chatting about a book they had to read or a mathematical problem they had to solve. It always aroused envy inside him. He should have been there but he had been denied it. He ground a few shellfish under his boot in anger.

Chapter Eight

The lone walker stopped. A long stake net lay in his path, blocking his way over the stretch of firmer sand. He considered for a moment, then veered to the right for a hundred yards. On reaching the end of the net he carefully removed one of the stakes. This would be useful when he came to the shifting channel of the River Kent and the uncertain sands around it: he could use it to test any potentially dangerous spots.

Walter envied the life of the fishermen. Their life was hard and hazardous but at least they had the freedom to come and go as they pleased and spend their life in the wide outdoors, not stuck in some shop or small factory as he had been for so much of his life. His misery at having to learn his trade in that draper's shop had pervaded the whole household throughout his early teenage years.

* * *

Walter had left school at twelve, much to his own sadness and that of Mr McIntosh and his mother. The former had given him as much encouragement as he dared, although he realised it was against the wishes of the boy's father, and had pointed out that Walter could continue his education at the Mechanics Institute. Tosh had offered his final words in a short note that he gave to

Walter on his last day at school:

Good luck go with you, young man. Do not forget that any education and learning you gain is not wasted. Should you need any advice on any such matters, I would be only too happy to help on any occasion in the future.
D. McIntosh

So began Walter's work in the draper's shop, under the ever-censorial and critical eye of his stepfather. For the most part life was uneventful, but the dull routine was broken by adventures with his friends and the celebrations that were part of northern tradition. As Bowling, in common with many such suburbs, was thriving and expanding, the opportunities and events got bigger and better as the years went on. The township even gained its own swimming baths, and Walter and his friends took full advantage of them. For once the agile Albert did not prove the most able; in fact he struggled to gain mastery of anything other than the ungainly and slow breaststroke. Walter proved the outstanding performer, better even than Arby or Tom Pickersgill, who was a year younger than the others but already a head taller than Walter. Walter was occasionally inclined to give his cousin a ducking or a sly push under.

Such was the spirit between them, a friendship that was always tinged with rivalry. This rivalry made Albert wilder and more reckless as he grew up, and Walter was not averse to joining him in his escapades, partly through boredom and partly to revenge himself on his stepfather – to make life for him as awkward as possible. His one regret was the pain it caused his mother, but he was determined to give life a poke in the eye and make the most of the few opportunities he had for enjoyment.

The greatest opportunity was Bowling Tide in August, which had grown into the highlight of the year. Walter and his friends always wandered across from West Bowling to East Bowling, where the fair took place. By now the fields and wastelands between the two villages were no more: houses and streets had sprung up in the years of Walter's childhood, and around Bowling Hall a new park had been laid out for the benefit of the local population.

To Walter and his friends there was no more exciting sight than the traction engines, carts and caravans winding up Wakefield Road on a warm Thursday evening, to set up on Tide Field. The gang always went over to watch the procession making its way up the hill, taking the turn into Paley Road, then struggling the last few yards on to the site. They gazed at the long-haired youths and men who drove the creaking wagons and caravans, shouting and encouraging the horses to one last effort. Amid the drab and uniform surroundings of terraced houses, mills and ironworks it was a blaze of colour, with the brightly decorated caravans and the wagons piled high with painted boards and signs. But best of all were the fairground engines, smart in black, red and blue, grinding and hissing their way over the cobbles, flywheels whizzing round, and whistling and hooting to the cheering crowds of lads and lasses.

The bigger boys helped the men and women of the fair set up their stalls, carry coal and water, spread sawdust and generally fetch and carry. The payment for such help was free tickets for some of the rides, and Walter's gang was always there to take advantage of this bounty. The fair opened on a Friday night, when the workers had been paid and the mills had been closed for the Tide holiday.

One particularly memorable Tide Fair, when Walter was fifteen, stood out above all the others. It was a cloudy but dry evening when the gang set off, armed with their pocket money and some free tickets. It seemed as if the whole of Bowling was making its way to Paley Fields. On the way down Mill Lane they caught up with a group of girls that included Emily Lumb. She still stood out from the crowd, taller, darker and more striking than ever. For three years she had been working in Horsfall's Mill, yet the grinding work in the weaving shed had not diminished her beauty, and a few coppers in her purse had afforded her a cheap 'Sunday Best' dress, which she wore with her usual individuality and flair. Teasing and flirting between the two groups lasted all the way up Bowling Park Drive, across Wakefield Road and to the fair. As they passed the brandy snap stall, where for one penny you could have a bag bursting with the sugary delight, Walter immediately offered a piece to Emily.

'My, my, Walter Clough, you're certainly spreading your brass around tonight,' she joked. 'Your dad must pay you better in t'drapery than I get in t'mill.' She smiled and took an extra piece. Walter reddened, and would gladly have given her the whole bag.

It promised to be the most exciting night of the year. Tide Fair was bigger and better than ever, with stalls full of every conceivable delight to eat and sideshows to test every skill you could think of. Joseph Lumb had already added chips to the brandy snaps and was undecided between pie and peas or ice-cream when the rest of the gang dragged him away, determined to win at darts, hoopla or the coconut shy. Arby twice hit the coconut, which failed to dislodge.

'Hey missus,' he complained, 'yon coconut didn't move. I hit it fair 'n' square twice and it hasn't come off. I reckon we ought to have it.'

'Refer complaints to the owner, lad. He's here now.'

A twenty-stone giant of a man with an evil scarred face appeared from behind the tent flap. The gang decided discretion was the better part of valour and quickly retreated, shouting to the belligerent stallholder, and anyone in earshot, that it was a cheat and that the coconuts were stuck on with glue.

They disregarded the freak shows – the fat woman, the two-headed calves, dwarves and the like – and made a beeline for the best rides, to test their bravado and daring. The cake walk was the first they found, and they laughed at their antics as they came off reeling and swaying like a drunk on his late night journey home. Herbert Craven, ever the mimic and comedian of the party, set them roaring with merriment as he imitated the girls and women who had dared to venture on the swaying, bucking pathway. They tried the spewpans next, which not only whizzed them round and round but attempted by sudden moves to throw them off if they did not hold on tightly enough.

Albert tried legging it on the flying horses, waiting until the showman was on the far side and then jumping on for a free ride. He was successful, and Walter and the others followed suit on the next turn, but the brawny owner was well aware of the tricks lads played and suddenly brought the ride to a screeching stop. Albert and Walter were too quick to get caught, but Tom Pickersgill failed to notice the man creeping up behind him. 'I'll teach thee a lesson, yer snivelling cheat,' he roared, grabbing his collar. Tom was dragged to the centre of the ride, where a large tub of water served the needs of the engine. Twice the burly attendant forced the head of the hapless lad under, then, holding him by the scruff of the neck, flung him from the ride. Fortunately he was none the worse for wear after this rough justice, apart from a wet jacket and a couple of bruises.

The gang gathered round the fairground organ to fill up with pie and peas or chips while deciding what to do next. To Walter the organ was a wonder. It had an ornately carved white frame and in its three central windows were gaily coloured carved figures in fancy hats and bright shorts. A sign at the front read 'Gassler Bruder'. Walter engaged the owner in conversation, and the delighted old man showed him round the contraption, explaining the workings of the machine. When he came back to the front the rest of the gang had wandered off, but an elderly woman helpfully pointed the direction in which they had gone.

Walter caught up at 'Fairclough's Famous Boxing Booth', where his friends were watching the boxers prancing and jabbing on a small stage outside. 'Two pounds I'll give thee,' shouted the portly showman. 'Two pounds for anyone who can last three rounds in the ring with any of these fighters. Come on, gentlemen, you won't get an easier chance to win two pounds in your life.'

Albert's face lit up, and he turned to Joseph. 'Hey, Lumpy, what about it? I reckon you could take on that little un at the end. He's nobbut a whippet and couldn't get near if thee fended him off at arm's length.'

The six foot mountain was uncertain. He had lost a lot of his podginess in the last few years and could perform tremendous feats of strength for a lad of sixteen. Work at the quarry had made him fitter and stronger, and his increased height had given him a manlier frame.

'Go on, Lumpy,' Tom Pickersgill butted in. 'You can handle any of us, two at a time sometimes. You're as strong as an 'oss. Yon tiddler on t'end couldn't hurt thee, even if he could reach thee. And think of it, two pounds: half for thee, half for thy mates; we'd be 'ere for two more nights.'

The thought of unending pies, peas, brandy snaps, chips and other delights was too much for an unimaginative youth like Joseph. 'Aye, I'll give it a try,' he agreed. 'Yer right, Picky, yon squirt on t'end couldn't do me much harm, even if he got near me.'

Before he had a chance to change his mind Albert, his new trainer and manager, was over to the showman. 'Hey, mister, yon lad reckons he can whip that one on t'end. Wilt thee agree?'

A sly look came over Seth Fairclough's face; his smile was hidden under his enormous moustache. 'He's a big lad for me featherweight. By rights he should take on someone his own size. I don't want my boys hurt by a lump like that.'

'Aye, but he's only sixteen,' argued the eager match-fixer, 'and thee's got no one wanting to fight right now. Thee's not doing much business and this'll bring them in. They all knows Mad Lumpy around here. He's got a fearsome reputation round Bowling. No one picks a fight with him, even ones a lot older.'

'All right,' agreed the showman with a dramatic sigh. 'I suppose I'll have to.'

What Seth didn't say was that Jack Quinlan, though small and light, was a former champion with arms, body and fists of steel honed through frequent training and years of experience and combat. And he was particularly adept at taking on much larger opponents. 'Ladies and gentlemen,' the exuberant compère announced, 'we have a contest between your champion here in Bowling and 'Wild' Jack Quinlan, Ireland's former featherweight title-holder. Threepence each to see this fight of the night, only threepence!' He went on in this vein for a few minutes and gradually a few spectators, scenting blood, started to trickle into the tent.

The now uncertain Joseph and his small band of supporters were ushered round the back. It was too late to back out now. Stripped to the waist, Lumpy did not present an awe-inspiring sight, as spare fat abounded round his middle and his arms. Ill-fitting gloves were thrust on to his hands, and he was pushed into the corner of a makeshift ring scattered with sawdust. From close quarters his opponent did not seem quite so small. In height he certainly was, but his body was a mass of muscle from his biceps to his shoulders and across his chest. His neck was short and thick and his face evil and intense. Fairclough announced the start of the contest, and before poor Joseph knew what was happening a bell was rung, the crowd bayed for blood and firm hands shoved him into the middle of the ring. His wily opponent immediately knew how to handle a large but leaden-footed victim. He feinted to the left and Joseph, his eyes open wide in terror, moved his arms to block. Immediately he felt a crunching pain in the stomach as a bolt of lightning hit him from the other side, right in the midriff. He doubled up groaning, offering his chin as a clear target. His Irish executioner was not one to refuse such a kind gift and landed a haymaker, which seemed to come from way back behind him and ended right on the chin of his adversary, knocking poor Joseph right off his feet. He did not even hear the count or the booing that rang out around the tent. The unfortunate punters had spent threepence for two seconds of mayhem but no torture, slaughter and blood. They were none too pleased.

The showman had a bucket of water to hand; he was adept at reviving the unfortunate victims of 'Wild Jack'. Eventually Joseph came round and, though groggy and unsteady on his feet, was ushered straight out through the flap at the back of the tent. It took a further fifteen minutes in the fresh evening air to bring him round to anything like his full senses. He moaned constantly thereafter, touching his swollen face with little cries of pain, taking no further interest in the proceedings.

Earlier Walter had eyed a sideshow that he thought might offer some amusement, and as they passed it he pointed it out to the others. 'What about trying the ghost show? It might be a bit of fun.'

The gang agreed, paid their tuppences and filed in past the sign that advertised 'Strange Apparitions, Drama, Out of this World Experiences, Horrors beyond Imagination'. They were the first in and were directed to the front row, where they sat on wooden benches facing a small black stage skirted along the front by black cloth. The tent was dimly lit by oil lamps. Walter sat in the middle and his friends filled the bench to the left. Out of the corner of his eye he noticed some girls entering from the other side and being directed to fill the bench on his right. His heart jumped. Leading the line of girls, to the seat next to him, was Emily Lumb. She stopped to giggle with Charlotte Whitaker further back in the line, and Grace Naylor, a small plain girl with mousy hair and freckles took the lead and began to move along the front row towards him. He had to think quickly. Fortunately he had saved some brandy snap, and took out the bag. He looked at Emily and offered her the delicacy. To his delight she stepped round Grace and sat down at the end of the adjoining bench, with just a small gap between them.

'Ooh, Walter, you're a one who knows how to tempt a girl,' she laughed. 'I'll bet our Joseph hasn't got any left.'

In the dim light she had not noticed the state her brother was in. Walter's heart was pounding fast. There she was right next to him. Supposing she was frightened by the show? Secretly he hoped she would be; he would be there to comfort her. What if she swooned or fainted? He would be there to catch her in his arms. Walter edged further to his right until the gap between them was no more than a few inches. The auditorium grew darker. He became bolder and offered her another piece of brandy snap, which she readily accepted. The flap on the tent was closed and the oil lamps doused one by one. He edged closer still, until he could feel the sleeve of her dress rustling against his arm. Then out of nowhere Albert appeared, and tried to squeeze between them.

'Hope I get a better view 'ere,' he said. 'I was right at t'end. I couldn't see a damn thing there. Hope you two don't mind.'

The manoeuvre was too obvious, but Emily didn't resist. She was determined to play off the two rivals to the best of her ability, as she loved to be the centre of attention; this was too good an opportunity to miss. 'We'll just about squeeze you in,' she giggled, moving a little to the right.

Walter was seething with anger, but the show was starting and he could do little about it. Why hadn't he moved closer to her before Albert appeared? Why hadn't he anticipated his cousin's clever ploy? Not for the first time he regretted his lack of decisiveness.

The first part of the show came as a surprise for the whole audience. The master of ceremonies, dressed in top hat and frock coat, appeared from behind a curtain and the centre of the stage was lit with a narrow beam, to reveal the disembodied, pale, ghostly head of a child. The master of ceremonies spoke slowly and solemnly. 'Here you see, ladies and gentlemen, boys and girls, this unfortunate child. It has a head and yet no body. But you will see by miracle of miracles it is alive, as I will demonstrate to you. Oh strange and mysterious head,' he commanded, 'look to the right!'

The head slowly rolled its eyes and turned them to the right. There was an audible gasp from the audience.

'And now look to the left.' The head obeyed. 'Open your

mouth!' the master cried, and the head duly followed his command. 'Speak to us, oh wondrous being!'

The mouth moved slowly, and an echoing voice recited a sad and poetic lament. After several other tricks the head concluded its act by smoking a cigarette, which was placed in its mouth by the triumphant master of ceremonies.

To many in the audience it must have been a marvel of magic and wonder, but to Walter, who was in the best position to observe the dismembered apparition, it was clearly a trick. He had noticed a rustle in the black cloth that curtained the front of the stage and guessed the body of the boy lay below stage level. As the beam that lit the head dimmed at the end of the act he stretched his leg out and kicked the cloth. The apparition gave a sudden, unearthly yelp that shocked some of the audience even more. Walter withdrew his foot, craftily noticing that Albert's leg was still stretched out in front of him. He awaited the disturbance and the removal of Albert from the tent. But he waited in vain: his revenge did not come. The master of ceremonies gave Albert a hard and vicious stare, but as the second act was beginning he did not want to stop the show.

It restarted with a short drama about the death of a small child named Florence, whom Walter guessed was really the boy of the first act. As she died the stage darkened, and it seemed as if her body rose in the air to angels who were waiting above, accompanied by the sighs and oohs of the enraptured crowd. Walter guessed that a trick or two were involved, but even he could not work out that the apparent levitation was stealthily accomplished with mirrors.

The final part involved the magical appearance of ghosts past and present, whose heads appeared at various locations around the stage and vanished just as mysteriously. Walter could tell from his seat at the front that most were papier-mâché figures, though some may have been people quickly costumed. The more horrific ones drew screams and cries, and the image of Bonaparte was roundly booed by the audience. With a final flash and explosion the show was over. The door-flaps were opened, the light streamed in and they got up to leave.

Outside they were met by the stern face of Emily Lumb. All airs, graces and smiles had vanished. 'I've had enough of you and your lot. You, Albert Dowgill, for the tricks you got up to in t'show. I'm a good girl and I'll have none o' that. And you'd have tried the same, Walter Clough, if you'd had the opportunity.' She turned to the bruised figure of Joseph. 'And what have you let my brother get up to? I know you crafty lot. He hasn't the gumption to try fighting in t'boxing booth. It were you lot that got him into it, I've no doubt. And God knows what my mother will say when she sees the state of him. I've had my lot with you, once and for all!'

With that she strode off, accompanied by her coterie of chattering and sniggering girls, one or two of whom turned back to give Albert and Walter a sly look and furtive giggle.

Later Walter heard that the Lumbs had moved to Manningham, where they had all found employment at Lister's, the biggest mill in the city.

* * *

It was as if a light had gone out in his life. He always remembered the dark-haired girl with the beautiful gypsy looks, down the years and into the middle of the wide wilderness. He took the stake in both hands and drew her name out there on the sands. Each letter he drew carefully and lovingly, finishing it with a delicate heart. He knew his mark for a love long lost would, in a few hours, disappear with the incoming tide. That's how life was, but it would be her memorial.

Chapter Nine

Most people can say with certainty what they were doing on one momentous day – perhaps when they heard of the death of a monarch or celebrated a Royal Jubilee. For Walter, however, and for most of the folk of West Bowling, it would be 28 December 1882, when he was eighteen years old. It was then that the massive chimney at Newlands Mill fell, killing fifty-four souls and injuring more than seventy, many of whom were Walter's contemporaries and friends. Not an overtly religious man, Walter stopped, stood on a small outcrop, took off his hat and paid a silent tribute to those who died. He remembered all of them, but one dear friend in particular.

It was an irony, he thought, that such a tragedy occurred on Holy Innocents' Day, as most of the victims were children, youths and young women, forced to work from an early age for a pittance in filthy and inhuman conditions; the prosperity and industry of a thriving city was bought at the price of misery and grief. Walter had eventually realised this when he met Reuben and the other fishermen some two years before, during his stay with his family on the edge of the bay in the village of Arnside. The gnarled, sinewy fisherman and his friends lived a precarious but satisfied existence in communion with their surroundings, in contrast with many city-dwellers. That is not to say that the fishermen did not confront unexpected tragedy in their working

73

lives. 'Crooked sea's a dangerous place,' Reuben had warned Walter, after telling him the tale of two mussel gatherers lost on the incoming tide the year before. 'Bay changes from one tide to the next, and any man who thinks he can ever know her or tame her is a fool.'

* * *

Newland Mill was a tragedy on a far greater scale. The mill housed the spinning sheds of Haley's, Greenwood's and Horsefall's and had been built by the industrialist Sir Henry Ripley before Walter was born; it was still known as Ripley's Mill long after other businesses took over the premises. The MP and industrialist truly dominated the area: the mill was on Ripley Street, which ran past Ripley's sidings to the Ripley Dye Works, and various other undertakings he owned were nearby.

Both locals and contractors had warned Sir Henry not to build such a tall chimney, as the site chosen was over former coal workings, but he ignored their advice as he wanted it, at 300 feet, to be the tallest mill chimney in Bradford, dominating the whole city and proclaiming his wealth and influence. In the end he was persuaded to limit it to 256 feet. Ripley compounded his folly by insisting on a decorative stonework plaque near the base, which further weakened the structure. From its earliest days the chimney had shown signs of movement and instability, which necessitated much remedial work. He did not live to see the tragedy, dying two months before the fateful day.

Walter got up early to dress the draper's shop window. It was a wild morning, as it had been all over Christmas, with a howling wind and squalls of beating rain. He could not remember afterwards whether he heard a crash or felt a slight rumble beneath his feet, as he was intent on finishing his tasks before opening the shop. At twenty past eight there was a loud beating on the front door. He opened it to see the wild and distressed figure of Albert, dressed in his butcher's apron.

'What's up?' he asked. 'You look as if you've seen a ghost.'

Albert could scarcely get his words out, even less convey any sense to their meaning. 'It's happened,' he gasped. 'What us feared. After all these years it's happened.'

'What's happened?' asked his exasperated cousin. 'What's going on?'

'I was along Newton Street by the school with my meat cart when I heard it. The whole ground shook. My God, I was right next to it ten minutes afore. It could have been me!' Walter was perplexed. He stared at his cousin trying to catch a clue. At last Albert regained his composure and was able to tell his tale. 'Ripley's chimney. It's fell down. Right on top of t'mill.'

'My God!' Walter froze for a second, hardly able to comprehend the news. 'We've got to get help,' he blurted out.

Albert nodded: the shock had stunned him into silence. After a few seconds he recovered and dashed back up the street. Walter followed, grabbing his jacket from behind the door. They were up Old Lane in a flash and cutting through the area known as Little India, along Bengal Street and Bombay Street and past the hundreds of small back-to-back houses that lay in the shadow of the mill.

The sight that met their eyes on turning into Upper Castle Street was worse than either of them had expected. It was as if a giant's hand had smashed through the mill frontage, leaving the ends undisturbed yet turning the central five-storey gable into a crushed pile of bricks and rubble scarcely more than one storey high. The street, pavements and houses were covered with what seemed like grey snow, which still hung in clouds, stinging the eyes and choking the throat of anyone who ventured near. Bleeding and broken souls were being helped out of the buildings to the left and right, where stray bricks had smashed through the thin asbestos roofing. There seemed little hope of pulling anyone alive from the mountain of rubble.

One man was taking charge amid the filth, chaos and confusion. Lines of volunteers were being organised by Sergeant Laycock from the local police station either to pick at the debris with their bare hands or pass the stones, bricks and broken wood down a chain, in a frantic effort to clear the rubble, so that the desperate, hopeless, search for survivors could begin.

The two young men approached the grimy, dust-covered policeman. 'Can we help?' asked Walter.

'We need all the help we can get. There may be survivors under that chimney. But tread carefully: much of that rubble's loose. We don't want to lose two more.'

'Where do you want us?' asked Albert, his face sombre.

'Join that gang over there,' the sergeant ordered, pointing to the far side of the street, 'and try not to disturb owt below.'

The two volunteers scrambled up the pile of smashed stonework and balanced on a ridge; they were soon passing the rubble down to the street below. The work was strenuous and dirty but they toiled on, encouraged by the severe policeman, his once-smart blue uniform now a dusty grey and brown. As he went from team to team he helped them dig, and found them spars of wood to lever out lumps of concrete or sections of brick wall. Occasionally he called a halt. 'Stop work!' his voice boomed above the mêlée. They all obeyed, and a deathly hush descended. Nearly two hundred people froze as if in an eerie photograph, each one straining to hear the faintest cry or whimper. 'All right, continue!' their leader called after an agonising wait of a half a minute.

If ever the people of Bowling needed a man of ability and leadership to turn to in its hour of need it was now, and that man was Joshua Laycock. The brave men and youths under his command worked on, building up a rhythm in their back-breaking toil and sweating profusely despite the cold wind that blew around them. Luck was with them. At eleven o'clock a gang of men pulled aside a slab of wall to discover underneath a metal girder that had held up the rubble above, creating a small space. There they found a young girl, who had scarcely the breath to call out for help or even give her name. Her right leg was crushed yet she was still alive. Sergeant Laycock called a halt.

'Bring over that plank,' he shouted to Walter and Albert. 'Now lie her on it. Careful, like: take your time.'

Slowly and cautiously the team of burly men lifted their precious cargo on to their makeshift stretcher and gently carried her down to the street below. This encouraged the rescuers and they set to with a greater will. In the middle of the devastation, where the chimney had less distance to fall, it had not crushed all below it with the same force. The pile was higher in this part and more gaps had been found underneath the masonry. An enterprising miner from Holme Top led a party under the rubble and by shoring up their passage with abundant spars of wood, a skill he knew well from his daily work, had effected the rescue of an overlooker and his mate. A cheer rose from the crowd below when, as if by a miracle, they were brought out bruised but without terrible injury.

Some of the teams lifted a mass of stones only to find broken gas pipes slowly hissing out their poison. They informed their commander, who immediately stopped all work and warned the brave volunteers. 'Lads, don't light any cigarettes or pipes. There's escaping gas around.'

Every team nodded its assent and they resumed work. The sergeant had been joined by a couple of his constables, who tried to push the gathering crowd back to the end of the street, giving room for women to tend the injured and for the mounting piles of rubble from the ruined mill. Bodies were now being recovered, as the top layers of shattered roofing and brickwork had been removed: they were respectfully covered and carried down to the street. Cries of anguish broke from the crowd as those who could be recognised were named. Two chapels had been commandeered as temporary morgues, while nurses and doctors were already arriving from hospitals in Bradford. Relief teams of rescuers had been brought together, ready to take over when the first heroes of the day started to flag. From the early chaos order was emerging.

Walter and Albert had been helping some older men move some planking and stonework when they heard a cry below. A small hole appeared beneath them, no bigger than a drainpipe. The moaning became louder and the two lads summoned their leader.

After inspecting the crevice and listening for a while, he called the small gang together. 'Can't see what's below,' the sergeant said. 'Someone needs to try to get down there.'

The gap was too small for the older men, but not for Albert Dowgill. The recklessness that had always been such a vice became a virtue in the hour of need. 'Aye, I reckon I might get down there,' he volunteered.

'You be careful, lad,' commanded the policeman. 'First tell us what it's like below, who's there and in what condition. Don't try to move anything yourself: we don't want this lot coming down on you.'

Albert carefully squeezed down the hole feet first. There was a pause of half a minute or so while his eyes became accustomed to the dim light. 'There's a lad down 'ere,' he called. 'I thinks he's all right. I thinks I can free him, then I'll try to push him out.'

'All right,' his anxious superior shouted back, 'but don't do owt daft.'

There followed an eerie silence, broken by the sounds of exertion and a soft moan, then banging and crashing.

'What's up lad? Are you all right?' Sergeant Laycock called down.

'Aye,' came the reply from the darkness below. 'Summat's hit me in t'face and I'm bleeding a bit, but I'm all right, honest. T'lad's free. I'm going to try and push him up through t'gap.'

Walter and the others waited patiently. Gradually a small head, grey with dust and red with blood, poked through into the light. The boy was carried down to the pavement, where he was attended to by a group of women. Suddenly there was a disturbance at the end of the street and a small woman, dressed in a black headscarf, broke loose from the crowd and rushed down to the prone figure, flinging her arms round him and crying uncontrollably. Albert appeared above the rubble a few moments later, his head bleeding but none the worse for his venture.

'You're a very brave young man,' announced the sergeant, clapping him on the back. The rest of the group stopped and applauded, and they were soon joined by many in the crowd. For once in his life Albert did not know what to say, and beneath the mask of dust he turned red with embarrassment. 'You lads go down and get your mate attended to,' ordered their commander. 'You've done a real good job and you can be right proud of yourselves, but everyone's getting tired. There should be other volunteers we can get now, so stand down and take a break. You deserve it.'

They would have worked for him all day and the next if he had so ordered, but they followed his instructions. Relief gangs were already armed with shovels, crowbars and planks. The noble policeman did not follow his own advice, but continued to welcome volunteers and explained the best ways of working. Albert had his head bandaged, and together the cousins tramped back through the dusty streets, their grime and blood a testament to their effort and bravery. People acknowledged them as they passed, and one rather bewildered little boy asked his mother,

'What's up with them two? Has t'chimney fallen down on them?'

On arriving at Walter's home, they discovered that news of their exploits had already reached the shop. Harriet hugged them both, glad to see her son back in one piece. Even Enos shook Walter's hand, and did not seem perturbed that he had ruined his working clothes.

The after-effects of the disaster dawned on West Bowling in the next few weeks. Mill villages were close communities and there were no strangers among them. At first there was a succession of funerals that went on day after day, and the people took on a solemn, quiet demeanour. Then they started to examine the horrific details of that day. Amid the tragedies and injuries stories abounded of rescues and lucky escapes. There were many terrifying accounts of the disaster, some more fuelled by imagination than reality. Several families from the lane had seen their children badly injured, and one child had been killed. Other households escaped with lighter injuries, but would carry the trauma with them for many years to come. Walter was relieved to hear that his former classmate Frederick Bendig, had escaped with only cuts and bruises, but later that evening was devastated when he learned of Herbert Craven's death. He grieved for the quiet lad whose wicked sense of humour cheered up the gang when they were miserable and kept them entertained with his infectious talent for mimicry. Amid the tragedy he heard stories of amazing luck, such as the girl who ran home during the morning break for something to eat, leaving her mother and sister to perish at the mill.

Grief gradually turned to blame and judgement as Bowling's citizens tried to make sense of the awful disaster that had blighted their lives. Matters were not helped by the morbid curiosity of strangers, who came from all parts of Bradford and surrounding towns to gaze on the disaster. Disgusted, local people began to attack them as the days passed.

It was generally agreed that the chimney had been in a perilous state for some years, slowly bending several feet out of true. Many would not work at the mills for that reason and had sought employment in other factories. From her friend Fanny Grimshaw Harriet heard a very disturbing tale. 'They began work to secure the chimney on the 27th of December,' she told her friend. 'That was the day before the collapse. And the workmen didn't turn up on the morning of the tragedy.'

'Why was that?' asked a puzzled Harriet.

'Because they knew the state it was in, and with the strong winds getting worse they were scared. I tell you, they knew it would come down but they've been sworn to secrecy. I'm sure of it.'

Harriet ignored the tittle-tattle and gossip of many a customer, but knew that Fanny was not inclined to pass on rumours or repeat the latest scandal without a thought to the consequences, as she was a woman of principle and intelligence. The story disturbed her greatly.

The village's mood gradually turned to anger when the inquest did not name Ripley's as responsible, returning verdicts of accidental deaths on all fifty-four victims. Enos, reading the proceedings in the *Bradford Daily Telegraph*, professed disgust, and declared that the jury were men of straw, too easily influenced by their lords and masters. Whether this was righteous indignation or because one of the jury had a rival drapery business on the Manchester Road, Walter could not be sure. Enos, however, benefited, as folk subsequently shunned his rival and took their custom to Enos's shop.

Walter could see, looking back seventeen years, that if any good came from the tragedy it was that it brought together ever closer the good folk of West Bowling, and inspired a strong desire to improve the lot of ordinary working folk. People also recognised the efforts so many had made. Sergeant Laycock still had to deal with criminality and drunkenness, but he achieved great respect and lasting gratitude from the people, not least some of his more frequent customers – who considered it a privilege to be locked up by the hero of the disaster. That heroism was also rewarded with a medal from Bradford Council.

As for Walter and Albert, they did not gain any tangible award, but together with the many who risked their lives in the rubble of Newland's Mill received an unspoken recognition especially from those most affected by the tragedy. They had grown up a lot in those few weeks, seeing danger, death, mutilation and grief, and had taken it in their stride, as a rite of passage into manhood. It left in Walter, however, a greater dissatisfaction both with his lot and with the conditions in which he saw many others. They were victims of a system that left them powerless, and limited their opportunities.

* * *

The walker stopped and looked around. He picked up a few large pebbles and laid them in a pile, then hunted for more. Some he had to dislodge from the sand with his boot; others he prised out more easily. Fortunately the flat outcrop provided him with all the material he needed. When he had collected fifty-four pebbles of varying sizes he piled the small stones into a cairn and laid the large ones in the form of a cross, trying to remember as many of those who had perished as he could. Faces flashed across his memory: young pale-faced girls, grimy boys, and women whose features were ravaged by the years of poverty, work and childbirth. He remembered a rubber-faced youth with a constant cheeky grin and eyes brighter than the shiny pebbles at his feet. Walter hoped that for the next few days the weather would be kind and the tides gentle, so that others might look on the memorial. He finished his deliberations with a silent prayer and, with a tear in his eye, replaced his hat and walked off the shingle towards the beckoning horizon.

Chapter Ten

There are some parts of your life that you want to forget, sometimes because of boredom but often because of embarrassment. They keep returning, though, either prodding your conscience with gentle reminders or biting back with intense discomfort. As Walter strode on across the lonely wastes he recalled his years as a young man, which contained many such episodes. Others, though, were amusing, all part of the adventure of growing into manhood. It was not that Walter was shy or awkward with the opposite sex, rather that, stuck in the stifling confines of the draper's shop, he did not have as many chances as those who worked in factories or larger businesses for dalliances or flirtations that might lead to further opportunities.

Certainly the young ladies of his age who attended St Stephen's Church were not much of a bunch to get excited about. Normally membership of the church or chapel and its various dependent organisations gave a respectable young man the opportunity to find a kindred spirit, a romantic friendship or even perhaps a future partner. For Walter, however, the young ladies there were as dull, plain and pious a crowd as you could ever hope to meet or, in his view, avoid. His mother regularly came up with sly suggestions. 'I'm inviting Amy Greenwood and her mother over on Saturday,' she would inform him. 'She's a very nice girl, and her mother says she's a wonderful cook. For once, Walter, do try to make conversation with someone.'

'I know her, Mother, and the less I have to do with her and her boring conversation the better.'

He found no talent, adventure or imagination among most of the girls he knew, while those who had a slightly sharper intellect and more interesting conversation were without doubt the ugliest and most unappealing for miles around.

Classes at the Mechanics Institute, which gave Walter an outlet for his creative and intellectual needs, gave him no opportunity to further romantic associations. He would probably have had to join cookery or secretarial courses to make any useful contacts, and he was sure he would not have been welcome at either.

What galled him, besides the obvious physical frustrations, was that many of his friends, Albert and Arby included, were neither as naïve nor as inexperienced. Albert in particular often regaled them with his exploits when they met in the Mason's Arms.

'There's nowt gives thee a better chance to get some experience with women than to do t'rounds with t'butcher's cart,' he boasted one night, when a few rounds of beer had passed down his throat, 'especially in t'daytime, when there's not a lot of folk around.'

'How do you meet young lasses doing that?' enquired Sam Varley, a jolly, tubby youth who had joined their drinking group a couple of months before.

'What do you mean, "young lasses"?' laughed Albert. 'I'm talking o' young married women. They know how to give their favours out, I'll tell thee, especially if there's going to be a bit of extra stewing beef on their plates. There's a lot I've learnt since going out on t'cart, and it's not about selling meat!'

'But thee'll get into trouble with their husbands if they find out,' Arby said.

'Nah. Them women knows how to keep their gob shut and if I've spawned any kid in Bowling or around husbands will think it's their own – and she'll not tell another tale, eh?' He winked at his audience. 'And a bit more for dinner will keep her keen for another time. Father never checks too close and I can swizzle t'other ones a bit to keep my books straight.'

They roared with laughter, Walter too, but deep down there was envy in his heart toward his libertine cousin, already experienced with women before he had even made a start.

'Hey, keep thy voice down,' warned Arby, 'There's some mill-women over there and they can tell owt that you say.'

'Nah, they're too far away.'

'I'm telling thee, they doesn't need to hear thee. In t'clatter of t'weaving shed you can't hear owt anyway, so they learns to lip-read. They can talk one to t'other over a dozen looms with no sound made.'

'All right,' asserted the ever-confident Albert, 'if thee knows all about these mill lasses, what are they like? Does they give thee a chance to get out thy Prince Albert?'

The oblique reference to the male member raised a guffaw. Arby was not to be outdone and, turning away from the bar, he moved into the corner, so that his tale could not be overheard or lip-read. 'Thee knows I'm an overlooker's apprentice,' he began, 'and I don't have as much chance as t'overlookers themselves. You'd be surprised what some women will do for t'gift of a bit of overtime or bonus work.' A ripple of suppressed laughter ran round the group. 'But I always gets t'chance to have a good look where none but their husbands can. They sends me to clean out under t'looms: scraps, fluff, spare bobbins and shuttles.' He gave a knowing wink to the assembled pals. 'It's a right mucky job, I'm telling thee.'

'How come?' asked Tom Pickersgill.

'Them women doesn't move out of t'way, you know. You have to crawl right under their skirts and they don't see if you have a crafty look up. There's black coms, and white uns, and grey uns and plenty with none at all.' Arby's voice rose to a crescendo. 'I reckon I've seen more *fluff* under them looms than you lot have had hot dinners.'

They broke into hoots of laughter. Faces turned to look at the young men, some of whom were rendered helpless by the joke. Albert spilt his drink, and even Walter was reduced to fits of choking by the infectious hilarity.

If the genteel folk of St Stephen's Church and Sunday School had known that Walter and his friends spent the odd night each week at a drinking den like the Mason's Arms they would have tutted with disgust. But the pub was not in West Bowling: it lay a mile further toward the centre of Bradford, far away from the prying eyes and wagging tongues around Old Lane. It was originally a beer house, unlicensed but permitted, set up some fifty years before to supply beer instead of spirits to the local people. It was argued that such a scheme would render the working people of Bradford slightly less unfit for work in the factories and weaving sheds than if they drank gin, and would also relieve them of the hazardous practice of drinking the local water. Although it had its usual assortment of villains it was a well-run public house, and despite being described by the police as 'indifferent', neither bad nor good, the magistrates had never sought to refuse the publicans a licence. The pub's unusual layout meant that although its rooms were cramped and low it had space to sell food, offer some simple entertainments such as darts, skittles and dominoes, and serve as a meeting place for workers' groups and fledgling trade unions, which were springing up thanks to the squalid working conditions in Bradford's factories. It afforded the luxury of a separate bar and parlour: the latter, a much larger room, had seating around its walls and a few tables, forms and stools scattered around the centre. The dim rooms were lit by gas, and a few pictures and mirrors adorned their smoke-darkened walls, while spittoons were provided in profusion. The crowning glory was a badly stuffed moose head. The creature had a curious, melancholy expression and looked as if it had drunk an excess of the establishment's strongest brew; even worse for wear than some of the customers at chucking-out time.

When Sam Lodge, the landlord, called 'Last orders' he followed it a few minutes later with 'Time, gentlemen, please!' It was a foolhardy customer who ignored these polite invitations to vacate the premises. Under Sam's eagle eye the pub was better run and had lost some of its wild and violent reputation.

Even so, the Mason's Arms was not in the same league as the Prince of Wales on Bowling Old Lane, one of those recognised by the licensing authorities as well-run premises where any criminal element was kept out, men and women were served in separate rooms and any client too worse for wear was not humoured. The Prince of Wales was run with impeccable morality by Bertha Mahoney, a small, fierce, grey-haired widow who would hold no truck with rowdiness or depravity. She was assisted in her management by Liam, her large slow-witted son who lived in dread of her, as did most of the customers. If ever, on a rare occasion, a stranger tried to disregard the rules of the house and had the temerity to ignore the orders of the fearsome landlady, then she would call on her son for assistance.

'Liam, I think the gentleman over there can't decide whether he wants to leave or not. Can you help him make up his mind?'

It was then that the formidable bulk of her offspring came into its own, and the foolish individual was propelled swiftly and with little ceremony on to the street. Bertha had a keen social conscience and would only allow a man one or two drinks if he was on his way home on Friday night with his wage packet. She recognised that a man was due some refreshment after a day's hard toil in the mill, but also that his money had to feed his family. She sent them home with the gentle reminder, 'I'm sure your wife and bairns will be waiting for you. I know they haven't managed too well this week and those wages will be welcome. She'll cook you a good tea, I expect, with that bit extra you've got for her.'

It may seem surprising that such a pub did good business, but it did. The grey-haired tyrant looked after her beer, the food was tasty and wholesome and the place was always bright and clean.

Walter never claimed to visit the Prince of Wales, as it was too close to home, but he maintained the lie that the only pubs he and his friends visited were such premises as the redoubtable Bertha Mahoney's. Enos saw through this deception, but even he did not divulge his suspicions to his wife, partly through his last vestiges of feeling for her and also through a disinclination to cast a spotlight on his own drinking habits.

One night, when Walter and Albert were at the bar in the Mason's Arms, Albert made a proposition – having noticed Walter's reluctance to admit his sexual adventures, and guessing the reason. 'What about us two going into Bradford one night?' he suggested. 'I've heard there's one or two rum places where we can have a right bit o' fun. Bring some brass with thee, mind.'

'What kind of places are you talking about?' asked an inebriated Walter.

'Oh, right respectable establishments, you can be sure of

that. Mind you, the girls there might not be as prissy and unwelcoming as you find at a St Stephen's Church social!'

Walter readily concurred, and one fine May evening the two of them set off down the hill and into the city. Walter was filled with a sense of excitement, tinged with apprehension and a nagging guilt. He had a fairly good idea what his cousin had planned. As they neared the centre, Albert turned off down a side street into a part of town Walter had never seen before. It had a strange mixture of large and small buildings, some run-down and dingy and others relatively new. In Brunswick Street they passed several pubs and lodging houses and even a building that claimed it was a temperance hotel, though this seemed unlikely. It was set between two noisy public houses and a couple of women hung round the entrance. Drunks abounded, even at this early hour, and there was the noise of singing and shouting in the background.

Albert turned into the doorway of a larger building that announced itself on a finely painted board as 'The Brunswick Saloon – Singing, Dancing, Music Hall and Fine Entertainment'. Walter followed, not knowing what to expect, and was pleasantly surprised to find a smart, ornately decorated entrance hall. The burly doorman demanded a shilling entrance fee and showed them through a pair of heavy wooden doors. In the dim light Walter could make out what seemed to be part theatre and part public house. A small stage framed by plush red curtains faced them and a few gilded figures of naked women were displayed against elegantly papered walls. Tables faced the stage, with red upholstered chairs round each one, and a bar ran along the wall to the right, backed by more gilding and mirrors.

If the initial impression of the room was of opulence and elegance, this was soon taken away its occupants. A large, brassy singer in a tight and revealing dress was offering a loud rendition of a popular music hall song, but with lyrics far coarser and more suggestive than Walter had heard before. No sooner had they sat down than they were joined at the table by two young women who emerged from the shadows at the back of the room. One was a dark, plump girl whose dress scarce seemed able to hold her bosom, which danced merrily before them. The other was thinner, blonde and a good deal taller than her companion. Both had bright lipstick, dark-painted eyes and thick pale make-up.

Despite this make-up and their attire, Walter guessed they were little more than seventeen or eighteen.

'Would you fine gentlemen care to buy some drinks?' wheedled the plumper of the two, laying her arms round a welcoming Albert. She announced herself as Sally. The thinner blonde girl, Daisy, perched on the arm of Walter's chair and leaned over him, revealing far less but not for want of trying. She gave Walter a squeeze and nuzzled into his neck, taking him by surprise with her unexpected physical familiarity. Albert was evidently not a newcomer to such advances, and quickly settled into the mood. Walter, though not unaware of such establishments and their reputation, was at first reticent. The blonde whore was obviously used to this response, and encouraged his confidence and ardour. Gin was ordered, and after bringing the drinks the girls settled down at the table in close proximity to their customers. More drinks followed, and as their familiarity increased the conversation became more ribald and the laughter more raucous.

'I think we've got a fine pair of turkeycocks here tonight, Sally,' Daisy began.

'Hope they're more than a turkey's,' Sally replied.

'I'm sure mine is,' her companion replied, plonking herself on Walter's lap and wiggling her behind. 'You can be sure, gentlemen, that we'll give you a real good time tonight.'

'And you as well, you can be sure of that, and with a little present to boot,' added Albert.

'Together with another one that comes by second class post, nine months later,' roared Walter, a little drunk.

'No chance of that, darling,' Daisy countered. 'The gentleman may want to go all the way to Blackpool, but we make him get off at the South Shore.'

'Don't tell me he has to make his own way to the Tower under his own steam,' replied Albert.

'You've got it,' said Sally. 'We can't leave the train standing in the station too long. It's got to pull out sooner rather than later.'

'When it gets the signal, you mean,' laughed Walter.

'Yes, and before it's had the chance to discharge its bloody passengers!' interrupted Albert.

They all roared again with laughter, and in the hilarity

Albert overbalanced his chair, sending Sally tumbling drunkenly on top of him. "Ere, you 'aven't even bought your ticket yet,' she shouted.

Thanks to the alcohol Walter began to enjoy himself. The cavortings of couples around them, encouraged by some suggestive dancing and crude renditions of popular songs, with choruses from the audience, continued. Daisy began kissing Walter passionately, and his member began to respond to her shuffling and wiggling. It began to respond even more as he thought of what the evening might bring.

Together with the other couples, Walter, Albert and the girls slipped on to a small dance floor and proceeded to pull each other round in tight and drunken embraces. Walter felt his partner's bosom pressing into him, and his hands wandered, unhindered, as he gripped his partner tightly in the strange and wanton waltz.

After a hazy, drunken hour, Walter's companion suggested that they might like to end their evening in what she called her 'little love nest'. He agreed, and together they left the saloon, not before Albert had given him a knowing wink. Daisy led her bemused client out into the street. Whether it was the cool, sobering breeze or the underlying feeling of remorse and guilt that drink can sometimes bring, Walter knew not, but as they reached the steps of the temperance hotel his enthusiasm had waned and he was beginning to feel a little uneasy.

The room was dirty and had an odour that was only partially masked by cheap, pungent perfume. The appearance of his companion, whom he now could see in the unforgiving light of the lamp, was not as appealing as it had seemed in the low, warm lights of the saloon. Her features seemed more pronounced and the make-up seemed pale and obvious, no longer covering the physical flaws of her young but brassy face. No sooner had they entered the squalid room than she began to pester him for the money. 'It'll be two shilling if you want a to and fro,' she informed him. Sensing his reluctance, she was determined not to lose her customer. 'Only one and six if you want to try a below job for the first time,' she simpered, and started to kneel in front of him.

Mixed feelings of guilt, memories from his past and physical discomfort now welled up inside Walter. This was not how the first time should be. He rushed past her, almost knocking her over in his bid to escape the abominable room and its equally ghastly inhabitant. In a few seconds he was down the wooden stairs, through the front door and into Brunswick Terrace before the keeper of the house could move from his chair. Walter ran, and did not stop running until he reached the Manchester Road. He spent some time sobering up at a horse trough and arrived back at the shop at about midnight – a much-chastened young man.

In the days that followed he did not dare admit his non-consummation to Albert, but craftily played to his innuendos.

* * *

The lone traveller was on firmer ground now, walking boldly on. The white limestone headland of Humphrey Head was just visible on the distant horizon, jutting out from the northerly foreshore. There was a long way still to go and he knew that there were dangerous tracts still to cross, uncertain sands and treacherous dykes that might make him doubt his judgement and memory. Beneath the bravado and confidence he displayed there still existed the guilt and uncertainty that had filled his life when he had learnt of the real circumstances of his birth all those years before. It had stayed with him until today, as he walked across the bay. At times it had seemed to recede, but it always remained to taunt him from the deep recesses of his mind.

Chapter Eleven

One person had not been in Walter's mind during that trek across the sands. He had deliberately kept Annie out of his thoughts, partly through misgivings about leaving her, despite what had become a near loveless marriage, and partly because he still remembered their chance meeting, their eventual falling in love and the good times they had shared. He did not want these memories to cloud his judgement or weaken his resolution.

* * *

It was on a fine Saturday afternoon that his mother told Walter and her husband that she was going to St John's Church in East Bowling to support their autumn bazaar. Such money-raising occasions, known as 'at homes', fetes, fayres and the like, were common among the poor churches and chapels of northern cities. A social gathering for Christian folk and provider of mutual support, they were also a chance for gossips and mischief-makers to compare, criticise and pass scandal far and wide. As Saturday afternoon had become a quiet time for the drapery and other small businesses in the village, with more and more people making the trip into the city where choice was so much greater and prices were lower, Walter was given time off by Enos, so he was sitting in the parlour.

'Why don't you come with me?' his mother asked. 'It's a long walk for me and Mrs Hobson is poorly so won't be able to come. I'd be glad of the company.'

Walter looked up and smiled. 'Oh well, I suppose I can't let you go over there on your own,' he sighed, with a look of amused resignation.

They set off together, dressed in their Sunday best, along New Cross Street. Since a park had been laid out on the other side of the railway there were numerous short cuts between the two halves of the township, and it was an altogether more pleasant stroll. They duly arrived at the church hall and Harriet busied herself renewing old acquaintances, leaving Walter to trail in her wake. At two o'clock the assembled company was invited into the Sunday School, where there were dreary speeches from the vicar and other notables in anticipation of the official opening by the deputy mayor of Bradford.

Thanks were extended to various helpers, and then the vicar cleared his throat. 'I would like to call upon Miss Annie Ackroyd, who has organised the Young Ladies' Group flower stall, to welcome our distinguished visitor.'

Now, thought Walter to himself, finally roused from his indifference, she's a bit of a bobby-dazzler. The young lady had strawberry blonde hair, pale eyes and elfin good looks. She was of average height and had a trim figure that fitted neatly into a smart, lavender-coloured dress. Her welcoming speech to the large and pompous deputy mayor was eloquent and appropriately brief, and showed a confidence that sprang from obvious intelligence – in stark contrast to the boring monotone of the invited guest, whose speech wandered round all Bradford, congratulating every aspect of the council's work and by implication himself and his self-important colleagues.

Finally there were the longed-for words, 'Hereby in my official capacity I declare this event well and truly open.' It was like the starting gun at the beginning of a road race. A large crowd, mainly women, rose up in a body and moved directly to the hall, jostling, elbowing and discreetly pushing to get to the front of the stalls, most notable of which was the white elephant. That there was no-one hurt in the mêlée was truly a wonder. Walter sidled down the quieter side of the hall. A few children were crowded round a sweet stall stuffing their faces with every possible concoction. Next to it was a pathetic affair, a table half-covered with tools, knick-knacks and miscellaneous unwanted objects. It was served by a couple of earnest, bespectacled young men from the church's young men's group, who had all the selling skills and personality of the stuffed moose that adorned the wall of the Mason's Arms.

Walter was most interested in the Young Ladies' flower stall, not its attractive array of flowers arranged in bunches for the parlour, in posies for ladies and in buttonholes for gentlemen, but its principal organiser. The stall was crowded for a time, so he held back, proffering feigned interest in the remnants of an old toolbox at the adjoining table. Then he spied his chance: the blonde girl was free. He quickly stepped in before anyone else had an opportunity.

'I'd like to purchase a buttonhole,' he said, and gave a warm smile.

'Certainly, sir,' she replied, smiling sweetly in return. 'They're twopence each.' He handed her a threepenny bit. 'Oh dear; we've run out of change. It always happens at the start of these events. I'll have to go and get some.'

'No matter,' Walter remarked. 'I'll pay the extra penny. It's all for a good cause. Mind you, I'll expect the best buttonhole you've got. I'll let you choose it for me.'

'Then it'll be this one,' she said with a smile. 'I made this one up myself, specially.'

She had caught his mood and was playing the same sweet game as he was. He smelt the delicate flowers, then pretended to have difficulty pinning them to his lapel and begged her to help him. She duly obliged, looking up into his eyes as she deftly pinned the buttonhole in place. He caught the scent of her delicate perfume. Up close she looked better than ever. Although she was not a classic beauty, her elfin features, pale but sparkling eyes, high cheekbones, petite nose and thin but sensual lips, crowned with those blonde ringlets, made her stand out above everyone else in the room.

'I've not seen you before,' she said, 'not in the village or when we promenade after church. Are you new to the area or from other parts?'

He ignored her question and replied with one of his own. 'And where do you promenade of a Sunday?' The sweet art of flirtation had never seemed easier, but it was hard to tell who was casting the line and who was taking the bait. Finally she swallowed the hook.

'Most of us promenade to the park, as far as the bandstand,' she admitted. 'And now, young man, I've got other customers waiting.'

Walter was not to be deterred. 'Ah, but I've got another purchase to make. I'll have one of those delightful posies at the back.'

For the first time she looked uncertainly at him. He detected a slight coldness, or doubt. Did she think it was for another girl, or that he was being too bold and was buying it for her? He tried to allay her uncertainty. 'It's for my mother, over there. It was she who persuaded me to come,' he explained.

She heaved a sigh of relief, and he paid the twopence. She smiled again and blushed. As Walter stepped back to let other customers make their purchases he kept his eyes firmly on her for a few seconds. He could see she was flustered, and she made a mistake with the next purchase before apologising and resuming her duties.

As he wandered off, Walter noticed the girl on the adjacent bookstall gave him a hard stare. She had similar features to the pretty blonde but they seemed more austere. Her dark hair was tied back in a bun and she wore a plain black dress. He stopped to look in curiosity at the books and pamphlets, but gave them short shrift: they had titles like *The Demon Drink* and *Mother's Ruin – Society's Ruin*. The banner above announced 'The Band of Hope'.

As he and his mother finally left the room, Walter stopped to look at the notice-board in the corner. A bright poster announced the St John's Church Fellowship Dance on the 14th of October, two weeks hence. A plan began to form in his mind, but as he wandered home on his mother's arm he still did not know how to execute it.

'I hope you didn't find it too boring, Walter,' his mother said, interrupting his thoughts. 'Thank you for the lovely bunch of flowers. You seemed to spend quite a time at the flower stall choosing them for me,' she added in a meaningful tone, and gave a wry smile to herself. 'Thank you for accompanying me today.'

'Oh, it was all right,' Walter murmured nonchalantly as

they reached the door of the draper's shop. 'It's passed the time away.'

Going straight up to his room, he lay on the bed. The delightful flower-seller seemed to appear wherever he looked, on the ceiling, round the walls, even framed in the picture opposite. He couldn't get her out of his mind, and he began to make plans.

Albert, he thought; there's always him around. One person not to tell was his errant cousin. The wrong word or a hint of his thoughts and actions, together with Albert's knack of deliberately spoiling things, might upset everything. Walter resolved to approach Isaac Buttershaw, his long-time friend and like-minded companion. The one-eyed joker had an intelligent sense of decorum and diplomacy, and could be charming, lively and funny, but he was also perceptive and adaptable to the needs of others.

When Walter suggested to Isaac after evening service the next day that instead of walking up Manchester Road they should stroll round Bowling Park, he readily agreed.

'What's up, Walter? Got your eye on someone and you want me to play gooseberry?' Walter said nothing but gave a half-smile. 'I'll bet you haven't mentioned anything about this to Albert,' Isaac laughed. 'She's either a decent lass and you don't want her frightened off, or a good-looker and you don't want him sniffing around.' They gave each other knowing looks. Butty was something of a mindreader, and could see things more clearly with one eye than most can with two. They walked on in silence for a couple of minutes.

'Aye, all right,' he chuckled. 'I'll go along with thee.'

That evening they wandered over the railway, past the almshouses and on to the tree-lined drive that had once been the grand carriageway to the hall but now served as an entrance to the recently built public park. At the end of the drive numerous paths and gravelled walkways branched in all directions. To the left ponds were visible and further away a series of steps led up to an elaborate water fountain. Only a few couples and small groups wandered around this informal part of the leisure grounds: it was a cool autumn and the nights were beginning to draw in. Walter immediately took the path ahead, which led over a small knoll and ended at the bandstand. Behind this imposing feature were flowerbeds set around an oval lawn. The last autumn roses made it an attractive setting even so late in the year.

They had no sooner settled themselves down on the bandstand steps when they spied a group of four young ladies making their way towards them, oblivious of the pair. As they passed, Walter stood up and raised his hat. 'Why, Miss Ackroyd, fancy meeting you here!' he said with feigned surprise.

'And you, young man, still sporting my buttonhole, I see,' said Annie in the same manner.

'That's because it was a very special one, hand-picked and definitely the best one on show.'

'Aren't you going to introduce yourself and your friend? I can't keep on calling you the young man with the buttonhole.'

Walter obliged, and she introduced her sister (the prim girl from the Band of Hope, as he had already guessed) and two other friends from the church group. Her sister had obviously not been party to the 'surprise meeting', and gave him the same hard stare he had received in the church hall. Isaac played his part to the letter, full of charm and polite, witty conversation, diverting the attention of the other three girls to give Walter an open field with the receptive Annie. Even her sister, Nancy, warmed to the affable Isaac. She showed great sympathy and concern when she heard how he had lost his eye in that unfortunate accident so many years before.

'Ah well,' he sighed, 'it does leave me with one terrible disadvantage.'

'What's that?' asked Nancy.

'It means,' he said dramatically, 'that I can only wink at lasses with one eye.' He gave them a demonstration, which brought fits of giggles from the other two.

As the girls turned for home Walter suggested that he and Isaac should accompany them, as it was getting dark. Annie craftily engineered a route that would drop off the other two girls first, leaving herself and her sister alone with the two young men. Nancy was charmed by the gallant Isaac and began telling him of her work in the church and the Band of Hope and the perils and evils of the demon drink. Isaac dutifully pretended to be interested. Meanwhile Annie and Walter fell behind.

'I was wondering,' Walter asked, 'if you would like to accompany me to St John's Fellowship Dance?'

'Oh dear! A young man from our church asked me more than a fortnight ago.' Walter's heart sank. She left him in a state of abject disappointment for a few moments before continuing. 'But as I've not given him an answer yet, I suppose I'll have to tell him I've made other arrangements.' She smiled. It was not a nice smile but a wicked, teasing smirk. Walter smiled back and shook his head: for once he had met his match.

After they had left the girls, Isaac turned to Walter and said, 'Oh, if only Annie had a twin sister! I'll do anything for you, Walt, you know that, but don't try to pair me off with that holy horror!'

* * *

For Walter the dance was a great success. He and Annie talked and danced all night. Only Nancy spoilt the evening by hanging around from start to finish like an over-protective chaperone. When Walter gave Isaac's excuses she seemed hurt and resentful, but Annie softened her mood by suggesting that Walter might ask him to join them in helping with the Christmas concert. The Young Ladies' Group drama was going well (under the dynamic leadership of Annie herself – although she would never admit this), and the Band of Hope choir had made a promising start under the direction of its demanding and able pianist and conductor (who else but the formidable Nancy?), but the Young Men's Group's attempt to create an entertaining revue was heading for disaster.

Walter readily agreed, and after much persuasion Isaac promised to lend a hand, provided he was kept well away from the earnest attentions of Annie's older sister. Not averse to producing or performing, Isaac had worked with Walter on entertainments when they were both at Sunday School; indeed, had he not suffered his unfortunate accident, he could have made a career on the stage, Walter thought.

The St John's Young Men's Association was as dull as could be. It consisted of half a dozen witless individuals, two of whom Walter had seen behind the stall two weeks before: to call them as spineless as jellyfish would have been an insult to jellyfish, in his opinion. They had no idea how to put on a light-hearted show, and the organising committee was rudderless. Eventually Isaac and Walter, who so far had kept low profiles, could stand it no longer and offered to write material and give guidance for its performance. The jellyfish clutched at their suggestion with relief.

For the next few nights the two friends busily reworked sketches they had seen on the music halls and in pub entertainment, but toned them down for their new audience. Also included was some original material, mainly from Walter's fertile imagination. The items included a funny monologue, a poem in local dialect and a witty song, which the other members could perform without too much difficulty. The two producers performed a series of fast-moving sketches and jokes, interspersed among the other acts, to keep the show running at a good pace.

The Christmas concert was duly performed on the 15th of December in a packed church hall. The Band of Hope choir opened the proceedings, and Annie's short play was competently performed by the young ladies of the church under her careful direction; but it was she who stood out in the leading role. Like her sister's effort, it received rapturous applause. It was the revue that the audience liked best, however. The young men from the church group rose to the occasion and performed their pieces word-perfectly, but it was the two comedians who stole the show. Everyone agreed that the highlight was a sketch in which a temperance speaker was harangued by a drunken bystander: Isaac knew it would not go down well with Nancy, and secretly hoped it would put some distance between them. He played the part of the preacher with more than a passing resemblance to the bumbling and witless vicar of St John's, much to the delight of his congregation and the vicar himself, who was too stupid to realise that he was being parodied. Another piece was a traditional music hall act, in which Walter and Isaac dressed as mill-women and mouthed jokes and patter across the stage. These included old chestnuts such as, 'My husband's very good. He does the washin' up when I ask him and dries up when told to.'

Local references were included as well, including one to Bowling's rag and bone man's elderly and doddering horse. 'I've just seen t'rag 'n' bone man's 'oss Lightning go down t'street.'

'Why dost thee call 'im Lightnin'? He's slowest 'oss fer miles around.'

'Ah, but thee hasn't seen him when he goes past t'knacker's yard.'

They ended the show with the old joke of the man collecting horse manure in the street. A schoolboy, brilliantly played by Isaac, asked the old man, 'Hey, mister, what's thee doing with that 'oss muck?'

'It's to put on my rhubarb, sonny.'

'That's funny,' concluded the boy. 'We put custard on ours!'

The rafters of St John's Church Hall rang long and loud with the cheers and shouts of the audience. At the end of the evening the stars took their bows and Annie cast a sideways glance at Walter – a look that spoke of admiration but was also that of the maiden in distress who sees a knight on a white charger approaching. For Walter it seemed that a new and better part of his life had begun. Successful in the eyes of many, and perhaps beginning to fall in love, he felt that nothing could now go wrong. Remembering the episode long afterwards, he realised how wrong he could be.

* * *

With no one to see him, the music hall artiste performed his repertoire one last time to the sands, sky and distant hills. This time there was no rapturous applause. The audience of gulls and terns wheeled above him, shrieking their displeasure. They had no interest in his performance: he had disturbed their feeding and they were none too pleased.

Chapter Twelve

As Walter strode on across the flat featureless landscape he whistled the song 'Meet me Gwen in Shipley Glen' to the seagulls and the open skies. He remembered the lyrics of the number that was popular in the music halls of Bradford, and also the more ribald version that he had heard in the Brunswick Saloon, and smiled. In the latter a lot more happened to Gwen than a kiss and cuddle in the woods or under the shelter of Nine Rock.

* * *

The Glen was a beautiful spot indeed, nestling on the edge of Baildon Moor – a steep wooded valley that rose from the River Aire and ended by the ancient circle of Bracken Rocks. So popular had it become at Whitsuntide and summer weekends that many refreshment kiosks and diversions had sprung up, all the way from the hotel at the bottom to the top of the valley path. When Walter was in his twenties it was a favourite outing for working folk and various stalls abounded, but people came principally for the fine views and exercise in the pleasant surroundings. On that memorable day in 1887 it still felt like a park, rather than the funfair it became later, despite the cable tramway that was being built to take crowds up the lower slopes.

Forgoing the Whitsuntide walks and processions, the gang had agreed to make the Glen their destination and had arrived early. The pleasure ground had a strong temperance influence especially on religious holidays, and was often the culmination of a march or rally. On this occasion Annie had been cajoled by her enthusiastic sister Nancy into the Band of Hope contingent. Any hope that Walter might join them had been dashed by a hurried excuse that he had an earlier engagement: if anyone he knew had seen him marching under a banner that declared 'Beer is Best – Left Alone!' he would have been a laughing stock for months – and if one of the marchers had seen him going into or out of any of the watering holes that he and his friends frequented and had told Annie, or even worse her evangelical sister, it might have nipped a promising romance firmly in the bud.

Arby, Tom, Sam, Albert, Isaac and Walter spent a little time among the stalls and cabins on the lower reaches and soon scrambled up to a clearing that afforded a commanding view of the Glen. From there they individually explored the surrounding area or made further progress to the top to view Nine Rock, Sentinel Rock and the Bracken Stones. They returned for a picnic of ham sandwiches, eggs and ginger beer that they had purchased earlier from the Glen Hotel, and the meal was interspersed with horseplay and joking as usual.

'Do any of thee remember t'firm that used to sell lemonade, ginger beer and the like from that horse and cart?' piped up Sam Varley. They all knew the joke that was coming.

'Aye, it were Thompson and Pearson's,' answered Albert.

'Well, you all know what folks say,' went on Sam, labouring the punch line.

'Aye,' broke in Albert. 'Drink T and P lemonade!'

They settled down after their picnic to enjoy the warm sunshine, and to keep an eye on any girls who walked past. Walter, however, decided to move on.

'What's up with thee?' asked Albert. 'Has thee got tired of our company?'

'Thee'll miss any lasses that come up this way,' said Tom. 'This place is a good place to spot them, and a good bit o' chat and snicking won't come amiss today.'

'Nay,' Albert butted in. 'Yon Miss Ackroyd's got him right

under her thumb, or he's too smitten to even look at another lass.'

'I reckon she's coming along here after all her marching and banner waving,' laughed Sam. 'They're going to have a secret rendezvous deep in the woods.'

'If you must know,' explained a smiling Walter, 'I'm going to have a look at the new camera obscura. They say it's amazing what you can see from it. Is anyone else coming?'

This was met with cat-calls and the inevitable comment of 'old clever clogs', but Isaac decided to join him and they set off up the path. They followed the signs to a point near Sentinel Rock. The camera obscura was on a platform of land that jutted out over the whole valley: brush and scrub had been cleared and the site had been levelled to provide a flat base for the small building that housed the instrument. Walter was intrigued by the small mirror mounted on a spike above the black octagonal shed and wondered if it might be the key to this unusual device.

A small, fussy, bald man was standing outside the door next to a sign that read 'Obadiah Jennings's Camera Obscura – The Scientific Wonder of the Age'. He was taking money from the few customers who had ventured up the steep path. 'That'll be threepence each, young gentlemen,' he announced, giving them each a small roughly printed blue ticket in exchange for their admission fee. 'I'm so glad you've come to see this wonderful diversion, gentlemen. I'm sure you'll be fascinated by the views it affords. You'll see Shipley Glen in a totally different light.' He laughed heartily at his joke, although he must have told it ten times already that day.

Walter and Isaac smiled weakly and entered through a narrow door. In the gloom they could make out the features of another half-dozen souls whose curiosity had led them this far.

After a few minutes' wait the proprietor came into the hut. 'The programme will begin in one minute.' He adjusted the apparatus and turned to the small crowd. 'Ladies and gentlemen, for the camera obscura to work perfectly we must be in total, I mean total, darkness. This means you will not be able to move around once the door is shut and the curtain drawn. Please ensure you have a clear sight of the viewing table. Children should be allowed to the front and taller gentlemen should stand at the back.' The fact that there were only eight customers and each one had an excellent view was of no consequence: he had his little speech to make and no circumstance would allow any variation to the rigid routine. 'I will now close the door and curtains and you will be plunged into darkness,' he announced, with the drama of a Shakespearian actor. The door shut with a bang. They heard curtain rings squeaking along a rusty rail. What he had said was true. You could not see a hand in front of your face. 'And now,' he proclaimed, 'nature's scientific wonder, the camera obscura!'

He pulled a lever, and the table was covered in a milky light. As their eyes grew accustomed to the surroundings, the audience could see it was a picture of Shipley Glen, not a photograph but a moving picture that showed people walking and climbing and children playing in the glades and on grassy banks. A collective 'ooh' went up. Walter was impressed. It was like the largest telescope you could imagine, but showing a clear image over three feet wide from over a mile away.

'With this amazing instrument', continued the showman, 'we can see not only one view but many scenes in this area, and the pleasures and entertainments it affords.'

He cranked a handle and the contraption panned round to show the switchback railway at the bottom of the valley. A little red train crowded with children and their parents was chugging up the line. He cranked the handle again and the scene changed again. The picture was blurred, but the little man turned a wheel above him and it came back into focus to show the Aire Valley with the model village and factories at Saltaire, looking indeed like models on the table before them. Another adjustment and the Glen Hotel came into view, with the food cabins, stalls and amusements all around. The view moved on, and they could see the half-completed towers that would become the new cable ride in the following season.

As they came round the valley the focus became shorter and the details clearer. The camera stopped, alighting on groups picnicking or playing. It lingered a while on a young couple holding hands and then briefly on another pair well away from the others, lying in the long grass and kissing passionately, oblivious of the power of the remarkable camera obscura. Stationary for a few seconds it then whizzed away, like a peeping Tom caught in the act. 'I'm afraid discretion and decency dictate we must quickly move on,' the showman announced – a well-rehearsed ploy that Walter guessed he used often. It brought laughter from the audience and giggles from a couple of lads at the front.

The camera moved round. Before it finished its three hundred and sixty degree journey the little man had one more trick up his sleeve. It finally rested on the refreshment kiosk halfway up the valley which, on this warm day, was doing a roaring trade in ice-cream. The maestro gave one more adjustment to the focus wheel, and to the amazement of the group they could see faces at the kiosk in great detail, though they must have been nearly half a mile away. The wily operator picked on a fat young man holding a child and attempting to eat an ice-cream. His invisible audience roared with laughter.

Except Walter, that is. He immediately recognised the face: it was Joseph Lumb, accompanied by an equally plump wife with a babe in arms. Nearby were Mr and Mrs Lumb senior, older now but clearly recognisable. Walter's heart skipped a beat. Was there any chance that Emily would be with them? He stared hard at the picture. Yes, behind them, in a queue at the kiosk, was the tall, unmistakable figure he knew, her jet-black hair and elegant neck clearly recognisable, although he could only see her profile. She was with a small brown-haired woman; no young man accompanied her. Walter felt a strange, uncertain mixture of feelings, among which was the desire to look, just look, at the most beautiful girl he had ever known.

The show finished, and Walter, having edged to the back, was out of the door first, forgetting all manners and conventions. He half-walked, half-ran down the path with Isaac in his wake. 'Come on, Butty, hurry up!' he shouted. They reached the others, who had finished their picnic and were strolling slowly down the glen.

'Why the hurry?' asked Albert, seeing Walter's headlong rush down the path.

'Caught sight of Lumpy,' Walter shouted. 'He's got a fat missus and two kids in tow. If we hurry we might catch him before he gets into the crowds at the bottom. It'll be nice to see him after all this time.'

The rest joined the rush down – but Albert didn't entirely believe Walter's story. When they reached the kiosk they found

Joseph easily among the mass of people thanks to his colossal girth and frame. The gang crowded round him, but Walter took no notice of his former friend and pushed further into the crowd, where he caught sight of Emily, as tall, dark and elegant as ever. She had her back to him and was talking to the girl he had seen in the camera.

For a second he choked, then blurted out, 'Emily, Emily Lumb, fancy meeting you here!'

She turned to face him, her eyes as dark and sparkling as they ever were and warm to his greeting, and she smiled. But it was a different smile, not the full red lips he remembered, but a swollen, distorted mouth covered by ulcers and blemishes.

'Why, Walter,' she called in the same confident manner he always remembered, 'how grand to see you after all these years. My, what a fine bloke you are!'

Walter gulped. 'It's lovely to see *you*,' he replied quietly.

For a few seconds they stood there among the crowd, not knowing what to say. Something in Walter stirred: whether it was bravery or hidden nobility he did not know. Going up to her, he kissed her boldly and slowly on the cheek – and became aware of a damp tear transferring to his face. He did not care that some in the crowd were staring at them. Eventually Emily took his hand and led him away to a half-hidden spot behind some trees.

'I can't say how sorry . . .' he began.

'Then don't,' she interrupted. 'What's done is done. There's no need to wonder about it or ask why.' She paused for a few moments, trying to find the right words. 'It's a canker,' she explained. 'I found out a month ago I'd got it, in my mouth 'n' throat. A few girls get it in t'mill. Most spend their whole lives there and don't catch it.' She wiped another tear away and faced him confidently, but he could tell it was bad enough to have affected her speech slightly, for not all her words were clear. 'They say you get it from kissing t'shuttle, when we use our mouth and teeth to thread it through. They reckon you get it from t'oil they use on t'machines. It affects blokes worse, them that looks after t'looms 'n' spinning frames.' She moved nearer to him and rested her hands on his shoulders. 'Just think,' she said softly, 'I could have had my pick of any lad in Bowling. Now I can't have any, and in a year or less I won't need any.' Emily bowed her head and quietly cried for a few seconds, then looked him straight in the eyes again. She spoke softly and warmly. 'I always knew you carried a torch for me, Walter Clough, and I know I've made a right fool of myself. You were t'finest lad around and you'll make something of your life. I should have set my cap for you and no one else. Just think, I'd be a fine young lady working in a shop, not one of God's hideous creatures.'

They stood staring at each other, wondering what to say, and both imagining what might have been.

Eventually, with tears running down her cheeks, she whispered quietly, 'Goodbye, Walter. I'll never forget thee. Don't thee ever forget me.'

She moved close. Walter shut his eyes and imagined the face of years before, unblemished, perfect in its beauty. She kissed him full on the lips. Oh how he remembered that kiss: even a dozen years later he remembered it was the sweetest kiss he'd ever known, and he wished it would go on for ever. He bent down to nuzzle his face into her neck, but she quickly detached herself and was gone.

Walter wandered slowly down the hill and joined the others, who were in a cheerful, rowdy mood having swapped tales and memories with the indomitable Lumpy. For them it had been a good day and a jolly laugh. They caught the horse tram into Bradford and started the long walk up the hill, on the last stage of their journey home. Walter tried to hide his intense sorrow by joining in the banter and merriment that he knew would last all the way along Manchester Road, but Isaac could see something was troubling him.

As they recounted the events of the day the conversation turned to Emily Lumb, and Arby passed comment on her appearance. It stung Walter to the core and Isaac, sensing his friend's unease, tried to pour oil on the troubled waters.

'Poor lass,' he sighed. 'She got that from working in the mill. It's when they suck the thread through. They call it kissing the shuttle.'

Albert, ignoring the feelings of those around him, thought of a joke. Regardless of the consequences he was determined to tell it. 'Ah reckons with a face like that she must have caught summat kissing t'overlooker's shuttle.'

For once no one laughed. Albert did not even see the blow

coming. Walter had never hit anything or anyone that hard: he could not say where his strength came from. His fist caught Albert square in the face, smashing his nose and sending him spinning to the ground. Walter walked off, his face turned away from the rest to hide his tears. He did not see the others raising the dazed Albert to his feet and wiping away the copious blood. This had been the worst day of his life. He had been devastated by his meeting with Emily and now he had lost his friendship with Albert, but with regard to the latter he had little care.

For a week Walter waited. He was expecting some enquiry from his mother or some reproach from Enos regarding the assault on his beloved nephew, but none came. He feigned illness over the weekend as he was too confused and distraught to want to see Annie. At last he managed to send her a letter, and received a charming and beautiful reply in her elegant hand. It made him feel even worse. At last his lonely weekend was interrupted, by a visit from, of all people, his cousin – who was still in a sorry state: his nose was misshapen and he carried bruises on both cheeks. Having claimed he had got into a fight with a youth from Shipley, Albert had not breathed a word of Walter's involvement. Enos told him that if he got hold of the ruffian who had perpetrated such damage he wouldn't walk for a month. The irony of his comment was not lost on the two young men.

'Ah wonder if you'd like to go a walk over t'railway this afternoon?' Albert enquired. 'A good walk in t'fresh air will do us both a bit o' good.' He seemed quiet and contrite, not the Albert that Walter had known before. The two walked along in silence for a while. Finally Albert spoke. 'What I said weren't right, ah knows that. It were rotten through and through. I don't blame you, Walt, but ah can't understand you. I know you really liked her. We all fancied her. She were t' best lass in Bowling, there's no doubt.' Walter tried to butt in but Albert was determined to say what he wanted to say. 'Why, Walt?' he implored. 'Why carry a torch for her all these years? You've got a lass, a real classy one, good-looking and plenty of style, not from t'mill but one that'll suit thee right. Why lose it all over a memory from long ago?'

Walter could stand it no longer. He stopped in the middle of the lane and faced his lifelong friend. For a second Albert drew back, fearing a repeat dose of the medicine he had received a week before. But Walter's hands were deep in his pockets and his voice was soft, not angry. 'It's not that, Albert,' he began, 'it's not that at all. They were poor, Emily's family, not two ha'pennies to rub together, tatty clothes, rotten jobs, but she had one thing, her beauty. It was her one great virtue and she wore it like a queen, with dignity and style.' His voice rose to anger at the skies above, the trees around and especially the city laid out below them in the far distance. 'This life in Bradford, it's taken it away from her. It was all she had, and this bloody life has robbed her of it. I'm sick of this existence, aren't you?'

Albert stood perplexed, unable to understand or answer his cousin. Walter took a deep breath and relaxed once more, placing a hand onto the shoulder of his lifelong friend. Slowly they wandered back into the village, determined to drown their sorrow and anger in the bar of the nearest pub. As they reached the door Walter stopped and gave his final parting shot on the matter to Albert, the street and the whole of Bradford. 'You know, there must be something better out there, and I'm going to bloody well find it.'

* * *

But Walter hadn't found it, or if he had it had slipped from his grasp. The walker thought that perhaps he had a chance to discover it at the end of his journey. Perhaps it might eventually mean a happier and better life in a place far away, one like this, with wide-open spaces, clean fresh air and the wonders of nature all around.

Far out in the bay, where he guessed the main Kent channel lay, a small group of people were gathered, crowded together, intent on their activity – cocklers perhaps or even cocklers' children. Even at this distance they seemed small for adults . . . The largest of them flapped its wings and rose up into the sky. The other cormorants, having finished their dipping for flounders, followed him. He had been deceived again.

Chapter Thirteen

Walter recalled some words from Shakespeare that he had learnt at classes at the Institute. He always found solace in England's greatest poet. Turning to the distant Lakeland hills, he recited the verse, 'When sorrows come, they come not in single spies but in battalions.'

* * *

And they did. Two weeks after the visit to Shipley Glen he tried to re-establish contact with Annie but received no reply. Surprised, and not a little bewildered, he took the now-familiar walk over the railway and across the park to her house on Wakefield Road. It was a much grander house than the draper's shop, double-fronted with stone steps leading up to a large door, with exquisitely coloured tiles patterned in a large mosaic in the recess on either side. Annie's father, some years deceased, had been a successful butter and cheese factor, supplying some of the best shops in Bradford. The house spoke eloquently of his relative wealth.

The door was opened by Nancy, and for the first time for months he received the frozen stare she had given when he first became acquainted with her. 'I'll see if my sister wants to speak to you,' she said coldly, and closed the door abruptly, leaving him perplexed on the step. A couple of minutes later Annie appeared at the door, her eyes red with crying and her face set in a frown.

'I must speak to you,' he implored. 'I don't know what's wrong. How have I offended you? Please tell me.'

Annie's expression turned briefly from anger and sadness to puzzlement. 'If you wish, we'll take a walk to the park.' She vanished into the house, and he heard the sound of raised voices: Annie's mother and, more stridently, Nancy, who came with Annie to the door. Her cold, hard stare had become a look of pure venom.

The busy Wakefield Road and its surroundings were no place to start a conversation. Annie stared straight ahead, and Walter's sidelong glances were steadfastly ignored. They must have looked an odd couple to any passer-by. Finally they reached the park, and found a quiet sheltered spot that looked out over one of the ponds. They sat down on a bench, and Annie placed distance between herself and Walter. Seeing her mood, he did not try to move any closer to her.

After a while she spoke. 'Oh, Walter, how could you? I thought you were different from so other men; that you were honest.'

'But I am, my dearest Annie,' he protested.

'You were seen at Shipley Glen,' she interrupted, 'kissing that tall, dark-haired girl.' His face red with embarrassment, Walter nodded his head. The truth was beginning to dawn. 'Sarah Waterhouse from the Band of Hope went on with her family to the Glen in the afternoon,' Annie continued. 'She recognised you immediately from the concert and told Nancy. She's a good sister and would never want me hurt. It was the hardest thing for her to tell me about it. Can you deny it happened?'

Walter could have made a sarcastic comment about Nancy and her jealousy, but now was not the time. 'Yes, it's true I kissed her,' he began, and, brooking no interruption, went on to tell her every detail of the meeting, of his life and love before.

She listened in silence, then said, 'But you kissed her on the lips passionately. Sarah Waterhouse watched you.' Walter would gladly have wrung the neck of the nosy, interfering Miss Waterhouse.

'No, Annie,' he insisted, '*she* kissed me, and if Nancy's little friend had told the *whole* truth she would have said that the dark-haired girl walked away, leaving me on my own. It was a goodbye kiss, Annie. The next time I see Emily Lumb will be at her funeral.' His voice became a hoarse and emotional whisper. 'But you can't stop me remembering her. I loved her once. It was a kind of puppy love and it's taken all these years to find out she felt something for me. That's over now, but I'll never forget her. She was a fine lass, the most beautiful girl I've ever seen, with a fine spirit that lifted her out of her wretched surroundings. I rather think you would have liked her too, even though she worked at the mill.'

Tears welled in both pairs of eyes but for different reasons. They sat in silence.

At length Annie spoke. 'Oh, I don't know what to think, Walter. Everything seems so true, yet . . . I've been hurt before by someone who could weave fine words like you. I heard this, and then you didn't want to see me for so long. What was I to think?'

'If there was one untruth it was that I was ill,' began Walter, 'but I couldn't face you in the state I was in. You would have known something was wrong. The rest is God's honest truth, I swear to you.'

She rose from the bench and he started to move, but as he raised his hand to take hers she abruptly declined it. 'No. I'll make my own way home. You must give me time to think. I'll write to you when I'm ready.'

Annie slowly walked away, leaving Walter standing alone in the park and as desolate as he had ever been. He wandered back home, and for three days he waited. There was nothing.

Even Albert noticed Walter's despair on Friday in the Mason's Arms and enquired sympathetically. Walter drew him aside and emptied his soul to his cousin. None of the gang realised the grand irony of it all: Albert, the listener and confidant you turned to when life was at rock bottom!

For two more days Walter heard nothing, and was tempted to cross the park and to see Annie for what could be the last time. He had lost all hope of winning her back and his mood was of gloom and desolation. His mother realised something was wrong and guessed the source of his trouble, but polite enquiries were met with equally polite rebuttals and silence. Enos trod carefully, not wanting an argument with his stepson while he was in this sombre, tetchy mood. Then out of the blue a letter arrived. Walter could tell from the perfume and the style of the envelope that it was from Annie. He left it beside his bed all day, fearing to open it lest it contained the final *coup de grâce*. That evening, after tea, he ventured upstairs and lay there staring at the envelope for a full half-hour. With trembling hand he opened it, and read the contents.

My dearest, dearest Walter, How can I be so wrong about you. Please forgive me for the hurt I have done you. I realise now what a noble spirit shines in your heart. It sometimes takes another to point this out and clear away the poison and doubt that cloud a mind and deceive a heart. I cannot wait until I see you again, my darling . . . Your loving Annie.

It was as if a massive weight had been removed from Walter's mind and body. He was both elated and shocked by the frankness and openness of the letter, yet mystified by the oblique reference to a third party. He rushed out of the house, realised it was raining heavily, popped back in for his coat and umbrella, then ran at full pelt down the streets and through the park to Annie's house. She must have spied him from the window above, for there was a clatter of feet on the stairs, a stern warning to Nancy to go back in the parlour and the frantic turning of a door handle. The door was flung open wide and a tearful but happy face stared into his eyes.

'What took you so long?' Annie implored. 'I feared you weren't coming.'

'I was so scared what your letter might say that I dared not open it.'

Despite the rain they hurried out, this time huddled close together under an umbrella. Reaching a bench in the park, well sheltered under the heavy leaved trees of an early summer, they sat down close together. There was not another foolish soul to be seen in the pouring rain. Walter did not need to make a move, for the demure, self-controlled Annie lost all inhibition and embraced him in a long and intense kiss. Eventually approaching footsteps called a halt to the proceedings, and they resumed more normal communication.

'I couldn't believe it when I read the letter,' he began, 'but why did you suddenly realise what really happened?'

'And do you know who to thank for pointing out the truth, which should have been as plain as the nose on your lovely, funny face?' she asked.

Annie was teasing him again, as always. He was going to have to think this one out for himself. Suddenly the penny dropped. 'Not Albert!' he gasped. She slowly nodded. 'But you hate him,' he protested. 'You think he's the devil incarnate.'

'I've been wrong about that too,' she admitted. 'I'll never get taken in by that lecherous, handsome snake. He'll always be trouble for you, Walter, he can't help himself. But he has a deep regard for you and your feelings when he stops and thinks. It must have been that right hook to the jaw you gave him!' She laughed as she tried to imagine the scene. He had never dared to mention his actions that night on the road home to Bowling, but here she was imagining the fight, and enjoying it. 'He knew you'd stuck by him through thick and thin,' she explained, 'despite all the rotten tricks he'd played, and he didn't want to lose your friendship. Amid all the wicked things in his wild, wanton life, it's the one thing that's precious to him.'

Walter sat open-mouthed and silent. The thought of his madcap, lascivious cousin baring his soul in a kind of religious confession to the girl *he* loved did not bear thinking about. He had known from early on that Annie despised Albert. She had told him that Albert had attempted to steal her shortly after they had started walking out. Turning up one evening in the park, attracted by her good looks, he had flirted with her behind Walter's back; but she saw through him immediately and gave him short shrift.

Annie stood up and turned to Walter, carefully relating the events of the past days. When Albert had turned up on her doorstep two days earlier her first inclination had been to boot him out without any due ceremony. But there was something strange in his demeanour, an earnest innocence she had never seen before. She was intrigued but, playing it safe, had insisted that he speak to her with Nancy present. Albert had baulked at this, knowing the delicacy of the situation, but was eventually obliged to follow her wishes. In the end he had made a good fist of being the honest broker, and had been straightforward in everything he had said about Walter, Emily and himself. When he had described his cousin's kiss on the poor girl's distorted face even Nancy was moved to tears. Annie saw at last that Walter's actions were truly noble, and not inspired by lustful desire.

When Annie finished her account she sat down again on the bench, resisted Walter's attempts to kiss her and looked at him intently. 'Don't think I approve of your cousin,' she explained in an earnest tone, 'I feel that what was once a roguish mischief has turned into a life of depravity. But in everyone God has planted a seed of goodness, and on occasion even the most wretched sinner can follow a virtuous path.' She finished her sermon, and her expression lightened into a mischievous rebuke. 'And don't think, Walter Clough,' she warned, 'that I don't know you go out drinking and carousing with your friends. They're not all that bad, I know that. Anyway, that's what my Uncle Sam who runs the Mason's says. I imagine that's a part of you I'll have to live with. Maybe,' she said slowly, 'it's something a good wife can change.'

Walter was totally thunderstruck. She smiled a little smile. The die was cast and he hadn't had a chance to say a word. For the first time in years he was tongue-tied and embarrassed. He finally blurted out the words, 'Darling Annie, will you . . . will you m . . .'

He hadn't even time to finish speaking before the diminutive, impetuous girl had grabbed him in a tight embrace, from which he couldn't and didn't want to break free. As he came up for air he heard the words, 'Of course I will, you silly man, I thought you'd never ask.'

* * *

A broad smile crossed the face of the lone walker. The sun broke through a small, threatening cloud and bathed the whole scene in a warm light that reflected in the pools and surface of the sodden sands. It cheered him, as did the memories of those happy months when he was young and in love, and when that love was so warmly returned.

Chapter Fourteen

To tell the truth, if those wonderful times before and after Walter's wedding had continued throughout his married life then he would not have been in the dilemma he was eleven years later, as he crossed Morecambe Bay. He brought to mind again those hectic but happy months, when everything seemed to go so smoothly, from his stuttering proposal, through the preparations for the wedding, to the ceremony, honeymoon and their return home. It was an exciting yet tense period, with every potential pitfall surmounted and each piece of a complicated jigsaw falling into place.

***

Walter's first task was to ask formally for Annie's hand in marriage. As her father had died some ten years earlier it was agreed that giving permission should fall on the shoulders of her Uncle Sam. Her two brothers, James and Victor, who ran the family business, were too young in status for this role, only a few years older than Walter himself. It was with some trepidation that Walter approached Sam, but he need not have worried. Mrs Ackroyd, having seen his help for and performance at the concert, approved of the match, while Nancy was now an enthusiastic supporter and Annie could twist her uncle round her little finger. Sam knew Walter, and recognised that just because a high-spirited young man goes out for a few drinks it does not preclude him from being of good character. He might have baulked had the prospect been Albert or Arby, but he recognised that young men like Walter, or indeed Isaac, were of a different mettle and more than suitable for his niece.

'Well now, young Walter, I hear of you wanting to marry our Annie,' he began in a serious voice, with a twinkle in his eye.

'Yes, sir,' the suitor answered politely.

'And what's this I hear about you going out some nights drinking with your mates and getting a bit noisy and boisterous?' he enquired.

'I'll obviously have to moderate my nights out when I'm a responsible married man,' Walter replied in a serious tone. 'My first duty will be to my future wife and any family we might have.'

Sam roared with laughter. 'Well, not too bloomin' much, Walter! Else what'll happen to my bar profits? Anyway, I heartily approve, young man. You may marry her with my blessing. But watch her, mind you. She's a cute girl that one. She'll have you tied up in knots before a few months is out, I know that for a fact.'

Walter relaxed and shook Sam's hand warmly. He jokingly admitted that he was already in such a state. How he would have liked Sam as a father-in-law or even as a father! He was a jolly, affable man, but nobody's fool.

Walter had some apprehension in breaking the news to his parents. This was not at all on his mother's account, as he was certain she would readily approve of his bride-to-be, but he was troubled by how Annie would view his stepfather and how Enos himself would react. He did not take kindly to change of any sort, and change there would be. For a start there was no way in which he and Annie could live over the shop: the house was too cramped as it was. Walter's moving out would cause some inconvenience for the awkward, obstinate draper: he had to take things a lot slower these days and expected his stepson to be up early to do those daily chores and jobs that he now found too onerous but were necessary before the shop could open each morning. This was especially true when he had been out the night before, to one of the local pubs or an Oddfellows' meeting:

on such occasions he might not surface until midday. If Walter lived elsewhere he could no longer be relied upon to complete these tasks each morning.

In terms of space, Wakefield Road seemed a much more viable alternative, indeed almost an ideal lodging, before the young couple eventually moved into their own accommodation. The house had been more than adequate for a family of six, and could have accommodated more. It now had two bedrooms unused, and as it had two reception rooms it would permit the newly married couple some privacy, should they wish to discuss their own affairs or seek each other's company of an evening.

Walter took Annie to tea at his own house a fortnight after their engagement. Enos was cool, and mostly polite and restrained in his conversation – although he did let slip the comment, 'Thee's a good-lookin' lass to be sure, but there's no doubt a couple o' good Sunday dinners would make thee a right bonny one an' all!'

Harriet tut-tutted and Annie blushed slightly, but laughed the remark off. There was no awkwardness in regard to her relationship with Harriet. It was obvious from the start that the two would become firm friends. When Enos had absented himself the three of them sat down in the parlour to take tea.

'You know, Mrs Clough,' Annie began, 'I've seen you a few times round our church at sales, recitals and the like, yet you go to St Stephen's here in West Bowling.'

'Well, as you know, my friend Mrs Hobson is a member of your church, even though she now lives on Old Lane, and so I often go with her. I like to get around and visit other places and meet new people from time to time. Mind you, it was a lucky coincidence that she was away three weeks at her sister's in Halifax and I got Walter to accompany me to your summer fayre, or you would never have met.'

Realisation dawned on Walter's face. 'Mother!' he butted in, 'you told me she was suddenly taken poorly and there was no one else to accompany you.'

'Well,' she continued, 'I'm sure the good Lord doesn't mind an occasional little lie, particularly if it's in a good cause. If I'd asked you a fortnight beforehand you'd have found a ready excuse to get out of it.'

A broad smile spread across Annie's face. 'Why did you

particularly want him to come over to our summer fayre, Mrs Clough?'

'Please call me Harriet,' his mother begged. 'I feel we're becoming such good friends, much more than mother and daughter-in-law.' She was teasing them both. Annie recognised not just her wit and imagination but also the sense of humour and deep mischievous streak that had attracted her to Harriet's son. 'You know, Annie, I've introduced him to lots of respectable young ladies from our church, had them round for tea, contrived to get him involved with them in work for the church and he never showed a ha'porth of interest. Not that I blame him. On the whole they're a dull lot, hardly an ounce of wit and imagination between them. And those that show a bit of life aren't exactly the prettiest girls you'd ever see. But when I saw the young ladies over at St John's . . . they're a different bunch indeed. Real sparkle, brains and common sense, and the personality and good looks to match.'

Walter blushed. He could not believe it. He knew Annie possessed her full share of feminine wiles and subterfuge, but had never suspected his mother could be devious and astute enough to manipulate him in such a manner. Annie was enjoying the conversation and Walter's discomfort to the full, and continued to tease him.

'And were there any girls at St John's you thought might make a particularly good match for your son?' she enquired nonchalantly.

'Well,' continued Harriet, 'I would have been happy with any one of three or four that I had my eye on, but if I could have made a bet on it, and gambling is a sin, I might have put some money on a certain girl to catch my son's eye. She seemed to have the looks, confidence, personality and wit to attract him, and the ability to organise him and keep him in check.'

They both sat, demure and silent, for a few seconds, wicked smirks on their lips. It was an understanding that no mere male could hope to outwit, and a meeting of minds. In marrying Walter, Annie had found not one soulmate but two, while Harriet had found the loving daughter she had always longed for. Walter was sublimely trapped between the two women he loved most in the world.

'I hope you don't mind me saying this,' Annie remarked, as

they walked home after one of the most sociable evenings she could remember, 'I'm glad, Walter Clough, that you're so much like your mother and not your father.' Her utter frankness startled him. 'I know this is a difficult thing to say, but you know me, I'm not afraid to say what has to be said. Perhaps it's my main fault. I noticed there isn't the same closeness between you and your father. You're quite cold to him, and he shows no affection for you. I don't think I could ever have married you if you were like him.'

Walter stopped, turned to face her and squeezed her hands. He was going to say what he had to say, and damn the consequences. If he was going to live the rest of his life with her he was determined not to live a lie, and if she saw it as a reason to break their engagement then it was not worth a candle anyway. 'Annie, he's not my father. He's my stepfather.'

'I guessed as much. Your father must have died when you were very young . . .'

'No!' Walter interrupted, then paused for a second, aware that what he was going to say might hurt his mother if she ever found out. 'Annie,' he blurted out, 'I don't know who my father is. Adams is my mother's maiden name, not her married name. There, you know it now. I have no more secrets to hide. If it makes any difference to us or our engagement tell me now.'

For her answer she kissed him as longingly and passionately as she had ever done.

'Don't ever tell my mother what I've said,' he begged. 'It would break her heart to know what I found out.'

'Your mother's almost as precious to me as you are, and who am I to judge someone for what happened all those years ago? You couldn't have a more loving mother than her, and I'd never dream of breaking such a sacred trust.'

Walter went on to tell her about his discovery all those years before, and about his hopes and ambitions that had been so cruelly dashed by the spiteful Enos. He did not spare her any detail, and Annie listened intently to every word. The light was fading and it was late by the time they arrived back in Wakefield Road. He scarcely had the time to tell her what he wanted to say. 'Dearest Annie, I won't stay in that drapery shop for ever. I've always wanted to make my mark in life, better myself and see more of the world. Marrying you makes no difference to those hopes. You can't take them away from me.'

'I'm marrying you for what you are, my darling,' she whispered, 'not for what I want to make you. It's your hope that makes you special.'

The door opened and Mrs Ackroyd appeared, worried and angry. No goodnight kiss but just a longing look would have to suffice tonight. Annie hurried up into the house, and Walter departed.

'Where do you think you've been until this hour, young lady?' Mary Ackroyd enquired.

'We had a lovely time at Walter's house. I got on really well with Mrs Clough and the hours just flew by. By the time we finished talking it was dark. You'll like Mrs Clough, Mother, she's got good conversation and a wonderful sense of humour.'

'That's as maybe,' chided her mother, 'but remember, Annie, you're engaged and not yet married – and there's many a slip twixt cup and lip!'

Annie pretended to be affronted by her mother's remark, but secretly smiled to herself. Though she would never defy convention and morality, the promise of the marriage bed did not hold any fears for her, and she was looking forward to the blissful union. She was glad it was only going to be a short engagement.

* * *

Walter stopped dead in front of a small, flat skear that poked out above the sand. Its sides were dotted with empty mussel shells. He guessed there might be live ones below the sand and even the odd starfish or two. He remembered bringing a few starfish back from an expedition with Reuben. Pulling them off the rocks was hard and had made his hands sore, but it was worthwhile to see the look on his children's faces at their strange gift.

He felt in his pocket and brought out a small bread roll, with a slice of cheese wedged inside. He had bought it from the baker's shop outside the station. Here was a perfect place for a snack and a moment to think again about his journey and his life as a young man in love, contemplating a happy marriage. After a few minutes he rose, threw a crust to some scavenging seagulls and went on his way.

Chapter Fifteen

The memory of those times seemed to put a spring in Walter's step. He found he was following the recent tracks of a cart, which had ventured on to the flat wastes of the open sands to search for cocklebeds. They seemed to be leading him the right way, so confidently he strode out in a northerly direction, still reading the sands for any dangerous pockets. The ebbing tide must have exposed a cocklebed, for as he trod he could definitely hear the spitting and hissing of the thousands of young shellfish beneath his feet. He stepped out even more firmly. Happy times flooded back into his mind, some ecstatic and dreamlike, others amusing and embarrassing.

* * *

It is all very well telling your family of your engagement and forthcoming marriage, but to tell your friends and drinking pals is an altogether different kettle of fish. The timing is particularly delicate. Too early and you may upset distant relatives and friends who have not heard but soon will, from other sources. Too late, and your pals will know beforehand, will be fully equipped with a barrage of jokes and comments – and will make you pay in full. In such circumstances the evening can become an hour or two of deliberate and hilarious humiliation. Walter laughed at the memory of his wedding announcement to his friends.

He had seen little of his pals since his proposal. Annie took up most of his time, and they had already begun to plan their life together with some thought and detail. That was Annie in a nutshell. Nothing was left to chance. She revelled in making the arrangements, drawing up lists and timetables and delegating various tasks to herself and Walter and also her sister and mother. Walter lovingly and dreamily concurred with everything.

It was some weeks later when the gang met again, at Walter's suggestion at the Marquis of Granby rather than the Mason's Arms. He fought shy of Sam Lodge's establishment, as he did not want him in earshot and embarrassed by wit and innuendo, some of which might be directed at his dear niece. In the event Walter's announcement was as embarrassing and uncomfortable as his friends could make it for him.

Albert had already got wind of how far the romance had progressed, and had primed the rest in anticipation. Walter suspected that his mother had let slip the information to Leah Dowgill, which was confirmed by what he overheard at the bar between Albert and Tom Pickersgill. Albert was laughing at his mother's dismay, which had been caused by Harriet's carefully chosen words.

'You know, Leah, Walter's got engaged. She's a Christian girl from a well-respected family.'

'Really,' replied Leah. 'I'm very pleased for the lad.'

But it was too much of an opportunity for Harriet to get one up on Enos's family and to twist the knife in. 'Hasn't Albert brought home any nice girls yet?'

Walter's anticipated announcement in the pub was swiftly followed with a succession of cheers, drinks and choruses of 'For he's a jolly good fellow', and an unending stream of jokes, wisecracks and bawdy songs, most referring to weddings, honeymoons, bridal trousseaux and such-like matters.

'I've heard that Annie Ackroyd's a real good looker,' announced Arby, deliberately loud enough for the whole pub to hear, 'Do we all get a turn to kiss the blushing bride?'

'Who's t'best man?' asked Tom. 'Does he get pick o' t'bridesmaids?'

'Aye, but only if he can take a strong dose of religion and straight lace,' joked Isaac.

The point was not lost on Walter or Albert, who explained the joke to the others. Walter was relieved that the focus of their baiting had turned from Annie and onto Nancy. But not for long. As Walter rose to go to the bar, Arby stopped him and offered to buy him another drink.

'Nay, Walter,' he cajoled, 'You're not getting your own drink. Sit down and rest a bit. You're going to need all the energy thee can get in t'next few months. You've been up 'n' down tonight more than a young bride's nightie!'

And so it went on for a whole evening, with Walter fending off a night-long barrage of jokes and wisecracks, until at last they helped him to his feet and supported him home through the dark streets to Old Lane, depositing him on the doorstep of the draper's shop. Harriet, occasionally used to dealing with her husband in such a condition, was surprised to see her son in like predicament, but guessed the reason. She assisted him to his bed, undressed him and tucked him in for the night, as she had when he was a little boy. Men, she observed, were at times no more than large children. She could not deny her son this rite of passage, and she hoped that his next nursemaid would be just as understanding.

In hindsight, Walter regretted giving his chums so much chance to make merry over his impending nuptials. The thought of them meeting the Ackroyds, the formidable mother, the prudish Nancy, and James and Victor, the brothers who ran the family business, filled him with foreboding. Isaac and Tom would probably pass muster, but how could he rein in his cousin? Walter soon formed a plan, and the next week called in at Dowgill's.

'Albert, you're my oldest friend. I've been thinking of asking you to be my best man. But it's no joke or opportunity to clown around. This is the most important day of my life and you've got to do it for real, no messing around, mind.'

Albert was taken aback. He had fully expected Walter to ask Isaac to perform this role, as he was capable, more serious and could speak in public with great ease. 'Aye, I'll do it,' he replied, 'and I'll do it proper for thee, Walter, never worry. It'll be the wedding day you can be proud of for thee and that right lovely bride o' thine.'

Walter smiled. His plan would work. The best man's duties and responsibilities should keep Albert in check, and he would be spending the whole day in his sight. He smiled to himself. When it came to being devious he could take a leaf out of Annie's book.

And it worked. Albert was true to his word. The wedding day passed off as well as it possibly could. Walter and his best man were at the church in good time, in such good time that Albert was able to offer the groom Dutch courage from a discreet hip-flask he had secreted upon him. It helped Walter calm his nerves during the long wait before the bride appeared, just a minute or two late, looking radiant on the arm of her uncle. It was generally agreed that Annie's natural good looks, her immaculate choice of dress and accessories and her happy, confident demeanour made her the most beautiful bride East Bowling had seen for many a long day, and that she was accompanied by the prettiest bunch of bridesmaids you were ever likely to meet. St John's Church was resplendent, decked with flowers inside and standing proud above the mills, houses and ironworks, with its tall, slim spire and golden brown stonework. The vicar, as expected, got some of the words of the service muddled, much to the amusement of the congregation.

'Do you, Walter,' he began, 'take this man Annie . . . no, I mean, do you, Annie . . .' He looked at the book and started again. The atmosphere was instantly lightened, and a weight was lifted from Annie's and Walter's shoulders: it would not seem so bad now if they stumbled or slipped.

After the ceremony the invited party retired to Wakefield Road, where the large house was an ideal venue for the wedding breakfast, leaving the rest of the congregation, the nosey-parkers and gossips to chew over one of the loveliest weddings ever to grace the village.

In a brief moment they got to themselves, Annie whispered, 'I do congratulate you, my dearest, on your choice of best man. I had misgivings, but I must say Albert has performed his duties admirably. Everything he's done has gone so well, and he's been so charming and attentive, particularly to the bridesmaids.'

'Yes,' answered her husband, 'even Nancy has been impressed.'

Finally the proceedings came to an end, and the happy couple prepared for their wedding tour. At Walter's suggestion they had chosen Morecambe. He hoped the beauty of the bay and its setting would complement their first, wonderful days together, and so it proved. Annie's aunt had suggested an excellent boarding house, and as it was early in the season they had no difficulty obtaining a booking. The carriage took them to Bradford station, and it was their good fortune to find a compartment to themselves all the way to their destination. Although a little weary, they were not too tired for a little canoodling when intervals between the stations allowed.

Finally the newly weds arrived at a smart guesthouse, Bay View, where they were welcomed by a smiling, cherubic lady, whose hands were still white from baking. She shook Walter's hand warmly, after planting a floury kiss on the bride's cheek. 'I suppose you'll be having the window table in the dining room,' she suggested with a twinkle in her eye. 'Now I know you asked for a room on the front, but I think you might find another one very much to your taste. It's at the back of the house and very private, and you'll have sole use of the bathroom on the passage.'

She led them down a corridor and opened a door. The view was not inspiring, as it looked out on to a blank wall some thirty feet away, but the room was bright, airy and spacious and had the impression of having been recently decorated. It was bedecked with three or four vases of fresh flowers, while on the bed was a new flowery coverlet. It appeared that someone had forewarned the landlady of their situation, and she was determined to make their honeymoon stay as perfect as it could be.

'You can use the small sitting room opposite,' she suggested. 'It's for me and Ted but we don't use it a lot. You'll find it private in this part of the house.'

She could see by the smiles on their faces that they were more than happy. Walter cast his mind back to his first meeting with a Morecambe landlady, and could not believe that two such different creatures did the same job. She informed them of the times for tea and breakfast but said, with a chuckle, 'You'll be tired after your journey, so we won't mind if you're not down right on time tomorrow.'

Neither realised how tired they were after such a tense, hectic but perfect day, but after a short but gentle attempt at their first lovemaking they fell fast asleep in each others' arms, and did not wake until the morning sun slipped over the wall and through their curtains. They resumed their tender exertions for a short while, before realising that breakfast time was nigh and hurriedly preparing for the day ahead.

Annie had wisely included a pair of stout shoes in her trousseau. The two spent many happy hours walking together, not just to view the pleasures of the town but also to the more remote and beautiful spots such as Heysham Head, with its small bays and fascinating rock pools, and north-east to the wider, windswept stretches of beach at Bare and Hest Bank. They took a carriage out to the pretty village of Arnside, and both were enraptured by the quaint fishing village with its stone cottages and small harbour set against the steep, grey fells of the Lake District.

It could not be said that their honeymoon was perfect harmony for the whole of the time, for when two strong personalities are learning to live together they have to find each others' limitations and boundaries. Annie was occasionally petulant and organising, Walter obstinate and lacking in common sense, but all differences were resolved before they fell asleep. As the week progressed their lovemaking became more sustained, skilled and enthusiastic. The prim and proper Miss Ackroyd had quickly become the sensual and indulgent Mrs Clough.

During the week there was some rain but the two retired to their sitting room, played cards, read some books and were totally absorbed by each others' company. Occasionally they dashed out between the showers on shopping expeditions or to the entertainments at the pavilion on the pier. The weather cleared on the last day, and Walter suggested a trip to Glasson Dock. The estuarine scenery did not impress them as much as the other places they had visited, but for Walter the sight of a magnificent schooner as it pulled out of the estuary and into the bay compensated for this. 'I'd love to take you on such a fine ship to a faraway foreign land,' he declared.

'Walt, you're a dreamer,' Annie sighed, and for a few minutes remained silent.

Arriving at their new home, arrangements seemed at first to work well. The couple resumed their intimacy in the privacy of what had once been Annie's own comfortable bedroom. One night, however, their enthusiastic lovemaking was interrupted by loud and rather obvious coughing. It was not from Nancy, who slept in the next bedroom, but from further across the landing. Pointed remarks were made by Mrs Ackroyd at the breakfast table. 'We must always remember to show proper decorum in a Christian household,' she observed. 'It helps promote a wholesome family life.'

Nancy, whom Walter would have expected to join in such a discussion and put forward strong moral arguments, remained silent and reddened slightly. It surprised him that although they had woken Annie's mother his sister-in-law next door appeared to have slept through it all.

After a couple of months the household slipped into an imperceptibly new routine. Annie and Walter became more circumspect and took opportunities to indulge their passion when the house was empty. Annie occasionally pleaded a headache to absent herself from work at the church, leaving Nancy to carry the burden. Surprisingly Nancy neither objected nor complained. The routine was finally broken by the joyous discovery of a change in Annie's condition. After her excited announcement to her husband he bade her sit down and rest, and took elaborate pains over the next few days to ensure she was comfortable and not inclined to exert herself. At the end of the week she informed her mother, and one evening, when she and Nancy were alone in the parlour, she decided to tell her sister the joyful news.

'Dearest Nancy,' she began, 'you may or may not have guessed from my happiness over the last few days that I have some wonderful news to tell you. I'm going to have a baby.'

There was silence. Tears welled up in Nancy's dark eyes, finally flooding out in a torrent of emotion and despair. 'Oh Annie,' she sobbed, 'so am I!'

Chapter Sixteen

The cart tracks veered off to the west. The cocklers had no doubt gone further out into the bay in search of their plunder. Walter was left to his own devices again, to rely on his own skill at reading the dangerous landscape. Ahead of him, across his path, lay a wide patch of darker silt. He approached it carefully and with some trepidation, plunging in the stake as far as he dared. It met little resistance and sank deep into the morass, with no solid rock or clay to be found. His suspicions were confirmed. It was a melgrave: a hole scooped out during a stormy tide and filled in thereafter with soft quicksand. The most dangerous feature on these muddy wastes, it was a sly and vicious trap to ensnare the foolish and unwary.

* * *

Walter arrived back at Wakefield Road late that evening. He had stayed on to have tea with his mother and Enos and break his happy news to them. Harriet was delighted and kissed her son warmly. She and her daughter-in-law had become quite close, and it was a blessing to look forward to a future that included grandchildren. Enos feigned congratulation and pleasure, but deep down felt resentment. It meant that another line would prosper and perhaps run his business, and reminded him bitterly of his own inability to father a family. But another problem immediately sprang to mind. 'Ah suppose that now thee'll want a rise in wages to feed the bairn. We'll have to see about that when t'time comes.'

In reality the draper's shop wasn't doing well, and Enos was not in the best of health: he often relied on Walter to take on the running of the shop for days at a time. He foresaw trouble: the lure of eventually owning the business might not be enough to keep his stepson in line. What he did not know was that Walter had already been making enquiries about better-paid work in Bradford.

When Walter eventually arrived home he found his wife red-eyed and crying, and for a moment he feared the worst. 'Whatever is up, dearest?' he enquired. 'It's not, it's not . . .'

'No, Walter,' she sobbed. 'It's not that. Our baby's all right. It's not me at all. It's Nancy.'

'What's the matter with her?'

'You might well ask!' interrupted Mrs Ackroyd. 'You may have been the source of happiness to one of my daughters, but you've been the cause of misery and ruin to my other one.'

Walter was aghast. What did she mean? What had happened to Nancy? He could not fathom the reason for so much upset.

Annie at length composed herself. 'Nancy is pregnant as well.'

A dozen emotions crossed Walter's face simultaneously. Part of him was shocked, part horrified, part puzzled and part of him wanted to laugh out loud, as he was sure Isaac, Albert and Arby would have done had they heard such news: it would have been a source of merriment for weeks to come. But it was different now. He was part of this family, and no matter how much Nancy might annoy him she was now his sister, his darling wife's closest family and friend, and therefore partly his responsibility. Her next words struck even harder.

'We believe,' Annie said without emotion, 'that the father is Albert.'

'Your wicked, lascivious, deceitful friend and cousin,' added Mrs Ackroyd, immediately twisting the knife. 'Just wait until her brothers hear about this: there'll be trouble an' all. He's sown his wild oats too freely this time, and in our garden too. They won't take kindly to that.'

Walter thought of James and Victor: Victor, in particular, seemed a quiet, boring man. Perhaps they would not exact revenge personally, but no doubt they had too many burly carters and farmers in their debt or workmen in their employ for Albert's safety.

'I'll go and see him now,' said Walter. 'I'll make sure he does the right thing by her.'

'You're too late!' triumphed his mother-in-law. 'The cowardly snake has upped sticks and gone. Sam says the rumour is he's gone to Liverpool. He'd better not show his face round here or he'll be sorry.'

'Nevertheless I'll do what I can,' Walter assured them. 'I'll go and see Aunt Leah and Uncle Josh: they may know his whereabouts. If he doesn't return soon I'll go to Liverpool, and try to persuade him to come back and do the decent thing. If he'll listen to anyone he'll listen to me.'

'You're wasting your time,' went on the embittered mother. 'He just sees my dear daughter as another notch on his walking cane. Sam knows all about your despicable cousin. We know his like, but he's tried it on with the wrong folk. We Ackroyds never forget.'

For once Annie had heard enough. 'Walter's right, Mother!' she insisted. 'I know the kind of life he's led, but there are a few good things about him. If there's one person he cares about it's Walter. So give him a chance, Mother. But if I were you, Walt, I'd wait a couple of days before chasing off after him. Give him a chance to come back and make amends of his own accord. And if he doesn't we'll have had time to find out where he's gone.'

After much argument it was decided to leave the matter in Walter's hands, but he agreed to Annie's suggestion. It was a decision that proved to be of some consequence.

Walter recalled Annie's account of that meeting when she'd first heard from her sister's own lips of her 'fall from grace'. It was so ironic that the words Nancy used so often in her preaching could be turned against her. Oh, how he would have loved to have been a fly on the wall when she told Annie!

'Albert!' Annie pleaded unbelievingly, 'Tell me it isn't him. How could it be Albert Dowgill?'

Nancy nodded slowly.

'Oh, Nancy, how could this have happened?'

Nancy, weeping, collected her thoughts. She explained that the first seeds of the flowering romance had been planted when Albert had visited their house in the role of honest broker. 'After that meeting at the house, when he told you the truth about Walter's feelings for you, I knew there was some good in him. I felt he was a soul who could be redeemed, so I looked for a chance to save him from his wicked ways. Oh, Annie, he had the face of an angel. I've never seen anyone who looked so like a saint!'

Annie scowled. All thought of the precious burden she carried inside her, and the joy it would bring, was gone. There before her was her silly, naïve sister, who thought that by the power of her persuasive tongue, her evangelical zeal and feminine wiles she could convert Satan's ultimate sinner and libertine.

Nancy's feelings for Albert would have remained hidden, and eventually withered, had it not been for the wedding. Annie realised that by asking Albert to be his best man Walter had, in part, triggered the sequence of events that had led to this tragedy. It was one of Albert's duties to look after the bridesmaids, and from these attentions Nancy's hidden hope had sprung. She had been chosen as chief bridesmaid, with two of Annie's friends also in attendance. In essence Nancy was not an ugly or even a plain girl; it was just that she normally dressed and acted in such a severe, even puritanical, manner that her beauty and femininity were well hidden. At the wedding, however, one of her duties was to look attractive – which she managed to perfection. Annie was surprised that her sister concurred so readily in the choice of bridesmaids' dresses, which, although in plain muslin, were sumptuously adorned with ribbon and lace trimmings matched by plain tulle veils; she did not even resist Annie's attempts to loosen and style her hair. The casual observer who had seen Nancy at church meetings might have guessed that Annie had not chosen Nancy at all, but had a secret sister who only appeared at weddings and other special occasions. The sight of a beautiful, elegantly dressed principal bridesmaid, with a handsome figure and winning smile, surprised many a guest as well the bridegroom.

Nancy had her most notable effect, however, on the best man, and a plan for the ultimate conquest slowly formed in his mind. Chance and occasion had thrown the two together, and

Albert was not going to waste the opportunity. It was he who offered to present the bridegroom's gifts to the attendants, which he did with all his natural charm. He paid consideration to each one, but reserved special attention for the last recipient. As Albert slowly fastened the delicate locket round Nancy's neck he planted a kiss on her cheek. This was not the brief peck he had given to the other bridesmaids, but a slightly lingering, moister contact, which raised an unseen blush on the cheek of the surprised, but secretly delighted, maid of honour.

Whether it was because of the headiness and romance of the whole occasion, or her secret longings that had burst suddenly to the surface, Nancy had responded in kind. Although she had distributed the bride's favours impeccably, the best lilies and white roses going to the closest and most honoured guests, the smaller, white ferns to more distant relatives and friends, she had saved the best rose in her sister's bouquet for Albert. She added it to his buttonhole at the end of the wedding breakfast. 'There!' she said. 'I dare say that will make you look finer than ever.'

Nancy was careful not to bore Albert with conversation about her work for the Band of Hope and other church committees, having been warned by Annie beforehand, but kept her conversation to the light chatter and pleasantries common on these occasions. Albert was careful to model his behaviour on hers in order to win her favour, following her lead in taking up lemonade to toast the wedded couple and introducing her good works into their conversation. He studiously avoided her uncle from the Mason's Arms. Had Sam seen the two together so often, and knowing Albert's reputation, he would surely have smelled a rat.

It was with some difficulty that Annie extracted from Nancy the details of her meetings with Albert. They started a week after the wedding when Albert turned up unexpectedly at one of her Band of Hope meetings. He delayed her with chatter about the wedding and flattered her, praising her appearance and the role she had played in making the occasion so successful. She reciprocated, and said how much she had enjoyed his company and attentions.

He then surprised her by remarking, 'You know, what you said about your work for wicked people and sinners started me thinking. I'm one of 'em, you know.'

'I know you're not as bad as some people paint you,' she replied. 'There's a lot of good in you, Albert. I saw it when you came to our house to tell Annie about Walter's true feelings. It took a lot of courage to do that. You must think a lot of him to be a friend like that.'

'Aye, but it took a good thump on t'nose to make me realise.'

'I'm sure it was God's work. I've heard of him coming in bolts of lightning and the like, but never on the end of a fist!'

'Aye, but thee knows I go drinking, get into trouble and do daft things. Mind you, I've never done owt criminal, mind. I make an honest living as a butcher, so perhaps there's some hope for me.'

'There's always hope in God's love, Albert; Walter told me what you did when the mill chimney fell down. You risked your life to save that child. You may not have got a medal for it, but He knows, and you'll get your reward in heaven for that.'

'Ah, but *He* knows about me wicked ways an' all,' murmured the sinner, 'and I bet you've heard too. I've sown my wild oats, but not half as often as some folks think. Young blokes boast about such things, you know, and you don't have to believe half of what they tell thee.'

Nancy laughed and blushed slightly.

Albert, careful not to be seen, as they were approaching her house, and mindful of not being too forward, gave her hand a squeeze and muttered, 'Thanks for listening. You're an understanding lass, one of His best.'

He gave a shy smile, turned and walked away. She stood there for a few seconds watching him, then skipped dreamily up the steps to the front door. She was totally under his spell.

Each week their meeting was almost the same, but every time Albert ratcheted up the romance, first giving her a quick peck on the cheek, then slowly extending his embrace and increasing the passion. As an experienced and skilful seducer, he was able to release longings and desires she didn't know existed within her. One warm, summer evening they detoured by the Roughs and found a bank on which to rest. Whether she was jealous of her sister, who had found fulfilment in the sanctity of marriage with Walter, and whom she could hear occasionally engaging in her passion through the adjoining bedroom wall, or whether she liked to imagine that she too was married and enjoying the fruits of the marriage bed, she could not be sure. But she had gradually fallen under the spell of the handsome, beguiling young man, and she succumbed to his gentle but accomplished lovemaking.

For Albert it may not have been his first virgin, but it was his greatest conquest ever, perhaps more difficult than he could have ever imagined but eminently satisfying. For the hapless Nancy that moment of pleasure became a long night of regret, as she lay awake and realised the enormity and shame of what she had done. She tried to comfort herself that their consummation had been a precursor to an offer of marriage, but deep down she realised that she had been tricked; like a score or more mill girls, shop assistants or young housewives she was just another conquest. Like many before her she had fallen too readily into an inviting trap. Her fears were compounded when Albert did not turn up to the next meeting, and all attempts to contact him proved fruitless. Her guilt and shame reached new depths when some weeks later she realised she was pregnant, and it took several days of weeping and desolation before she plucked up the courage to tell her sister. Annie had been left to ponder on her sister's foolishness and inform their mother; something Nancy could not face herself.

Two days after Walter had been informed he decided to take action. He stopped off first at the draper's shop. Harriet's surprise at seeing him was dashed when he broke his shocking news. She took it calmly, but his stepfather seemed devastated. He had spent his life making excuses for his errant nephew, and now, suddenly confronted with the truth, he could not face it.

Harriet immediately put on her shawl and accompanied her son to the Dowgills' house. They found Albert's parents shocked by his sudden disappearance, but totally unaware of the cause. They had feared the worst and were surprised when Harriet told them of the reason. To her amazement they seemed somewhat relieved.

'Give it a month or two and he'll be back and it'll all be forgotten about,' declared Albert's father. 'After all, it won't be t'first lass that's got into trouble in this town. It gives gossips summat to blaht about, then it'll be over like a storm in a teacup.'

'No it won't!' stormed Harriet. 'Ackroyds are well-off folk and won't let it rest.' Walter saw a side of his mother he had rarely seen before, a strong determined woman who was not to be deflected by her brother-in-law's bluff excuses. 'What Albert's done is wrong and it's got to be put right. It's not any poor mill girl or floozie he's seduced this time . . .'

Joshua began to protest vehemently, but Harriet was unrepentant and not to be cowed.

'It's the sister and daughter of respectable business people with important friends in this city,' she continued. 'Albert must do the right thing or stay away from Bradford for good. We think he's gone to Liverpool. Walter's going to try to find him. Enos has given him the week off with pay.'

She delivered her final blow to the stunned couple. 'I trust that if Walter does persuade him to come back and do the right thing by this respectable girl, then *you'll* remember the sacrifice your brother-in-law's family has made, Joshua Dowgill!'

Cowed in the face of this onslaught, the two parents sat silent for a time, then Leah made a suggestion. 'You'd best look for him in the importers' and wholesale meat markets. Albert said that with the amount of meat coming in from America and Australia there are prospects in Liverpool for a good butcher – and he always was a good butcher, just like his father.'

Harriet would have loved to make a cutting comment about the other traits he had inherited, but now was not the time or place. She turned on her heel and abruptly departed, with the bemused and admiring Walter in her wake.

Thereafter Walter observed the changes that gradually occurred in the draper's shop and his parents' household. With Enos's health and moral authority weakened, his mother's star was in the ascendant. No longer would she be cowed by her thoughtless and bullying husband. Albert's transgressions had given her a convenient weapon, and she was not afraid to use it.

* * *

The lone walker stopped and roared with laughter to the seagulls wheeling above. Walter had not laughed at the time but now, looking back over the years, it seemed so funny to imagine the most unlikely lovers in history. Yet when he thought about it he could see, possibly for the first time, the reason for this impossible love match.

Any man likes to make his mark on life. The mountaineer sets foot on the highest peaks where none have trodden before. The explorer tracks unknown wastes or hidden jungles. Others strive to make discoveries and inventions unknown to man, or by their writings bring to public attention thoughts and philosophies previously undreamed of. It was clear to Walter now that the seduction of a pure young woman, whose aim was to save his soul, must have been for Albert the ultimate conquest, requiring all his skills and patience. Perhaps he had finally grown tired of his easy conquests: the young wives he met on his daily round, the willing mill girls or the women of easy virtue he met in the saloons of Bradford.

The lone walker set his foot down on the edge of the morass. It squelched and moved as if he were stepping on a jelly. He laughed, and turned sharply to the right to skirt the yawning trap before him. The darker sand of the melgrave would not tempt him to risk all in order to save a few minutes on his journey. What to the unwary might seem a sensible route over dry sand, which swayed and heaved as if you were walking on the thick skin of a rice pudding, could lead to a slow and agonising death if that skin was broken. He would not be tricked and ensnared like the hapless Nancy, at least not for a long time yet.

Chapter Seventeen

As he reached the middle of that endless expanse the walker stopped to admire the spectacle around him. The grey-blue Lakeland hills had come into view above the thin, darker, grey-green strip of shoreline, made up of rocks, pinewoods and salt marsh. The brown sand paled to a deep gold in the rays of the sun and the blue and white above was reflected in the distant sea, and the pools and watery silt around him. The white headland was now much clearer. It was dotted with trees and shrubs of different shades of green, among which he could see patches of sharp colour from the flowers that abounded on its slopes.

* * *

When it came to scenes created by the hand of man it took a lot to impress Walter Clough, but the view from the entrance of Lime Street station certainly did. He recalled the first time he ever saw it on that late August day. The heart of Liverpool was bigger, grander and more awe-inspiring than any city he had ever seen, at least in its magnificent centre. Like his own city it had its own St George's Hall, built some thirty-five years before, but this one dwarfed Bradford's, as if the latter were only a Roman temple to some lesser deity. Not only that, it stood in the widest street he had ever seen. The building was set in the middle of open space so that its scale and grandeur could be fully appreciated. In front of it was a raised, paved area, on which people wandered to and fro, chatted and relaxed, while behind lay magnificent public gardens.

The view stretched out before him. Large hotels and banks resplendent in the morning sun lay to his right. There were decorative railings and elegant lampposts along the street, statues abounded and in the distance rose a large triumphal column. Golden sandstone gleamed in the autumn sunshine, only slightly tarnished by the smoke from the industry and homes of the city. Walter could never understand why the people hurrying and scurrying like ants, crowded on the horse buses or dashing along this triumphal way in their cabs and carriages, never stopped to gaze at the scene's magnificence. He seemed to be the only person who was considering the beauty that man could achieve.

After a few minutes Walter turned his mind to other things. Where was he to find Albert in this giant, bustling city? He wandered along in what he sensed was the direction of the waterfront. When he saw a butcher's shop, with a window displaying as wide a range of delicacies as he had ever seen, he walked in and nodded politely to a small, dark man dressed in a striped apron and straw hat.

'Excuse me,' he began, 'I wonder if you can help me. I'm looking for someone who's moved to Liverpool to work in the butchery trade.'

The little man eyed him suspiciously. 'You'se a workin' jack or a bizzie?' he asked.

'Sorry, what do you mean?'

The assistant hesitated, realising he was speaking to an innocent. 'I mean the scuffers.'

'Pardon?'

'The police. Lord above, where do you'se come from?'

'I'm from Bradford and I'm looking for my cousin.'

'Hear this, Mikey, this fella's looking for a butcher here in the Pool. I hopes he's got a week's holiday owed, 'cos it's gorra take him that long at least to find him. There's hundreds of butchers in this city, wack, and you'se wants to find just one?'

'Actually,' said Walter, 'I think he may be working with one of the meat importers or factors, not just in a shop.' He knew he had said the wrong thing the moment he opened his mouth. The little man took instant offence.

'Listen 'ere you'se, there's nuthin wrong with working in a butcher's shop, and you'se better know that for a start, before I . . .'

Walter was about to apologise, but the older man interrupted. 'Don't get on at him, Jack. Poor bloke's doing his best. Pool's a big city, if you're from away.' He addressed Walter in a friendly manner. 'Don't mind him, wack. He often takes offence, but he don't mean no harm. Most meat importers and wholesalers are either on the docks or the streets just behind. You gorra start round there, but it'll be a long search. You'se best starting at the Princes and Wapping Docks, but they've started taking refrigerated meat from the Americas and Australia up to Bootle, and there's a lot of trade with South America over the water.'

Walter stood perplexed. He knew that his native Bradford dialect seemed strange to people from other parts, but some of this was incomprehensible.

'He means Birk'nhead,' put in Jack, keen to get back in his boss's good books.

'And if you're still stuck, try the Chamber of Trade in Lime Street,' added the manager. 'They have a list of all meat firms that are members.'

Walter thanked them, and made his way towards the docks. He was amazed by the sights. For a man whose only experience of a port was Glasson Dock on the mouth of the Lune, it came as a shock. Docks, warehouses, cranes and ships spread out before him as far as the eye could see. People were walking along pontoons to a floating pier, where ferries and steamers were tied. A goods train hooted and clattered along the street amid the crowds. Grand buildings looked out on to the docks and the river, where ships of every size and type, sailing barques, steamships and paddle-wheeled ferries moved graciously up and down or scurried backwards and forwards between the docks and city.

He stood there for a full five minutes gazing on the scene, then deciding he was hungry, he dived into a small café, just behind the wharfs. Most customers seemed to be enjoying a plate of delicious-smelling stew.

'Can I have the stew?' he asked the young girl who attended his table.

She looked puzzled for a second, then the penny dropped. 'Youse wants scouse then?'

'Er, yes please.' Walter desperately hoped he'd made the right choice.

'You'll like our scouse. It's not thin an' watery like the posh place up the street. Ours 'as got a lorra meat in it.'

It was indeed delicious, and after a treacle sponge Walter felt refreshed and ready to resume his search. He decided to leave 'over the water' until the next day if need be, when a ferry trip would allow him to view the whole waterfront from the river, and vowed there and then to come back one day and explore this exciting place further, unencumbered by his search for the wayward Albert.

Walter struck lucky halfway through the afternoon. The foreman at a meat warehouse on Wapping Dock told him that a firm on James Street had been taking on new butchers and packers, so he ventured down to a tall building behind Queen's Dock. An impressive brass plate at the side of the entrance announced the firm as David Elliott – Meat Importers. He opened the large mahogany door and walked in, to find an office that was no less imposing. Confronted at the front desk by an officious, older woman, Walter was questioned closely about why he was searching for his cousin. When she was called away to an inner office her assistant, a pretty, red-haired girl of no more than twenty, came over to help.

Walter politely explained that his previous inquisitor had been reluctant to help and the girl whispered in a giggle, 'You mustn't be bothered by Miss Mather; she's a real Tilly Mint.' He wondered if he would ever fathom this strange new language. 'Now, who is it you're looking for?' she asked, smitten by the tall, young stranger.

'His name's Albert Dowgill.'

She immediately giggled, then blushed a little. 'Oh yes, Albert. I know him. We took him on last week. Mr Hornby says he's an excellent butcher by all accounts, and he's impressed a lorra girls in the office as well. He speaks funny like you, only harder to understand.'

Walter smiled. Obviously Albert's famous charm had already started to work, even overcoming the language barrier: it was plain his errant cousin had picked up where he had left off in Bradford. 'When can I see him, do you think?'

'He'll be finished at five, and don't take all of his time, will you, mister? Tell him Doris wants a bit of the evening left for her!'

She gave Walter directions to Elliott's meat store, which was down by Salthouse Dock, and he thanked her and headed back to the waterfront. He gave a sigh, partly of relief. It had not taken as long to find Albert as he had feared, but the thought that his cousin was still continuing in his old ways filled him with foreboding. He had worried that persuading Albert to face his responsibilities in Bradford might prove difficult, but with Doris and who knows how many others on the scene it might prove impossible.

Walter passed an hour on the Pier Head, mingling with the passengers hurrying to and from the ships at the quayside. He noticed some families who were dragging large amounts of luggage and possessions towards a much larger ship berthed at the end of the floating dock, and guessed they were emigrants on their way to a new life in America or Australia. He would have loved to have taken a closer look at the ship, but had to make his way to Salthouse Dock for one of the most difficult meetings in his life.

To his surprise Albert came out of the building looking for him. Obviously Doris had passed a message to him, through an office boy or messenger she had under her thumb. Walter cursed his luck. He had hoped that the surprise meeting would catch Albert off guard, but now he was forewarned and would know why his cousin had come searching for him.

'Hi, Walt,' Albert shouted over the heads of a stream of workers making their way home. 'What brings you over here?'

Walter clasped his shoulder and shook his hand. He did not answer the question. Despite everything else he was glad his friend was safe, had got a job and was as happy and friendly as the Albert of old. They retired to a quiet pub down a side street off Lord Street.

'You know why I've come,' Walter began, when they had settled down in a quiet corner with their drinks. 'You've left quite a mess back in Bradford. Nancy's with child, and it's no use trying to blame this one on anyone but you.'

'I suppose thee's come to persuade me to go back and marry her, and I bet they all sent thee 'cos they thought as I might listen to thee.'

'No, you're wrong. It was my idea. Most of them have given you up. I thought you might change your mind and do the decent thing.'

'Walter, thee knows me and what I'm like. I'd be no good for Nancy. She deserves better than the likes o' me. I have some feelings for her, Walt. I know she's strong on religion and abstinence and all that, but that's not the reason why I shouldn't marry 'er. She were the one lass that took interest in me for what I am, and she made me think what a cheat and liar I am. But I can't change, and neither thee nor all the Band of Hope can change me.' His voice rose above the general hubbub, and a few people turned to look as they heard the heartfelt confession. 'I'd be up to my tricks in no time, and she'd end up an unhappy wife with a cheating drunkard of an husband who'd be no good for her. Can't you see that, Walt?'

Walter nodded. Secretly he had dreaded Albert as his brother-in-law.

'What'll happen to t'babby?' asked Albert.

'There are plans for Nancy to go and live with her aunt in Leeds for a time. When the child is born they'll either put it into a church orphanage or have it adopted. They'll ensure it's brought up by good Christian folk.'

Albert stared vacantly into space. For the first time ever Walter saw tears in his cousin's eyes. 'Let me know what it looks like,' he said, choking back the tears. 'I'll put some brass aside if I can, when it's grown up. But don't let it know or Nancy either.'

'All right,' whispered Walter. 'I'll see what I can do. I'll come over to see you, if I can. Keep in touch and give me an address to write to. All the best, lad!'

They shook hands, and Walter walked slowly up Lord Street back towards St George's Hall. As Enos was paying he decided not to travel back that night but to stay over in the Railway Hotel. He was determined to take that ferry ride the following morning and enjoy the sights and sounds of the busy port before he took the train back to Bradford.

As Walter journeyed home the next day one thing worried him. Should he or should he not tell Annie, Nancy and the others that he had found Albert and managed to talk to him, but not persuaded him to return to Bradford? He gazed out of the carriage window and pondered. 'No,' he said to himself, 'I'll tell them I couldn't find Albert.'

* * *

The flat fields of the Lancashire plain on that journey home so long ago were almost as wide and empty a horizon as the overwhelming, muddy vastness on which he now stood. Walter remembered the landscape changing to the endless terraces and factories around Manchester and then to dreary narrow valleys, hemmed in by bleak northern moorlands. Like the train he could now see pulling up the main line to Carlisle, it had chugged slowly upwards past grey villages and small cotton mills on its way through the Todmorden Gap, then dived in and out of the short tunnels that made up the greater part of that journey across the Pennines.

The sun had gone behind some dark clouds that had appeared in the south-west. They streamed quickly on the north-east wind to cover the tops of the Lakeland fells in a grey mist; there was a bleakness and sadness to his surroundings, just like the scene he recalled. Had he made the right decision then, or had he set wheels in motion that brought darker consequences?

Chapter Eighteen

That lie would come back to haunt him. Walter realised this now as he looked back over those last eleven eventful years. It was done with the best of motives, to save Nancy the heartache of renewed hope and to put an end to the matter, at least in the eyes of her family. It was perhaps this deceit that brought about the first crack in what he had looked on as a solid marriage. Did it sow the first seeds of doubt in Annie's mind? If he had lied in such a matter, could he and would he lie in others? After all, she had been crossed in love before they met – although he could never prise details of this from her.

Walter racked his brains as he strode across the sands, trying to understand why a bond that had once been so strong and loving had withered into embitterment. In recent times it had still occasionally flared from its embers in a moment of passion, kindled perhaps by the spark of feeling they still had for each other.

Thinking back, from his vantage point in time, the lone walker wondered if it was their married life that was partly to blame. For Annie it meant its attendant duties of childbearing and rearing. Their family, born of passion, had come too soon, and his own situation had not helped. His need to change his job, his nights away from home, all isolated her. Perhaps they brought to the surface once more those suspicions that had lain dormant ever since his chance meeting with Emily Lumb so early in their courtship. The thought also crossed his mind that she had found out about his one liaison, the affair that had led to his present predicament.

In the distance Walter could see the glistening waters of the Kent as it flowed out across the estuary. He could just make out two horses dragging a shrimp trawl down each side of the channel. Instinctively he veered to the left to keep well away from the activity, and in doing so came upon one of the bay's charming surprises – one he had heard of but never seen. A grey seal lay stretched out on the sandbank. He had seen it first as a dark lump, silhouetted against the bright horizon and had wondered what it was. As he drew near it turned its head to watch him and its profile became clearer. It did not move but eyed the walker warily as he passed. The abundant whiskers and self-satisfied expression reminded him of a certain person who had come to have a great influence on his life, for both good and ill.

* * *

Lemuel Metcalf was a bluff but wily Yorkshireman who had served Ledger's Drapery (wholesale department) for over twenty years. He turned up from time to time with his samples and his wares, trying to tempt drapers and clothiers to improve their orders, increase their stock or try new lines. With Enos he had little success. The myopic old skinflint resisted all the salesmanship, unless it was a special offer that might increase his margins. He stuck rigidly to Ledger's basic range of bed linens, flax sheeting, flannels and towelling, together with the occasional purchase of handkerchiefs, shawls or undergarments. He liked to play one firm off against another but kept his choice simple, cheap and utilitarian. This suited him, but less and less did it suit his customers in West Bowling.

Walter remembered the occasion when an ebullient Lemuel had called with his case of wares and Enos, who had taken to his bed a week before, was too ill to come down, although he was gradually recovering from a fever and cough. Harriet had feared consumption, but his illness responded to rest, a mixture of medicine and home-made remedies and a couple of visits from the doctor. Enos grumbled at the cost of the doctor's calls, but Harriet had taken firm charge and would brook no argument. While his father was ill Walter had sole charge of the shop and Annie had come over to help him. Having renewed the standard lines, Lem was quick to see an opportunity.

'You know, Walter,' he began, 'this shop does less and less trade as the years go on, and your father can't see why. He's still selling the plain stuff he sold twenty year ago and folks has more brass in their pockets these days. They want summat with a bit more style, even working folks. And t'young uns don't want to be dressed like their fathers and mothers.'

Walter agreed, and went on to point out in detail the changes he would make if he were in charge. He bemoaned the opportunity they had lost when their rival on Manchester Road had shut five years before, following the owner's unpopular association with the mill disaster. 'We should have either moved there or opened a second shop,' he explained. 'There are more folks and shops in that part of the village and you get a lot of passing trade. I could have made a real go of that, but my father didn't listen. He never does.'

His complaint did not fall on deaf ears. Lemuel lowered his voice as he replied. 'Then why don't you come and work for Ledger's, young man? We're the biggest wholesale drapers in West Yorkshire. You've got good ideas and you know t'trade inside out. We could do with a bright fellow like you.' He paused for a second, then said dramatically, 'You can have *my* job.'

'Your job? How can I have your job?'

'Because Mr Ledger's making me chief sales supervisor when old Pratt retires next week. There'll be a vacancy on t'sales team. It won't be my patch in Leeds and Bradford: one of the older blokes will have that plum. I reckon Aire Valley and Lancashire area will come vacant. It's new for us, and I reckon a keen young salesman could do well round there.'

Walter hesitated. It seemed too good to be true.

Lem could see the doubt and continued to wiggle the bait: it would be a feather in his cap if he could appoint such a bright, well-spoken young bloke who would need little training. 'Basic wages are a bit better than t'old skinflint pays thee, I reckon, but commission's real good for a keen young feller like you, who could push up sales and bring in customers. You might have to spend the odd night on t'road, mind you, but you'll get expenses for that.' Walter was on the edge. The offer seemed too tempting to refuse. Lemuel Metcalf pushed him over. 'I reckon a good young 'un like you could double his salary in a few months, and all it needs from me is a word in Mr Ledger's ear.'

'Give me a little time,' Walter insisted. 'I've got to speak to my wife about this.' He nodded in the direction of the shop, where he had left Annie in charge.

'Fine by me, Walter,' agreed Lem. 'I understand. I can't see her objecting, though, when you tell 'er about more brass coming in and her with a bairn on t'way too. Oh, congratulations by the way.' He laughed and warmly shook Walter's hand. 'Here's my card, Walt. You'll catch me in the shop or office Mondays an' Friday afternoons. Let me know within a week. You'll have to go through an interview with young Mr Ledger, but if you want the job I can almost guarantee it's yours.'

'Now,' Walter said, pocketing the card, 'let's have a look at your samples: all of them, not just those we normally take. I think this shop needs some newer, smarter lines.' A plan was forming in his mind.

Lem opened his case and laid out a range of linens and clothing. Walter picked out one or two lines he liked. He was particularly intrigued by a stylish cream blouse that had a deeper scalloped neckline and some neat embroidery. As he looked at it Annie entered the room. 'What do you think of this, love?' he asked.

'That's nice!' she cooed. 'Much better than the plain stuff you normally keep.'

'I can let you have half a dozen at a special introductory price. And I'll tell you what,' Lem suggested, 'it's your size, lass. Why don't you try it on, then show us how it looks on thee. You're far prettier than any shop window mannequin.'

Annie blushed, but agreed to slip upstairs to change. When she came down a few minutes later both her husband and the salesman were of the opinion that she brought out the very best in the garment.

'Well I declare,' said Lem, taking more interest in the model than the item of clothing, 'I'm sure that when it comes to you and that blouse the two of you were made for each other.'

Then he added, 'Oh dear, lass, I'm sure there's a small mark on the back. It should wash out, but it's no use to me as a sample now. I'll tell thee what, Walter, let this young lady have it – compliments of the firm. After all, Cloughs have been customers of ours nigh on twenty years.'

He gave them both a sly wink. Walter placed an order and Lem began to collect up his samples and place them carefully in his case. They were interrupted by the return of Harriet, who went straight to the kitchen. Annie left to help her and Lem said his goodbyes, but not without a final reminder to Walter. 'Now don't thee forget,' he whispered, 'one week to make your mind up. I can't hold it for thee any longer.'

Woken by the voices below, Enos roused himself and dragged his aching body downstairs. He was not happy to miss Lemuel Metcalf, whom he had always regarded with deep suspicion. He picked up the order from the counter and studied it intently. 'What the bloody hell's this?' he shouted. 'What has that twistin' bugger foisted on us? You're daft, Walter, to let him push this stuff on you. Bowling folk won't pay these prices.'

Harriet rushed in from the kitchen, to see what the commotion was about.

'It's only six blouses!' protested Walter. 'And he didn't push them on to us. I chose them as a new line, and he gave a good discount as an introductory offer. They sell in Bradford shops for five bob, so you'll make a far better mark-up than you would on the plain, cheap stuff.'

Enos was about to answer back, but a fit of coughing stopped him.

Harriet intervened. 'Oh, they're lovely, particularly for the younger woman,' she said, taking her son's side. 'Annie's wearing the sample he gave her. Just have a look.' Annie walked in as she spoke. The blouse accentuated her still-trim figure and the lower-cut scalloped neckline showed Annie's slender neck and pure white skin to great advantage.

'I'm not sellin' that stuff!' Enos raged. 'Yon's fer trollops and hussies. It's not fer respectable Bowling folk.'

If Walter's plan was to upset Enos, make an argument and raise a pretext for quitting the shop, it worked too well and much too soon. Walter couldn't control himself and turned to face his father, his face twisted in anger. 'How dare you suggest that of my wife, you nasty old man? I've finished with you and your damned shop for good!' He held his breath for a few seconds, scarcely comprehending what he had said. Then the words rushed from his mouth as if he couldn't control them. 'Next week I'll be working for Ledger's as a sales representative, and at a far better wage than you'd pay your own son. You and your poxy shop can go to hell!' Enos slumped into his chair, aghast. Harriet and Annie stood open-mouthed, shocked by the sudden revelation. Walter calmed down. 'I'm sorry, Mother. I know you'll have to bear the brunt of this, and it's not the way I wanted it to happen. But it's for the best. We're not staying for tea.' He kissed his mother on the cheek and turned to take Annie's hand. 'Well, love,' he murmured, 'I think we'll be on our way home. We may have overstayed our welcome as far as some folk are concerned.' He shut the door quietly behind them.

Enos looked at Harriet, who turned away. 'I don't feel well,' he whined, 'not well at all.'

'Then you'd best get yourself up to bed!' she barked, 'and stay there until you're better. And don't expect me to come and work in that damned shop. I'll put a card in the window tomorrow for a shop assistant, and if that doesn't work I'll have to go into Bradford and you'll pay for an advert in the *Telegraph*. You can't blame my son, Enos Clough. You've had this coming to you for a long, long time!'

With that she slammed the kitchen door behind her. Enos was reduced to a lengthy fit of painful coughing. He retreated to bed, a sick and broken man.

Walter and Annie said little to each other on their walk home, or indeed for the whole evening. It was only when they retired to bed that she gave vent to her feelings.

'Why couldn't you have discussed it with me first, Walt?' I thought marriage was about making decisions together.'

'Lem made me the offer this afternoon on the spur of the moment. I told him I'd have to speak to you first. He gave me a week to think it over.'

'But why didn't you? You didn't have to argue with your father on my account. You could have kept your counsel.'

'Honestly, my darling, that's what I intended, but that nasty old devil pushed me over the edge. I couldn't let him get away with what he said about you. This has been coming for a long time. I know I've burnt my boats, but I'm no longer beholden to him.'

Tears welled in Annie's eyes. 'But you'll be away sometimes,' she sobbed. 'Sales representatives have to stay over when they're away from home: I know that from our family business. And I couldn't bear you not being there beside me through the night.'

'You'll be all right. The job's for the Aire Valley and Lancashire, so I'll be back on a late train and safe in your arms most nights. I'll only be away occasionally. And you don't want to believe all those stories you hear about travelling salesmen,' Walter teased. 'They're just jokes in the music halls.'

'I know, I know,' she murmured, and tried to force a little smile. She snuggled up to him, and tried in vain to fall asleep.

Despite Annie's confident and bubbly nature, deep down was an insecurity she could not fathom. Perhaps the seed had been sown by the sudden death of her dear father so early in her life. She knew her dear father had been smitten by the last and loveliest of his children, and had unashamedly spoilt her. She was his darling: happy, bright and innocently precocious. His sudden death had struck the ten-year-old like a hammer blow, and it had left in her a deep uncertainty that her bright, confident exterior could never overcome. Deception by a young man, who had meant much to her, had eroded her confidence further – and the shame of this episode, her sense of failure, had led her to keep the details from her family and her husband. The recent disastrous affair between Albert and her sister had further increased the nagging cancer of doubt. Annie cradled Walter's sleeping head in her bosom and wondered if he would always be true to her.

* * *

As the lone walker thought about the events in what had been a pivotal day in his life, he wondered again if they had sowed the first suspicion in his young wife's mind, and consequently the uncertainty that grew between them. He wiped a tear from his eye, and tried to convince himself that it had been caused by the stiff breeze that had suddenly sprung up. It had moved the clouds on, and Cartmel Fell to the north-west was already beginning to clear.

Chapter Nineteen

Walter had always been comfortable in his own company. Working alone or just being on his own was never irksome. Although a sociable and affable young man, he did not seek company for its own sake. He enjoyed lonely walks in inaccessible places, where he had opportunity to roam and time to think, just as he had now in the middle of this sandy waste.

* * *

For a time, being a sales representative for Ledger's Wholesale and Retail Drapery gave Walter a freedom and solitude that he had never known before, as he quickly adapted to the loneliness of travelling and the responsibility for organising his own day's work; in fact he thrived on it. He enjoyed watching the ever-changing scenery and exploring new towns, looking forward to the long walks and to meeting new people, even if many of them were provincial shopkeepers with narrow outlooks and narrow lives. He suited the firm and the firm suited him. They hardly had to train him in matters relating to the drapery trade, for his knowledge was as good as anybody's. He even had little to learn about tricks of the trade, for he had suffered his fair share of patter and promises from the other side of the fence and knew instinctively which methods worked and which didn't. Walter prepared himself for his new job by borrowing books from Bradford library, including some on the new science of psychology, so that he was aware of the subtle approaches and interactions that were needed.

At his interview Walter readily impressed Mr Ledger, who openly commended his sales director on his choice of successor. 'Well done, Lem!' he said. 'You seem to have found a promising young bloke for the Lancashire area. And we won't have to train you much, Mr Clough. You seem to know your stuff, and I can see you've brought no bad habits with you from other firms.'

Lem smiled with self-satisfaction. It was a feather in his cap too. 'Thank you, Mr Ledger,' he grovelled. 'Yes, I interviewed a lot of young men to find a salesman like our Mr Clough here. I'm glad you approve. But we must make sure that all areas are up to scratch. I'm going down to Miss Dobson in the office to pick up the sales returns, so I can see where we need to make more effort. You can rest assured I'll make sure no one's slacking in this firm.'

It was soon obvious to Walter that his predecessor *had* been slacking, getting by with just enough sales to satisfy his superiors. With the enthusiasm and energy of youth, Walter Clough made a flying start to his sales career. He spent a few days touring his patch with Lem and discovered that rail communications were good, even to the West Lancashire towns of Blackburn, Preston and Accrington. He was also pleased to learn that Lancaster and his beloved Morecambe were in his domain.

'Don't be put off by rival salesmen,' Lem warned him. 'They'll tell you that Lancashire isn't your area or that there's a gentleman's agreement or such lies. It's all tosh. If you've got right goods at right prices then t'drapers' shops will buy 'em. It's all fair in selling and war.'

Walter had bought a map of North Lancashire, something his predecessor had never thought of. He brought it to Lem that afternoon and both spent some time in the office looking at it closely, together with sales sheets for the area.

'First of all,' Lem warned him, 'don't go to any towns further south than Bolton. You don't want to antagonise the big Manchester wholesalers, and Handley's in particular. We do have an unspoken agreement with *them*. They don't touch us and we keep to the north of Lancashire. It would be a lot of travelling for little gain, and I don't want them appearing here in Yorkshire.'

'I'll need to look at these sales sheets for an hour or two,' Walter said.

'All right. You can use a corner of my office, but keep it tidy.'

Walter borrowed a pencil and pad and vanished into the office. He emerged later that afternoon.

'Well?' asked his boss.

'We don't seem to do much in Morecambe and Blackpool, and there are a lot of new shops opening up. If we get in there in spring they'll be stocking up for the summer. You know folk like to spend their brass on holiday. Clothing and gift lines should go well.'

'They're a long way away.'

'Which is why not many salesmen go there – but the trains are good. I'll also have to work out strategies for towns on my patch. They'll need different approaches and merchandise.'

And so Walter Clough began his career as sales representative for Ledger's Wholesale Drapers. Annie soon appreciated that his overnight stays were not as frequent as she had feared. He made every effort to return most nights, even if it meant taking the last train and returning to a cold dinner.

Walter quickly learned to prepare his sales pitch well, adapting his ranges to the areas he visited. Better quality lines always went well in suburban, fashionable towns, while the cotton towns of Lancashire needed a cheaper, more utilitarian range. Country towns such as Skipton and Clitheroe were different again, requiring quality goods but more traditional styles. Walter particularly loved the short run to Skipton, where the wide market street afforded a fine view of the old church at the top. This was not on market days of course: he tended to avoid these, when more trade was done in just a few hours than in the rest of the week put together. It was better to wait for the next day when the town was quiet, the shelves empty and shopkeepers wanted to break the monotony with a pleasant chat. It was like that in all the small country towns that he grew to love. If time permitted he allowed himself the luxury of a lunchtime walk up into the Dales or, if time was more pressing, around the castle or along the canal. His greater business and profit was in the crowded, smoky towns, but his heart was in the countryside.

Walter's plans worked well, and in the first few months – taking into account his sales bonuses – his income was double what he would have earned in Enos's shop. He was determined to make a success of his new career, and this did not go unnoticed by his employers. But, looking back over the years, he wondered if that success might have sown the seeds for his eventual downfall.

One evening he returned late, and as they sat together in the back parlour Annie suddenly remarked, 'It would be nice if we could have a house of our own, Walt. After all, with the baby coming we'd be a real family, all three of us together.'

The idea appealed to Walter. He had wondered about it himself, but had thought of delaying it until after their first child had arrived. His increased wages ensured there was no difficulty in taking such a step.

His wife broke into his thoughts again. 'I've been hearing about those new terraced houses being built over near Goose Hill. They're quite big and well away from the mills and ironworks. Shall we walk over this weekend and take a look?'

'Are you sure you haven't been to look already, dearest?' he joked.

'Well, your mother and I did take a walk down Rooley Lane,' Annie admitted. 'Moderate exercise is beneficial for a young lady in my condition, and we happened to notice some houses that they've nearly finished at the bottom of Bowling Park Road. It's such a perfect spot, backing on to the park and within easy reach of the new tramway that'll go right into Bradford. It won't be too far from your mother . . .'

'Stop!' Walter laughed. 'I can see you've worked it all out, and knowing you, you scheming little madam, I'm sure you've picked the perfect spot. Well, let's go and look tomorrow afternoon. To complete my sales schedule I'll have to miss my lunch, so as punishment you'll have to make sandwiches. So there!'

She flung her arms round his neck, like a little girl who has been given the best doll in the shop. Any hope poor Walter had of getting to sleep that night was forestalled by Annie's conversation about everything from the colour of curtains to the style of tablecloths and antimacassars.

And so they moved into a neat, new house on Bowling Park Road. It stood at the end of a terrace of a dozen, all identical. Slightly bigger than the norm, they had six rooms, three on each floor, and a capacious cellar below. They were faced in the same Yorkshire sandstone, a millstone grit, which when new offered a golden hue to any sunny day, though this darkened to a dark grey-brown after a few years' exposure to the smoky atmosphere. A small front garden was bounded by a low stone wall and gate, and in the back yard was a small privy connected to an enclosed drain. Annie, of course, paid close attention to every detail around the house, even planting pink roses in the small front garden.

Despite the fashion for dark furniture and curtains, the high ceilings and large windows made the rooms feel light and airy. With wedding gifts and loans from Harriet, Mary Ackroyd and other relatives, furnishing the new house proved no problem, and money saved from Walter's increased wages filled in the gaps that were left. Working for Ledger's also proved useful, as Walter could purchase many household items at a discount. Even Lem joined in the spirit of their venture, presenting him with a box of useful items gleaned from samples and ends of lines.

When the couple moved in, Annie keenly directed the gang of volunteers who were assisting them in moving furniture, fitting shelves, putting up curtains and carrying and unpacking tea chests and boxes. 'We'll want that tea chest taken upstairs and those boxes left in the cellar for the moment,' she ordered, as Walter's friends struggled under their heavy loads.

'Hey, Walt,' declared Arby, loud enough for Annie to hear, 'yon missus of yours is a right slave driver. I don't know how you manage to live with 'er.'

Annie had got used to comments like this, most of which had been directed jokingly at her.

'Aye,' muttered Tom, 'and with all this back-breaking work she makes us do I could drown myself in a pint of ale. But I don't suppose they'll have any in a teetotal household like this.'

Annie smiled: the crate of beer smuggled into the cellar by Walter had not escaped her notice. She had the sense to realise that moving house was thirsty work and required its own reward. The gang had shown a true spirit of friendship throughout the hectic day, and she valued this.

When the last helper had gone, and Walter and Annie had eaten a quickly prepared meal, they climbed the stairs and snuggled into the bed that Tom, Arby and Sam had carried all the way from Wakefield Road in a small handcart. She stretched over to kiss her husband, but he was already fast asleep.

In the following weeks there followed a hectic round of 'at homes': invitations were sent to relatives and friends so that the married couple could receive them in their new home. Two notable absentees were Nancy and Enos, for different reasons. Some months before, Nancy had gone to stay with her aunt and uncle in Leeds. Neither she nor her mother could face the shame of her condition. It was hoped that events would take their course with a minimum of fuss and in utmost secrecy, as far as the churchgoers of East Bowling and members of the Band of Hope were concerned. Arrangements were in hand for the adoption, and the story was circulated that Nancy had not been well and had gone to a relative in Scarborough to convalesce in the fresh sea air.

Enos, on the other hand, would not have been welcome, nor did his resentment allow him to visit his stepson. He had heard through the grapevine how well Walter had been doing, and this only served to rub salt into the wound. It was with some relief that Harriet turned up for tea on Sunday with her friend, Mrs Hobson. It was not the first time Harriet had visited the house, of course, for she had been popping in from time to time to keep Annie company, as well as helping with cleaning and other little jobs her daughter-in-law now found difficult – all of which was genuinely appreciated by the mother-to-be.

After finishing her tea Walter's mother looked round the room, and shocked the assembled company by declaring, 'Oh Walter, Annie, it's such a charming house! I wish I could have persuaded Enos to move into a lovely home like this, instead of putting up with that dump behind the draper's shop all these years – but he was too mean to spend the money.'

Annie suppressed a giggle, Walter turned his head away and Maud Hobson, who had known Harriet for a long time, had a bright twinkle in her blue eyes.

On the 12th of March Annie presented Walter with a healthy daughter, whom they called Hannah. Walter had suggested the name, Annie had happily agreed and Harriet was delighted. Hannah was not a placid baby but alert and demanding. Annie managed her with all the patience and love she could muster, but would have found motherhood a trying time but for the kindly intervention of Harriet. Her mother-in-law walked to their house in all weathers to help with the household chores, take over care of the baby when she cried and, in general, made life bearable for the exhausted young mother. She never bossed or tried to control but worked under Annie's direction, offering advice only when asked. She was glad she had decided not to help with the drapery, leaving her husband to bear the expense of an assistant, as her new granddaughter had given her a new lease of life and she was determined to enjoy it to the full.

To Walter, Hannah was the most wonderful thing that God had ever created. Mind you, it was easy for a man who was at work all day to come home, hug and play with his child, then go out again the following morning. In later years Hannah's kiss was the first to greet him when he returned home, and there was often time before bed when they could share a book.

The news came a few weeks later that Nancy had given birth to a healthy baby boy. Annie was determined to visit her and see her nephew before the chance was lost. Walter felt uneasy: he would have preferred all the arrangements to have been completed and Nancy to have returned home before he saw her again. Annie prevailed, and two weeks later the new family caught the train to Leeds and took a cab to the peaceful and elegant suburb of Burley.

The house was large, larger even than Annie's family house in Wakefield Road. It stood well back in a quiet, prosperous street where no children played and doors were kept shut. Walter opened the gate and they made their way up the path to the front door. After he rang the bell it took a few seconds for a maid to appear. She ushered them in quickly, and down the hallway to a drawing room at the rear of the house.

Nancy was standing in the large bay window, looking out on to the extensive manicured garden, which was secluded from any inward gaze by a neatly trimmed hedge. She was holding the infant to her, but on seeing them enter she carefully laid him down in his cradle and turned to Annie. For a few seconds they stared at each other, then embraced. It was a strange embrace, warm, but uncertain, as if they did not know what to say or how to act.

'Thank you for coming, Annie,' Nancy said quietly. 'And you as well, Walter.' She turned to look at Hannah, who was dribbling down Walter's lapel. 'She's lovely, Annie,' she whispered. 'She's God's perfect gift to you. I know she'll make you both very happy.' Nancy made no attempt to pick Hannah up or touch her, and for a minute there was an awkward silence. Annie's impatience gave way. She turned to the quiet baby in his cradle.

'May I?' she asked.

'Of course,' replied her sister, and took up the small infant from its cot. She looked at him for a second before handing him over.

'Why, he's beautiful,' murmured Annie. She did not know whether to enthuse or to compliment her sister, so her tone conveyed no emotion. She looked at the baby longingly for a moment, before swapping him awkwardly with her husband for Hannah.

Walter was keen to show his prowess as a father, and held the young infant before him in a secure, confident manner. He certainly was a beautiful baby boy, with a round face, clear blue eyes, wispy blond hair and an angelic expression. Walter looked at him intently and his charge stared back in an almost knowing manner. Was he imagining things or was this the kind of look he had seen somewhere before? He remembered Mrs Ackroyd's words about the spawn of Satan, and wondered what life might hold in store for the innocent bundle in his arms.

'I've called him Gideon,' Nancy said. 'One of God's soldiers fighting for truth, and watchful against evil.' Annie and Walter glanced at each other, not knowing what to say.

The boy whimpered softly. Nancy gently took him from Walter's arms and turned away to discreetly suckle him, mindful of her brother-in-law's presence. After a minute she stopped, buttoned her dress and turned back to them.

'He's a very good baby. He hardly cries at all. He sleeps through most of the night and only wakes me in the morning when he's hungry.'

'That's nice,' replied Annie. 'I only wish our Hannah was like that. She's always crying, and always wants my attention. As I told you in my letter, without Walter's mother's help I don't know how I would have coped.'

Nancy wasn't listening; tears were rolling down her cheeks. 'Oh, Annie, I love him and I'm going to have to give him up!' she wailed. 'I know he'll be well looked after, but I could give him so much more. It would have been so wonderful if we'd both been married, with new babies and new lives and having each other to turn to.' Nancy held the infant close and kissed his cheek, then placed him in his cradle and fell sobbing into the armchair. Annie hurriedly returned Hannah to the arms of her father and went to comfort her sister, she too in floods of tears. Hannah seemed to catch the spirit of the occasion and began to cry herself, wailing far louder than the others . . .

* * *

The lone figure out on the sands was beginning to feel colder, at least his feet were, as his socks and shoes had been soaked for a long time. He bent down to take them off, tied his laces together and, still deep in thought, hung his shoes round his neck. Walter could picture the scene as if it were yesterday: the two sisters and his daughter sharing their tears, the two males in the room remaining silent, too helpless and perplexed to offer any comment or contribution.

Chapter Twenty

Among the difficulties, obstacles and traps for the unwary, there is often a stretch on a journey when you can make good progress on firm unyielding ground. As Walter approached the Kent he crossed a stretch of firm sand that rose up in gentle banks and would scarcely be covered by an incoming tide. He walked steadily and safely for over a mile towards the crossing point.

* * *

The first five years of his marriage were a similar comfortable and sure period in Walter's life journey. They were perhaps the calmest, most settled time he experienced, predictable but enjoyable, like the early part of his childhood when he felt safe, certain and loved. His relationship with Annie had a familiar pattern. She was engrossed in raising the family, keeping house, the social round and church duties. But the passion and energy of their first two years together slowly began to dissipate. Within six months of Hannah's birth Annie was pregnant again, and thereafter wary of full commitment to her husband. Besides which, opportunities had become more limited. Hannah was a clinging child in her early years, and when she found it difficult to sleep she often sought solace in their bed. Walter, too, was often weary, because of the travelling.

Rose was totally different to her sister; a much more passive child. She had dark curls, a round cherubic face and a happy smile. She was an ideal baby, sleeping well and often, and as she grew up she became a contented infant, who loved to watch her mother at work or her energetic, impatient sister at play. Annie blessed this fact. Had Rose been even slightly like her sister in temperament, her mother would have found it difficult to cope. Harriet continued to help the young couple, looking after the two children for many hours a week and thereby ensuring that Annie and Walter could spend some time in each other's company, if church commitments permitted. Walter slightly resented this intrusion, but he did not let it show – realising that he was not around to help his wife during the week, and that she had to have social contact outside the home.

One summer's day Walter took his wife to Shipley Glen. As they reached the Bracken Stones after a tiring climb she turned to him and said, 'Deep down, Walter, would you have preferred it to be Emily on your arm this afternoon?'

He was stunned, and had to collect his thoughts. He hoped his hesitancy was not interpreted as admission. 'No, I don't. She was a beautiful lass, but I don't know whether she would have understood me as you do'.

'How do you mean, Walt?' Annie persisted.

Her husband pondered for a moment. 'You know what makes me tick, and how, though I may not be as devout as you, I love God's beautiful world and want to see more of it. I don't think she could have seen that part of me.'

But secretly he wondered how it might have been. Were there hidden depths to that beautiful, enigmatic, dark-haired girl? Would she have made the effort to understand him and his hopes and aspirations? With his encouragement, could she have improved herself? Might she have taken childbirth and family life in her stride and still remained a passionate and willing lover?

He sat down on the grass with Annie, and like a secret courting couple they kissed and teased and laughed. Such opportunities were few and far between; and all too soon they had to return home, as Harriet had to return home to cook Enos's meal. Although more subdued and acquiescent these days, her husband might be roused to anger if he had no supper on the table.

Enos's health was in steady decline, and he had passed the daily running of his shop to the able Mrs Booth, whose children had grown up and whose husband was long away at sea. He had reluctantly agreed to the changes she had demanded in stock and styles.

'You're going to need more household linens, Mr Clough. And those aprons don't sell well at all. Holmes's in Bradford have some much fancier ones, and they'll only be sixpence more at wholesale price.'

He had grumbled but eventually had given in. Maud Booth was, he knew, too valuable to lose. Shop assistants might be two a penny, but a woman who had the energy and ideas to improve sales and profits was an asset to be prized, despite her stubborn nature. Walter could see that she possessed the qualities of thrift and business acumen that Enos prized, but she also had qualities that Walter's mother recognised, such as a woman's sense of style and taste. Maud's welcoming sales manner attracted far more customers than the miserable proprietor had ever done, and in a short time she had transformed the look and running of the shop. Although Enos disliked her and her bossy ways, he couldn't deny the effect she had on his profits.

Walter had, on his mother's insistence, eventually made his peace with his stepfather, but it was a cold, formal relationship: both minded their ps and qs and said little to antagonise the other. When he visited for tea for the first time everyone was polite, and although the atmosphere was strained all passed off with no untoward comments or confrontation. Harriet was thankful for that.

'Aye, it's a right nice house thee has,' the old miser commented, 'and thee keeps it very nice, young lass, but them houses isn't as good as t'old uns. No fancy privy in t'back yard or running watter; you had to fetch it from t'well. But they was plain, solid dwellings with none o' this fancy stuff on t'ceilings and round doors. They did us all right, though. They made us tough, and them kids as weren't didn't last long.'

Harriet would have loved to have added her two penn'orth on the subject of old houses, but refrained. The evening had passed without argument and that was good enough for her.

Hannah's enthusiasm on meeting her grandfather was tinged with disappointment. He was not as she had hoped a grandfather might be, being neither playful nor interested in anything she might have to say. 'Grumpy grandad,' she confided to her father as he tucked her up in bed.

Nancy eventually made a visit to Walter and Annie's home twelve months after her return. She had stayed in Leeds with her son for two months after the birth, until arrangements were made for the adoption, and then spent a further two months with her aunt and uncle. No one suspected the real reason for her prolonged absence and she spent her first week back bravely thanking well-wishers at church and in the village for their kind and solicitous enquiries about her health. She was quiet and introspective, never mentioning the child she had loved, and any attempt by Annie to raise the subject was met with a cool but polite rebuff. When Nancy resumed her work for the church with greater evangelical fervour than ever, her family hoped that all would be quietly forgotten and her life would resume as normal. But no young man caught her eye; nor did she ever encourage such association.

It was on her first visit to her sister's house that Nancy surprised them all with a bland announcement of her plans. 'I'm leaving St John's Church,' she began. 'I'm going to work at the mission church in Silsbridge Lane. I'll continue my work for the Band of Hope there, working with the poor unfortunates and sinners and dedicating my life to God's work.'

Her family stood open-mouthed in shock. Silsbridge Lane was probably the meanest and most dangerous area in the whole of the centre of Bradford. It comprised run-down back-to-back houses, dingy and half-derelict hotels and boarding houses, pubs and inns of the most dubious reputation. It was home to the most evil and violent criminals known to the city constabulary: robbers, whoremongers, swindlers and drunkards, as well as the most miserable wretches who scraped a pittance on the streets.

'Do you know anything about those streets?' asked Annie. 'It's the worst area in Bradford.'

Nancy nodded. 'It's the Lord's work I've been called for, and there are more sinners to save and people to help than anywhere else in this town.'

'But it's dangerous,' added Walter, deeply worried. 'There are men there who'll slit your throat as soon as look at you. You hear about young women vanishing in those streets.'

'God will protect me,' Nancy replied. 'Pastor Robinson and his wife have worked among these people for some time and I'll be in their care. I'm going to help them in their charitable work, as well as offering salvation to those in moral and physical danger.'

'What do you mean?' asked her sister. 'Who are you going to help?'

'I'm no longer an innocent in the ways of the world and I'm fully aware of its wickedness. I speak of those young girls desperate for lodging and sustenance who turn to any form of depravity to keep a roof over their head or a crust in their belly. We're planning to build a refuge for such poor girls, so that they're not thrown in desperation into the hands of evil felons, to sell their bodies for the desire of men. That will be much of my work for God.' The two listeners stood dumbfounded, astonished by her frankness and single-mindeness: she was a different person, still as devout and zealous but stronger and more confident. Nancy turned to Walter, and shocked him further with her forthright words. 'My seduction by your cousin, for such I believe it was, was God's doing, I'm sure. It is this that has turned me to work for the Lord among the sinners of this city. You see, Walter, God even has a purpose for poor Albert. I hope in time that he may realise the folly of his debauched and licentious life and turn to God's true path. If I have served but a small part in that then God be praised; it has been worth the heartache.'

She turned and left the room, leaving Walter and Annie silent and stunned.

Annie saw her sister less frequently as the years passed. They remained friends, but Nancy's evangelical zeal put an invisible barrier between them that the years did not remove. It led to a deep resentment on Annie's part, not toward her sister but directed at the man and circumstances she judged had been the cause. At first she kept these feelings hidden from Walter.

Her husband had his own secret as well: from time to time he slipped off to Liverpool to see his cousin. Albert had not changed. He had not married and settled down, nor had he any inclination to do so. He had set up residence with a couple of his women, but these were short-lived, loveless affairs and for the most part he continued in his wanton ways. But the boyish charm had gone; the women were older and less innocent. The relentless drinking had made his skin redder and blotched, and his girth expanded as the years wore on. Away from the jollity of his drunken state he was more sombre and self-pitying, but he always enquired after Nancy, even before he asked about Walter and his family. Walter's visits became more infrequent as the years passed, not because he did not care about his cousin but because they seemed to have less in common; what had once been a jolly and pleasant interlude became a duty and a humdrum chore.

There were other things that Walter kept from his wife, not because he was ashamed but because he did not want to upset her or sow any seed of mistaken suspicion in her mind. From his earliest days as a salesman he became aware of the many opportunities that could arise for dalliance, or in the case of a married man for infidelity. His friends teased him about it, sometimes within Annie's earshot, and he tried hard to assure her that these beliefs were unfounded and grossly exaggerated by music hall comedians. Nevertheless, a handsome young salesman who visited shops used flattery and a little flirtation from time to time to establish a congenial atmosphere in which to display and sell his wares. Walter was not adverse to this, but that was where he drew the line; any advances from a shop girl or proprietress were politely and charmingly rebuffed.

He must have been tired or off guard when twenty months into his career as Ledger's sales representative he made his last call in Burnley, to Hindle's Drapery. It was run by Alice Hindle, a widow some ten years his senior, whom Walter had always found very pleasant to deal with.

'Would you like to stay for tea, love?' she asked, when they had finished their business.

'That would be very nice, thank you.'

'I've baked some scones and Eccles cakes this morning. I thought you might be popping round and it would be nice to have a bit of tea and a chat. Although the shop's doing well and I always have customers to natter to, when I shuts up shop it gets lonely of an evening, now that Herbert is no longer with us. Been gone these four year, he has.'

Walter was weary. He had missed lunch and the thought of a bite to eat, a cup of tea and the chance to put his feet up for half an hour appealed to him, far more than sitting in a cold waiting room on Burnley station. It would make his journey to Skipton and the last train to Bradford infinitely more bearable. Alice showed him through to the parlour and he eased himself into a comfortable armchair. She appeared with a plateful of delicacies and a pot of steaming tea. He helped himself generously, refilled his cup and warmed himself by the roaring fire.

Alice kept the conversation going, and Walter sleepily let her chatter on. He heard about her marriage to Herbert and his sudden demise. Matters then turned to her need for a man on whom she could rely, who would be available for advice and would be a shoulder to cry on. 'A kind, sensible man like you, or my Herbert when he was alive,' she hinted.

Walter smiled modestly in agreement. No alarm bells rang in his head; no warning signs of quicksands came into view. The conversation was taking a strange path and he naïvely followed. He did not find Alice at all attractive, and he assumed she felt the same way about him. It was only when he realised that time was passing that doubts started to cloud his mind. 'Thank you for such a lovely tea, Mrs Hindle,' he began, 'but I'm afraid I'll have to leave now. If I don't I'll miss my train.'

'Nonsense, Walter,' she answered, 'and the name's Alice, not Mrs Hindle. We get on so well together I'm sure we can be on first-name terms.'

'You really are too kind, but if I don't make a move now I'll get too comfortable to move from this chair.'

'But if you're settled,' she continued in a suggestive tone, 'you can stay here for the night. I've a spare room available if that's what you *really* want, and I can make sure you'd be nice and comfortable till the morning.' Alice came round the back of his seat as she spoke, and rested her hands on his shoulders, moving her fingers slowly along his collarbone, then inching them on to the front of his chest and round his shirt buttons. Walter sensed her breath and felt the distinctly soft, warm touch of what must have been her ample bosom on the back of his neck. He stared forward in terror, not daring to move his face to one side or the other.

'Thank you for your hospitality,' Walter gabbled nervously, 'but I must get my train home. My wife's expecting me. She worries if I don't get back of a night.'

'Nonsense,' Alice whispered coaxingly. 'Salesmen's wives know they have to stay over sometimes. It goes with the job. And it would be much cosier here than in a hotel.'

Walter tried to get up but it was no use. It was like pushing upwards into a deep, heavy but welcoming cushion. The forces of gravity and embarrassment were against him. He had to use guile and agility: strength was out of the question against such a powerful and determined temptress. He squirmed quickly under her grasp, and freed himself with a deft sideways movement. Alice's ample and voluptuous form precluded any chance of quick reaction, and she took a few seconds to recover her balance. This was just long enough for Walter to grab his coat and case and dodge her on his way to the door. He was in the back yard and down the alley before she could block his path. Out in the street he resumed a brisk walk, which turned into a gallop when he realised how late he was; and he made the train with no time to spare, opening the door and jumping on as it began to move.

Sitting in a compartment, Walter wondered how many unwary salesmen had succumbed to her ample charms and had willingly accepted such accommodation. He laughed to himself: it would be his last visit to Hindle's Drapery. Other salesmen would have to risk servicing the needs of the voluptuous Alice. He pondered what excuse to make when he explained the shop's removal from his sales lists. 'Change of trade!' he declared aloud to the empty carriage, 'I'll tell them it's become an ironmonger's.'

Annie gave him a warm kiss on his arrival home.

'Walter Clough, you've become a right messy eater,' she complained. 'Look, there are crumbs down your waistcoat and shirt front. What have you been up to?'

* * *

He hadn't the nerve to tell her what had occurred, and he had kept it to himself all these years, occasionally bringing it to mind when he needed a chuckle. Now there was no one to see this strange figure walking in the flat, muddy wastes, laughing and smiling to himself.

Chapter Twenty-One

The train rattled across the viaduct in the distance as it steamed out of Arnside station and across the wide river inlet. A flock of seagulls rose up in terror at the hissing, clanking monster. It reminded Walter of another railway, which ran overhead along the piers and docks of Liverpool. But trains on the 'dockers' umbrella' did not chug or hiss: their motors made no sound, but the wheels and bogeys clanged and clunked over bridges and points just the same. Passengers on either railway looked out on an estuary, some seeing the tranquillity of blue-green hills and wide empty sands, the others seeing ships, cranes, buildings, wagons and the industry of many, many people. It may have seemed strange to anyone who did not know him, but both scenes fascinated Walter.

* * *

On his next visit to Albert, Walter promised himself he would take the overhead railway its whole length, to see a complete panorama of Britain's largest port. It did not disappoint. Outside Lime Street station he took a horse tram in the general direction of Toxteth. On alighting, he asked for directions from the driver, who pointed him towards a set of steps that rose up from the street to a small station on the gantry above. It had been recently built and was bright and clean. Posters abounded, many offering journeys to and new lives in America, Canada or Australia via Liverpool's great shipping companies, Cunard, White Star, Bibby and numerous others.

One poster that caught Walter's eye proclaimed a 'Projected Party for Canada' on the Beaver Line steamer. It was recruiting 'strong country lads' to work on the farms of Manitoba. The journey cost eight pounds twelve shillings and ten pence. He decided to take a threepence ticket to Seaforth instead. After all, he thought, there's still the opportunity to change there for more exotic destinations – like Southport or Blundellsands . . .

Three carriages, with no visible engine, rattled into the station and the passengers emerged on to the platform. Along with half a dozen others Walter climbed aboard and deliberately settled himself on a hard ribbed wooden seat on the left. The carriages lurched forward and clanked slowly over a girder bridge that spanned a wide road, and he got his view of the older docks, including Salthouse Dock, where he had first met Albert after his flight from Bradford. To his left was the broad river, with the cranes and warehouses of Birkenhead clearly visible over the water.

The train made four brief stops before slowing down at the Pier Head station, from where Walter could see the floating dock and bridges. To someone who was interested in all things mechanical it was amazing and yet so simple, a long, floating, hinged pier that stuck out into the deeper river and fell and rose with the tide. No ferry, Irish Packet or passenger ship need enter a lock or dock gate and be marooned at low tide. The dock was just as busy as he had seen it before, with people and carts piled with luggage everywhere.

At the end of the pier stood a magnificent new passenger liner, admired by all who passed by. She was long and sleek with clean elegant lines. Two slim funnels rose amidships, and promenade decks ran virtually the whole length of her sides, painted a gleaming white in contrast to the jet black of her hull. Walter estimated she was at least four thousand tons, and recognised from the colour of her funnels that she was from the White Star Line. He caught sight of her name, which was perfect for a ship of such splendour: the *Majestic*. He imagined sailing on her with Annie and the children to a new, exciting, pioneering life in America or Australia . . .

He was awakened from his reverie as the train shuffled off again and a corpulent man, dressed in working clothes and wearing a leather cap, plonked himself down, occupying most of the seat and pinning Walter against the window. It was a good job he had chosen to view the exciting panorama that flashed by the carriage window, as in his current uncomfortable position there was no alternative.

Within seconds the liner had vanished between the warehouses and cranes. The train darted in and out between tall buildings, and at times skirted the dock edge so closely that Walter felt he could reach out and touch the ships. He passed warehouses as big as palaces, new earthworks and building projects that would form the giant docks for bigger and bigger ships of the future. The railway crossed the mouth of a canal, which he guessed was his beloved Leeds to Liverpool Canal, on the towpath of which he had taken many a country stroll. It had followed him across the country through Shipley, the Bingley locks, Skipton and through the rolling Pennine hills to meet him again. Here its canal boats discharged their wares on to wharves and took on goods from every part of the world.

Eventually the railway turned its back on the river. Since the enormous man had got off at the previous stop Walter could see to his right again, where, stretching into the distance, were thousands of small back-to-back houses crammed up against the docks.

Alighting at Seaforth, Walter took the train a few stops back to Sandon Dock, the nearest station to his cousin's home. He got directions from the stationmaster to Silvester Street and reached it after a brief walk. This building was not a back-to-back but a drab three-storey tenement, built of dark smoky brick with small windows and three short flights of stone steps leading to separate front doors. He chose the middle one because it looked less scruffy than the others.

The door was opened by a small, thin-faced, young woman. In earlier years she might have been considered attractive but her face was already careworn and hard. 'You'se wantin' sumten?' she asked sharply.

'I'm looking for Albert, Albert Dowgill'.

'Ooh, you've gorra be Walter,' she exclaimed, putting on a contrived smile of welcome. He had struck lucky, if that was the right phrase, first time. She led him down a hallway and into a dingy, meanly furnished room. Albert was lounging on a sofa. The room was untidy and dirty, the kitchen beyond in even more of a mess.

'Nice to see you, Walt,' was Albert's greeting. 'Thee's met Mary, Mary McGeechan. She's living with me. Good lass is Mary, one of the best.'

Walter would have begged to differ but was too polite to say. If Albert, in his younger and smarter days, had wanted to settle down with a girl he could have had his pick in Bowling, and all of them would have been prettier and nicer than this hard-faced hussy.

'I'm not working at present,' Albert told him. 'No meat ships in dock so they've laid us off. We expect some in next week, so we'll be back in t'meat halls to do some cutting up. In the meantime Mary keeps us going with a bit o' this and that.'

Walter could see through this for the lie it was. His cousin had lost his job and had to live on the wits of his companion. She winked at Walter in a way that made him cringe.

You'se can bet there's sumten I can turn my hand to, Walt,' she proudly announced. 'Some running at the Pier when the emigrants arrive, some dealing and trading. I can keep us going when things are tight.'

Walter did not enquire into what 'running' was or what exactly the dealing and trading entailed, though he was suspicious about their legality and morality. A few more minutes' chatter confirmed his suspicions. He had taken an instant dislike to Mary. After a long conversation, in which she seemed to do most of the talking in a fast Irish brogue that allowed little interruption, his worst fears were confirmed. Albert was entangled with an evil woman who would cheat, steal and sell anything, herself included, to gain a dishonest penny. What kind of life had his cousin been drawn into?

Walter was glad to get home that night. He had to lie to Annie, saying he had missed a connection to Bradford, but he felt no guilt. His marriage may have reached a plateau of respectability, family duty and predictability, but it was far better, he was sure, than anything his cousin was experiencing. Their marriage still roused itself into tenderness occasionally, with the consequence that Annie was pregnant again. Walter was not unduly worried: his wife had given birth to their daughters with relative ease and, with her mother-in-law's help, had learned to cope well. Besides, he thought, this time it might be a boy, a son to look forward to.

When he arrived home a couple of nights later Walter was met by his daughter's eager embrace. He lifted her into his arms, kissed her and was met by a dozen kisses in return, but he noticed something was wrong. Annie had been crying; her eyes were red and her skin pale. He put down his persistent daughter and looked at his wife.

'Oh, Walter, how could you? she said. 'All this time and you've been deceiving me.' She held a blue ticket in her hand. Stamped on it were the words 'Liverpool Docklands Railway: Three Pence'. 'I found it in the cupboard where you hang your coat. It must have slipped out of your pocket.'

'Mummy's been ever so sad today,' Hannah interrupted. 'She's been crying. Please make her happy again, Daddy.'

'You pop along to the parlour, darling,' Walter said, 'and see how Rosie is. She may want someone to play with. I'll follow in a minute and read you a story.'

Hannah obeyed. She instinctively realised her father knew what was best and always obeyed him in an instant, whereas she could be obstinate with her mother; although she eventually submitted to her will, it was often with reluctance.

'You've deceived me,' Annie said, picking up the thread of her accusation, 'and what I want to know is how long you've been lying and what else you're lying to me about.'

Walter was silent. As usual he hoped that the moment he took to collect his thoughts would not be construed as an admission of guilt. 'I *have* deceived you,' he admitted, 'and I've hid it from you from the beginning, but it's the only thing I've hidden, of that you can be sure.'

She burst into tears. He tried to embrace her but she pulled away from him.

'I did it for the best of reasons, for the right reasons; to save you and your sister from pain, in the hope that she might forget Albert.'

'But you kept on seeing him,' she protested.

'When I first went to Liverpool five years ago I found him

more or less straight away. I got a lucky break and was directed to the firm he worked for. We met and talked, but it was obvious he wasn't going to come back. I found out he had real feelings for her, but he knew he couldn't change. He realised that if he came back and married her he'd lead a rotten life and make her miserable.' Annie had stopped crying and was listening intently. 'I judged it was best to lie and say I hadn't found him, as that would cause Nancy less pain. I hoped that eventually she'd forget him, and never realise that he cared for her. Do you know, when I've seen him, and I've been half a dozen times over the years, the first thing he asks is how Nancy's getting on. I even tell him about her work down at the mission.' Walter did not mention his cousin's present situation or that, with the slut in attendance, Albert had for the first time been unable to ask after Nancy. 'Do you know, Annie, of all the women my cousin has met, flirted with, seduced, she was probably the only one that ever meant anything to him. Please don't tell her. It would probably break her heart. That's why I've kept silent over the years.'

She nodded in agreement, but she was not finished with him yet. 'But you kept on seeing him, and you lied to me to keep on doing it. How do I know what other lies you've told me? If I can't trust you in this, how can I trust you at all?'

'I had to keep seeing him. Despite everything he's still my lifelong friend, and he has to know I'd be there for him if he ever needed me. You don't desert your friends because they've done wrong. I may not see him much now, but he knows I'm there. He's no influence on my life any more, but maybe in some way I can influence his.'

Annie's anger subsided, but deep down her suspicion remained. She realised her efforts to change her husband, to alter his horizons and rein in his secret aspirations had foundered on the rocks of his own morality and ambition. It did not diminish her love for him, but continually wondering about Walter's commitment increased her insecurity.

It was a couple of months later and Walter had been away overnight. He had tried to get back from Barrow but had missed his connection, and he'd had to stay that night at the George Inn in Lancaster. He called at the office in Godwin Street to hand in his sales returns and then went home. He was met at the door not by Annie but by his mother. Her face was a grave and sombre mask.

'What's wrong?' he asked, but instinctively he guessed the answer.

'Oh, Walt, she's lost the child,' came Harriet's tearful reply, 'but don't worry, lad, she'll be all right – at least after some rest.'

She led Walter into the bedroom, where the curtains were half drawn. In the dim light he saw Annie's pale, sad face staring at the ceiling. Harriet left them alone, returning downstairs to look after Hannah and Rosie.

'Oh, Walt!' Annie cried. 'It happened last night. Why weren't you here?' She didn't wait for an answer. 'It was a boy, the doctor said, just what you wanted. I felt so alone, you being so far away . . . I wish you'd give up this job. I hate it!'

He tried to explain how he'd missed the train, but she wasn't listening. He sat holding her hand and eventually she fell asleep, partly through exhaustion but also because of the draught the doctor had left for her to sip.

Walter found out the details from his mother. There had been no fall, no accident. It had just been, as Harriet put it, 'God's way'. When the pain started Annie had panicked, but had the sense to send Hannah for her mother-in-law, in the company of an older girl from next door. The intelligent girl clearly remembered the way to her grandparents', even though she had only been a couple of times before, and guided her older companion up Rooley Lane, along Parkside and Woodroyd Road and straight to the draper's shop. Both girls ran all the way and arrived exhausted. Hannah told her worried grandmother that 'Mummy has poorly pains in her tummy,' and Harriet immediately realised the urgency of the situation. She called on the doctor in West Bowling, and all four took his pony and trap, arriving at the house not a moment too soon. Although the premature infant was still-born, the doctor was able to save Annie from further danger.

To the inquisitive Hannah, the death of her baby brother came as a shock. Her grandmother did her best to answer all her questions, telling her that the baby had 'gone to Jesus'. Hannah immediately asked her father, 'Daddy, will I go to Jesus one day?'

'We all do,' he assured her, 'but it'll be a long, long time before *you* go up to him.'

'Will I meet our baby there?'

Her father nodded.

'What will I call him?' she pleaded, ''cos you haven't given him a name.'

Walter smiled. He was tempted to say 'Albert', so that at least one Albert made it to heaven. But he was mindful of his daughter's inventive imagination, and her propensity to say anything that came into her head, especially at the most embarrassing and inopportune times. 'I think Baby Angel,' he said at last.

This satisfied his daughter briefly. About ten minutes later she asked, 'Will I get some wings one day, like my little brother?'

Chapter Twenty-Two

The narrow channel may have been gouged out by the last tide, by the one before that or even a week or two earlier. Walter's instinct was to jump it, but for some reason he held back: there was no point in taking a risk or making a rash decision. He recalled Reuben's advice. 'Every time tha goes out on the bay, be gentle with her. Treat her like a fine young woman. Be tender and patient with her. Get to know her moods and when to tread softly and when to take her generous bounty.'

* * *

Reuben was right. It had been like that with Eliza: their love had taken a time to grow. It was six years after he started at Ledger's that Eliza Smith breezed into the office in Godwin Street. Almost immediately everybody's world was turned upside down. She was not quite as tall as Emily Lumb, not quite as dark and enigmatic, but every bit as beautiful. In Walter's opinion she possessed that same mysterious gift of inner beauty, but with a quick wit and deep intelligence allied to her stunning looks.

Just like Emily she had come from humble beginnings. Ephraim Smith, Eliza's father, was a carter from Manningham Lane on the other side of the city. He had no formal education but a ready brain in business and a thirst for knowledge. When he cleared houses after a death or when he was moving households he always asked if this or that book were needed, and had thus acquired as good a library as you would find in the house of any vicar or schoolmaster. It was his middle daughter who had the good fortune to possess both her mother's striking looks and her father's natural intelligence, unlike some of her siblings, whose bad luck was to inherit their father's looks and mother's intelligence. Like Walter, Eliza was outstanding at school, and with the encouragement of her father and the generosity of a maiden aunt continued her education with book-keeping courses at the local institute. She made her mark in the offices of a local mill and a firm of accountants, and at the age of nineteen she obtained a post in the accounts department at Ledger's.

God knows what havoc she wreaked on leaving her previous employment, with broken hearts and tears shed, but this pattern continued among Ledger's tailors, drapers, clerks and travellers. Salesmen found any excuse to come back to the office and even filed their sales returns on time, hovering round her desk in the hope of receiving a glance or a smile. For junior sales assistants in the various retail departments she was an unobtainable goal, but that did not stop them dreaming about her every night. For the male clerks in accounts no pile of books was too heavy, nor message too far to run, in the hope of gaining her favour. She was skilful in the way she handled the men who flitted around her, sharing the odd dalliance and flirtation with the more acceptable young men, yet keeping the brash seducers and older married men firmly at arm's length.

Walter, like the others, was intrigued by her allure and charm, but did not fawn over her or seek ploys to gain her attention as many male employees did. He was friendly when their paths crossed, but that was all. After all, he had a young and pretty wife who after her fourth pregnancy had safely delivered him a dear and most desired son. His life, if not complete, had taken a turn for the better. He knew that after the birth, with the attention she paid to Thomas Harry Clough and her reluctance to risk another pregnancy so soon, their love life had descended again to temporary physical indifference. No matter. For the present his interest in his baby son and two growing daughters made him a happy man, and for him Eliza was no more than a beautiful picture that adorned the accounts office.

Eliza was intrigued: the most handsome and most interesting man around did not pay her any special attention. It was only when, in casual conversation, he began to wax lyrical about the beautiful scenes he saw every day, amid the daily grind of selling drapery, that she realised that of all the men who daily crossed her path this was the one who really interested her. Here was a thinking man who saw more to life than a quick female conquest or an extra shilling in his wages. She looked forward to Walter's calls in the office and engaged him in conversation about where he had been. His descriptions of the dark Lakeland fells, the pretty, Dales villages, old churches and castles and the sunsets over the expanse of Morecambe Bay were poetry to her ears. When he touched on his yearning to visit foreign shores and see wonderful sights, it awakened a desire in her for wider horizons and adventures.

Walter was surprised one afternoon when Eliza handed him a letter. It was addressed to him, care of Ledger's Drapers of Bradford, and had arrived with the daily pile of business post. She taunted him about it and would not hand it over immediately.

'Have you got a secret life that none of us knows about? she teased. 'Shall I let Mr Ledger know that you're using our office for your secret communications?' He was puzzled. Eventually she handed it over and said, with a laugh, 'You're all right, Walter. Your secret life is safe with me, and if any more turn up I'll intercept them so the office busybodies don't get a sniff. You salesmen are all alike. This life on the road gives you too many opportunities for romances and secret goings-on, and to think I thought you were different to the others, a happily married man . . .' Her laughter stopped: she could see by Walter's expression that it was bad news. She left him to read and returned to her desk, embarrassed at the distress she might have caused.

The letter was to the point. It was written in a simple, uneducated style and contained the broad speech and expressions the writer always used in his conversations: Albert had cared little for school. It was not a long letter, nor did it skirt delicately round the truth with polite phrases.

Dear Walt,

I'm writing this from my bed in the free hospital here in Liverpool. I'm dying, Walt, and it's from the pox. I think I picked it up from that whore Mary some time ago, but it's taken me this long to find out and now it's real bad. She's scarpered with all I owned and left me here to die. Please come as quick as you can before it's too late.

Your dear friend Albert.

As luck would have it, Walter was due to do a sales round in Accrington the following day. If he caught the early train out and missed some of the smaller shops he calculated he could get to Liverpool by three o'clock. Whether he could get home again by nightfall was not certain. Would he tell Annie? He wrestled with this all the way home. He decided to, but not the whole truth. On his way home he called at the Dowgills'. Aunt Leah opened the door and invited him in. She seemed worried, so obviously knew something.

'Well, this is a sad business,' she began. 'Albert knocked down by a runaway horse and taken to hospital. I hope it's not serious.'

Walter breathed a sigh of relief. He could use this as cover for visiting his cousin, and when he got home he could tell Annie the lie that Albert had told his family. 'Yes, I heard it from one of our pals. But it may not be as bad as we think, perhaps just broken limbs.'

'Would you go over and see him, Walter?' Leah pleaded. 'It's hard for us with the business, and especially for Josh. He's got heart trouble and can't travel far. And you're so used to travelling.'

'Yes of course, Aunt Leah,' he replied, relieved that they might not find out the awful truth. 'I'll be happy to do that.'

'You're such a good lad, Walter.' Leah smiled and patted his shoulder. 'I know Albert's doing well in Liverpool and has a nice young wife Mary from over there. But I wish he'd been more like you, attentive to his lessons, married a nice Bradford lass and given us a nice family of grandchilder to take on t'butchering business. But you can't have everything, can you?'

Walter swallowed hard. He was finding it hard to keep tears from his eyes, but he would rather Leah persist in her ignorance than learn the awful truth, even if she was Enos's sister.

'Well, at least he's doing well. This accident may only put him out for two or three weeks, and then things will get back to normal.'

She seemed reassured by his words, then disappeared into the kitchen and came back with five sovereigns. 'He'll need some brass with not working. It's our little store for emergencies. We don't trust banks and places like that. Give him that to see him over, will you, Walter?'

Walter took the money and said his goodbyes. He called in on his mother and Enos, and told them his aunt's story about Albert's unfortunate accident. Enos accepted it without question, but there was something in Harriet's eyes that made him realise she had guessed the situation was worse than he had related.

Annie believed his story and, seeing that he had Leah's money to hand over, could not really object to his journey. She was concerned, though, that he was contriving to deceive his employers. 'Why don't you ask Mr Metcalf for time off?' she suggested.

'Because he might say no. He can get funny about such things, and I had a day off when Thomas was born. Ledger's are all right with funerals and close family but they draw the line. If he refused and I went ahead and they found out I'd get the sack.'

'I suppose you're right, but I'm not happy about it. You've changed, Walter Clough. You're not as open and straightforward as you once were, with me or with anyone else.' Annie retreated to the kitchen, and was in a sullen, pensive mood for the rest of the afternoon.

Hannah, a bright and clever six year old who had made a good start to her schooling, was a perceptive child. 'Why are you and Mummy unhappy again, Daddy?' she asked. 'You're always arguing or sad these days. Why can't you always love each other?'

'We do, sweetheart,' he answered, 'but there are a lot of sad and difficult things in life, and they make people a bit grumpy from time to time.'

'Not like grumpy gramps,' she giggled. 'Now he's grumpy all the time!'

The Royal Liverpool Free Hospital was an imposing building. Its long wards were light and airy with beds arranged on each side down its length. Nurses marched up and down, attending to their patients with a kind but business-like manner. Walter's polite enquiry at the central desk in the main entrance was met with a prompt and helpful direction to a ward on the outer perimeter. He waited half an hour for the start of the visiting time, and when he finally entered the ward was scarcely able to recognise his cousin, who lay in a dazed state, breathing heavily. Albert's boyish good looks had totally vanished. The blond hair was darker and greasy, laid flat across his head. His face was grey and bloated, and his eyes had sunk deep. There were lesions and ulcers around his neck and probably, Walter guessed, over the rest of his body. He moaned from time to time and rambled in a mixture of unintelligible words and sounds. A nurse came over and mopped his sweating brow. Walter looked at her despairingly.

'This is how it affects them in the later stages,' she said. 'It's not just the rash, but the brain is fevered and there are swellings all over, inside and out. The heart can't beat properly. I'm sorry you've come so far and can't talk to him.' She turned away from the patient. 'It can't be more than a day or two now, I'm afraid,' she whispered. 'What's your name? I'll try and get him to understand.'

'Walter,' he replied. 'Walt to him. He's my cousin.'

She turned back to the living corpse. 'Walter's here to see you,' she said loudly, mouthing the words in an effort to make him understand.

It was as if someone had switched a light on in his brain, not a bright light but a small flickering one. He looked up and smiled. 'Walt,' he gasped. 'Walt, you've come. You were always my best friend. No one had a mate like you. I could always rely on you.'

'You can, Albert,' Walter whispered.

The dying man fought for breath in an attempt to speak. 'It won't be long now. Found out about this a couple of months ago.' He paused again. 'That Mary cleared out and took everything with her; evil bitch she was. I haven't touched a woman since. Got me wondering about my life and what I've done. Will you forgive me, Walt? I done a lot o' rotten things to you and your family over the years.' He smiled. 'But we've had some reyt good times as well, haven't we?'

Albert rambled on about the gang, their adventures and Emily. He even made a small joke. 'You know, Walt, if I do get to heaven by last-minute redemption, then happen I'll meet Emily. And thank God thee'll not be around to get in t'way!'

They both laughed as they always had done, but the effort took away his strength. He lay gasping for a while, then struggled to pull something from under his pillow. It was a sealed letter, but not in his writing. The envelope was addressed simply 'To Nancy'. 'Give this to her, Walt,' he croaked. 'T'nice nurse wrote it down, but it's my words. She did it for me a few days ago when I had the strength.' He fell back on the pillow again. Walter stayed for a few moments, took his hand and squeezed it. He could swear he felt a gentle squeeze in return.

It was the last contact he had with his cousin. He called at the hospital the following morning, and was informed that Albert had passed away in the night. He left them with his cousin's details and home address and took the train back. He called in at the Dowgills' straight away to break the sad news, then hurried home. When he informed Annie tears sprung to her eyes. She had never cared for Walter's wild and wanton cousin, but she knew how much he had meant to her husband. When he showed her the letter and told her of his intention to deliver it to Nancy, her mood changed.

'You can't do that to my sister! It would bring back the horror and shame of it all again. For God's sake, Walter, spare her that.'

For once he was resolute. If it meant a row with his wife and a bad atmosphere for days to come, so be it. 'You can't refuse the wish of a dying man,' Walter shouted. 'And I think, Annie, you underestimate your sister. It's not the first misjudgement you've made of people's motives, and it won't be the last!'

With that, he stormed out of the house and walked briskly through the park. It was a fine day, so he decided to walk into Bradford, thereby collecting his thoughts and calming his mind. He soon reached the city centre, and stopped off at Ledger's to hand in his sales returns. Lem was not his usual jovial self and took them from him in a perfunctory manner.

'What's this?' he complained. 'Two days messing around in Preston and Blackburn and that's all you've got to show for it?'

Walter gave a lame excuse about a rival firm moving on to their patch and left the office in a huff: he didn't even speak to

Eliza. He walked along Westgate and turned into the opening that was Silsbridge Lane, from the shops and fine buildings on the main street into another world.

The lane was narrow, and from it even narrower alleyways and ginnels sprouted. The houses were small and mean with dirty windows, and few had curtains. The small shop on the corner sported a couple of tatty placards, not for the *Bradford Argus* or the *Yorkshire Post* but for the *Shamrock* and *Hibernian*. Two burly policemen wandered past, giving him a casual look then passing on their way, looking into doorways and alleys and poking their noses into noisy pubs and squalid lodging houses. Walter had heard that the Bradford constabulary always went in twos down Silsbridge Lane and it was true, even in the middle of the day when it was quiet, compared with the mayhem of a Friday or Saturday night. To Walter, who had lived in the city all his life, it was a world he had never known, far meaner and poorer than anything he had seen in Bowling.

The stench increased as he wandered further down the vile street. Mixed with many foul odours was the distinctive smell of food cooking, and he soon came across its source. A scruffy eating house was on the next street corner, a rough sign outside advertising its simple menu: 'Grey Paes ½*d*, Potato Pie 2*d*, Penny Ducks 1*d*'. Walter stopped to look. Visible through the open door were five men, seated round a table. In the middle was a large dish containing a pie, which the hungry customers were picking up with their fingers: there was not a plate, knife or fork to be seen. Although he was hungry, no thought of stopping for a bite at such a filthy, disgusting place entered Walter's mind.

With relief, he realised he did not have much further to go, for round the next bend, between two lodging houses, was a simple stone building with a plain wooden cross affixed to the end gable. A small roughly painted sign announced it as the New Mission Church. It gave the times of services, and nothing else apart from the words 'Come and be saved by God's abiding love'. Walter opened the door and went in. The room was bare except for a few banners, and a cross on the end wall. Nancy was at the back of the hall, cleaning the chairs and benches. She stood up and stared at him in amazement.

'Why, Walter! What brings you down here?' Then, as if to

answer her own question, her face clouded into a look of worry and foreboding. 'I hope it isn't bad news.'

'Albert's dead,' Walter announced starkly. 'He died in Liverpool, and I was with him shortly before he passed away.'

'Oh, how sad,' she said, trying vainly to sound as if the news meant little to her.

'He wrote a letter, or should I say, a nurse wrote it down for him. He was too weak to do it himself. Anyway, it's for you. Please read it.'

Nancy took the letter from him and slowly opened it. She pored over each word, eventually resting it on her lap and sighing. Tears welled up into her eyes, but she didn't cry. Her head sank on to her chest. Whether it was prayer or anguish, Walter couldn't tell.

'Are you all right, Nancy?'

'Read it, please read it, Walter,' she begged. 'I don't mind. Being such a close friend you can probably guess what most of it says, anyway.' He took the paper from her and started to read.

My dearest Nancy,

I am writing this from my hospital bed. By the time you read this I may already be dead. First of all, I want to ask if you will forgive me for the wrong I have done you. If God can forgive me for all the wickedness in my life, please will you? I wronged you terribly. I know that. Everyone said that I should have done the decent thing and married you, but believe me, I would have cheated you and deceived you and caused you more pain if I'd done that. That's why I went away, 'cos I didn't want your life ruined even more by my wickedness. You can ask Walt about my real reasons. He'll tell you it's true.

When I knew how sick I was and that I would soon die, I went to this little church somewhere in the middle of Liverpool docks, probably something like yours. For the first time I went in to pray, proper like, not just pretending. This girl was there. She told me of God's forgiveness and how He loves us all, especially sinners. I didn't see her talking, only you all those years ago, telling me the truth. I should have recognised it then, instead of stringing you along for my own wicked ends.

Apart from my family, there are only two people that mean a lot to me. One is Walt who has been my one true friend and the other is you, 'cos you loved me for what I was, and saw something in me that others didn't. You wanted to make that one small, good spark into the fire that would guide my life. Eventually after all these years you succeeded.

Please pray for me Nancy, I know your prayers count a lot. I will never forget you.

Your dearest Albert.

PS. This is my only money. I won't be needing it. Use it for the church. I hope it can do some good.

Walter pulled out the two five pound notes from between the sheets of the letter. He handed them to Nancy, then took the five sovereigns from his pocket. 'I never had the chance to give him this. It was from his mother to tide him over while he was ill. No doubt he would have wanted it to go to your work as well.'

Nancy nodded, and took the money from him. She looked to the cross at the front of the church and then to Walter. She took his hand, held it firmly and bowed her head in prayer. Walter did the same. It was the right thing to do.

Chapter Twenty-Three

On the edge of the river Walter bowed his head and said the same silent prayer to his departed friend that he had said four years before.

Now he had to cross the Kent. It looked wide and gentle now, but it was still dangerous for the unwary. At its worst, when winter rains had saturated the hills around, it could be a raging torrent, scouring out sand in its dash for the sea, washing away the sandbanks, so that the broken edges stood like solid walls in the way of a desperate traveller. Walter had also seen the waters surge the other way, when a tidal bore, driven by a strong southerly wind, had rushed into the narrowing channel, a wall of water churning everything in its wake. But today it was its usual deceptive calm. He wandered up and down the edge for a hundred yards or so, then, satisfied he had picked the right spot, rolled up his trousers and carefully stepped into the water. It was warm, soothing and caressing his aching feet. He ploughed on for over three hundred yards, the water occasionally lapping over his knees. But because it was wide it was shallow, and its pull was gentle. He had done this a couple of times before, and he knew that providing he took care it held no fears.

Walter stepped dripping from the water and climbed to firmer ground. He felt he had overcome the most dangerous part of his journey. It was like baptism into a new life: there was no turning back now. With his new-found commitment to Eliza, he came from the river a new man, more determined than ever to go ahead with his plan.

Why was it he found Eliza so enticing and attractive? Why was she worth sacrificing his life for, sacrificing the family he treasured and the good opinion of all those people he valued? He had felt it during their first affair, when he had suddenly fallen in love with her. In the beginning it was a casual but intense liaison, but he and Eliza both realised that their feelings had changed, and the relationship had brought meaning to their lives. He remembered the months that had brought their first entanglement to its inevitable bitter end.

* * *

Albert's funeral had gone well, if you can say such a thing about such an occasion. To start with, Walter had spoken to the hospital doctor on the morning of his friend's death and he had named the primary cause of death as heart failure, agreeing to indicate the secondary cause as the infection *treponema pallidum*, not giving it its common name of syphilis. Walter thanked him for this consideration: it would save Albert's parents from knowing the true cause, and would save them embarrassment from its disclosure. It was his secret, to keep with him to the grave.

Much to Annie's consternation, Nancy insisted on accompanying them to the funeral. Nancy was a tower of strength to Walter, much more so than his wife. A bond of friendship and understanding had grown between them – a genuine feeling of companionship forged by their joint loss. She was introduced to Joshua and Leah as Annie's sister, and no more. Whether Leah had forgotten her role in her son's disappearance, or whether she had not realised the girl Albert had wronged was Annie's sister, they could not tell. She had, however, her brother's knack of making the most embarrassing comments. 'I'm so glad you could come and pay thy respects,' she said to Nancy. 'Yes, I do remember thee, lass, as t'chief bridesmaid at Walt's wedding. I remember thee and Albert together, and me thinking you made a right pretty pair.'

A look of embarrassment shot across Annie's face, and she and Walter turned to look at Nancy, who caught Walter's eye; he could swear that he saw a wry smile cross her lips.

It was at Walter's insistence that after Albert's funeral he and Annie started occasionally to raise money for the mission's hostel. Thanks to funds raised over the previous year, Albert's donation and help from public benefactors, many of whom were sought out by Walter, the project finally came to fruition. A modest extension was built on to the church, to afford cooking facilities and living quarters for six homeless girls, to save them from the dangers and degradation that might face them in the city. It was Nancy's concern from start to finish, and she was appointed to run it. Her determination and enterprise amazed everyone around her, and she looked after her charges with the fearlessness of a tigress and the tenderness of a loving mother.

Annie began to act strangely, seeming to resent her sister's success, Nancy's close friendship with Walter and particularly their visits to the squalor of Silsbridge Lane. It was a difficult period for Walter: despite all the attentions he paid his wife, he rarely seemed to receive her love and affection. He ensured he got back home every night when it was possible, instead of staying away, but his late arrival was often met with criticism and a cold meal. He rarely went out with his friends for a drink, instead striving to keep Annie company and endeavouring to do a share of the domestic and family duties. But the strain told on him.

Walter arrived at Godwin Street one day to be met by Lem Metcalf, who asked him into his office for his habitual haranguing about sales figures. Because he was trying to get back home most nights, Walter had let visits slide and sales were falling.

'It's only temporary difficulties, Lem,' he tried to explain. 'Come the summer it'll turn round. I know it will.'

'It's not good enough,' complained his boss. 'A few years ago you were the best salesman by far. Now you're like the rest of the lazy good-for-nothings.'

At least Walter always got a smile and cheery word from Eliza. As they passed on the corridor she greeted him with, 'How's my wandering boy today?'

'Not wandering enough, according to Lem,' he replied wryly.

'Well, you can help me then. I've got to go up to the attics to find some returns from two years ago. I'd welcome a brave

190

escort who'll save me from the spiders. Some girls say they've even seen mice up there.'

'I thought you were going to be the brave adventuress,' he joked, 'travelling to America, Australia and all over the world, facing deserts, jungles, snakes and creepy crawlies. And you're telling me you're afraid of a few spiders?' He laughed, and Eliza pretended to be scared. 'Oh well, I suppose I'd better go with you,' Walter sighed. 'You never know, there may be the odd tarantula or scorpion hiding in the papers.'

They climbed the winding stairs at the rear of the offices to a low room that spanned the building from front to back, under the roof. As in many such buildings, it had been floored to offer additional storage between the beams and joists. Walter switched on the dim electric light and Eliza closed the door behind them. In truth the room was not as dirty or as dusty as it might have been: it was used to store sheets and curtains, and some unfortunate junior had recently been sent up to sweep the area that held the soft furnishings.

In the dim light they searched the boxes, pleased to find them labelled. They quickly found the right one, for December 1893, and rifled through the papers closely.

'I think I've found them,' muttered Walter, and held them under the light.

She put her face close to his to check them. They stood there for almost a minute, cheek to cheek, reading the sheets of figures. What thoughts passed between them it was difficult to say. Then without a word she turned to him, kissing him slowly and passionately. Perhaps she caught him by surprise, or perhaps it was something he was hoping for or even expected; but her actions were not unwelcome. He responded just as ardently. Senses heightened by the danger of sudden interruption, their desire quickly mounted, and the kiss became a tight embrace. The adjacent pile of curtains made a soft and ready bed, and they tumbled on to it in an all-consuming passion. This was no one-sided seduction of an innocent office girl: Eliza may have been unschooled in the arts of love, but she responded willingly and readily to her lover's promptings. For Walter it was a moment of pure joy that had sprung from nowhere, and he welcomed all of it, to its consummation, without thought of the consequences. They finished their lovemaking, satiated and ecstatically happy.

Dressing hurriedly, for a minute they looked at each other, kissed again, then slowly made their way downstairs. Eliza checked that no-one was observing them leaving the attic together, and they parted in different directions.

For Walter it was an affair, plain and simple, but not a sordid, purely physical liaison. It was a tender, stimulating entrapment with a young woman whom he would grow to love deeply, not just for her undoubted beauty but for her whole being and spirit. There was no question of leaving Annie and the children; his sense of duty, love and obligation was strong. Eliza had found the one special man in her life, who interested and excited her, and she would defy convention and morality to have him. She knew he would not leave his wife and family and she would always be the mistress, but that didn't matter.

In the next few months their affair stuttered, not through a lack of commitment or passion but because of the force of circumstances. They deliberately avoided each other in the office, but met in a secluded corner of the park at lunchtimes or after work. Their encounters were confined to the occasional evening when Walter pretended to go out with his friends, and they met in some sordid hotel for intense but all too brief lovemaking.

One day, as they were strolling through the park, Eliza dropped her bombshell. 'I'm leaving Ledger's, next week.'

'Where are you going?' Walter asked, open-mouthed.

'I'm going to teach bookkeeping and accountancy at the Institute. It's only part time, some evenings and afternoons.' She smiled at Walter, who was still too surprised to say anything. 'I've not just been chasing men. While I've been at Ledger's I've been taking my exams, and I've passed them, so I'm well qualified. I intend to be a modern, independent woman, the kind you find these days living in London.'

'Will that be enough to keep you? After all, you like to spend on yourself. and you won't have a full-time wage coming in.'

'That's only part of it,' Eliza explained. 'I'll be working for my father as well, running his accounts, managing his paperwork and chasing his debtors. He's not a little two-cart business now, you know: he's bought out Turnbull's and their stables. They've got some big wagons and heavy horses, and Dad's got a contract with some mills, carrying raw materials. We're moving to a bigger house next week over Cottingley way. Mum's really looking forward to it. It's got a library where Dad can keep his books, instead of leaving them all over the house.'

'Will it be enough to keep you in dresses and hats?'

'Dad's going to find me some more firms whose accounts I can do, and he's having part of the stables converted into an office. Oh, I wish you could meet him,' she sighed. 'You'd like him a lot, Walter. He's rather like you. He can quote poetry, Shakespeare and the like. He knows nearly every fact known to man and he's interested in history and buildings and nature, all the things that make you such an interesting fellow. I think that's why I fell for you, Walter, as well as the other things you're good at!' Eliza giggled like a schoolgirl, and he joined in: it was fun to be with her. 'And it means we'll be able to see a bit more of each other. I won't be limited by office hours. Oh, it'll be busy to start with, but when things settle down I'm sure I'll be able to take up other interests besides bookkeeping.'

What she said was true. Ephraim Smith, who had once plied his trade with one cart, had become one of Bradford's most successful entrepreneurs. It was a far cry from when he used to ride the streets of Bradford, and at the end of the day would call to his horse, 'Hey, Samson, home, lad!' The horse, almost as intelligent as his master, could find his way back from any part of the city to Manningham Lane, and Ephraim would lie back, reading of course, with hardly a touch of the rein needed the whole way. It was a frequent sight, and a great source of amusement to the locals.

The two lovers continued to find opportunities to meet, though they were careful. Walter took no risks. Pretending he had to stay away overnight for work, he would travel back to Bradford then on to Leeds, where he booked a hotel for them for the night. Eliza told her family that she was spending an evening with a friend whom she had met in the course of her work, a Miss Jane Taylor, and that she was staying overnight at her house in Pudsey.

'I think Miss Taylor and I would like a short holiday,' she declared one day, turning to Walter. 'What do you say, Jane?'

Walter, with his best comic manner, took on the role of a

prim and proper young lady, put on one of Eliza's hats and pranced around the bedroom. 'I think, my dear,' he exclaimed in a high-pitched, affected voice, 'it would be an excellent idea for us to take the sea air. And who knows, we might even try a little sea bathing together.'

She roared with laughter at his antics. Walter was not only charming, a good lover and an interesting conversationalist, but he could also be ridiculous and funny. Though she was only able to have snatched moments with her lover, Eliza would willingly have shared her whole life with him.

So Walter informed his boss and Annie that, with the summer season upon them, it would take a two-night stay to visit all the shops in Preston and Blackpool. By missing lunchtimes and working harder than usual, he could make all the visits that were necessary and leave a day and a half free to enjoy a short but romantic holiday with Eliza. He chose Blackpool, thirty miles to the south, because it was safer than Morecambe, where he was too well known. At home quarrels followed his announcement.

'Just ask Lem Metcalf!' he explained to Annie. 'He's been on my back these last six months because I haven't spent much time there. The reason was, Annie, I was doing my best to get back to Bradford each night for your sake.'

'What do you mean?' his wife shouted. 'You've spent more nights away the last six months than you have ever done before.'

'But it's less than other salesmen,' he lied, 'and if I get Blackpool covered before the summer there'll be rich pickings and I'll keep the firm happy.'

'What am I to do for three days?' Annie complained. 'It's me who has to attend to the children, nurse them when they're ill and run the household while you're gallivanting off to Blackpool.'

'You don't want me to get the sack, do you? Because if I don't improve my sales that's what will happen. It's a once a year chance to sell some lines for the holiday trade. People will buy all kinds of stuff when they're away on holiday, and the shops want to be stocked to the ceiling. It's a real opportunity for us to get in as we did in Morecambe. If I do well it'll keep Lem off my back for the rest of the year.'

The argument descended into acrimony. Eventually Annie stormed into the kitchen and Walter stayed in the parlour, reading his newspaper. The children were in bed, but, woken yet again by the raised voices, Hannah was not asleep.

As he had predicted, Walter did good business. Blackpool was growing and thriving, and more and more visitors were arriving to see its new attractions. He concluded his visits by lunchtime on the second day, and carefully post-dated some of his sales sheets, as he had done for Preston the previous week. Eliza did not mind waiting around: she shopped extravagantly and took in some of the resort's delights. She was a brave and free spirit, and their time together was as wonderful as they had hoped for. They took the lift to the top of the new tower, from where they could see the whole of the Fylde coast, and they even ventured on to the Big Wheel, which had just been opened for the new season. At her suggestion, on their last afternoon they sat on the North Pier and composed a letter to be sent from Eliza's imaginary friend Jane, thanking Eliza for her company on their holiday in Blackpool. Walter agreed to write it down and post it on their return to Bradford. Oh, how they laughed and chuckled at their ingenious plans and subterfuges.

As they wandered back along the pier and down the promenade towards the hotel for the last time, they heard a band playing hymns on the sand below. A banner fluttering above it proudly proclaimed 'The Blackpool Christian Seaside Mission'. They strolled down the slipway to listen. Linking arms, as any happy lovers would, they watched the assembled crowd. When a young woman stepped from the band and accompanying choir with a collection box and wandered towards them, Walter froze. He turned to drag Eliza away, but it was too late.

'Walter, I can't believe it!' Nancy gasped. 'How could you do such a thing?'

Eliza dropped his arm and turned away in embarrassment. Walter was lost for words.

'Annie told me you were away for a few days, but you told her it was for business. How can you deceive her so cruelly?'

Walter's shame and guilt were on his face for all to see. He didn't try to excuse himself with lies. For the first time in years he felt those dark, intense eyes staring deep into him again, almost piercing his soul.

'I know things haven't been going well between you and Annie lately. A sister can sometimes feel these things. But Walter, this can never be the way.'

He turned his head away for a few seconds, then looked back at her. 'You're going to tell Annie?' he whispered.

Nancy stayed silent for a minute, deep in thought. 'If I do what will happen?' she asked. 'My sister will be devastated. She's become more and more anxious and uncertain in the past few months, and this would break her apart.'

'I won't leave her or my family. They're too precious to sacrifice. I swear to you, Nancy, that's the truth.'

'I think I believe you, Walter. You *are* a good and loving father to those dear children, but it's you who will have to decide. If you love them and have any vestige of feeling left for Annie you'll have to give this woman up. I will not seek to insult her by calling her the names that many would. She seems a presentable and attractive young woman, and one who has obviously fallen for you. You've always been a handsome fellow, charming and interesting.'

'This is the only other woman I've been with; you must believe me. Annie and I have been strangers these last few months, and I fell into temptation all too easily.'

'I believe you, Walter, and who am I to condemn when once I did the same? But the choice is yours: you know that as much as I do. You must give her up and make your peace with Annie. If you do that I promise you I won't tell her. It would ruin too many lives, and we've already seen so many destroyed.'

Walter remained silent. Nancy realised the struggle that was going on inside and looked at him intently, but it was no hard stare, just a gentle gaze. 'You leave me with only one choice,' he answered sullenly. 'I must do as you say.' He looked her in the eyes and slowly nodded.

'And please don't try to deceive me, Walt,' she begged. 'After all we've been through, we know each other too well. I'll sense if you've taken the right path: one look will tell me. If you lie to me I'll find out, and I'll have no compunction in telling Annie. You have a chance Walter. It's more than many have.'

She turned and walked away. Eliza, who had watched the proceedings from a little distance, was puzzled and wanted to ask all kinds of questions, but deep down, from Walter's sombre tone and taciturn manner, she knew their affair had come to an end. She accepted it with tears, having known it was bound to happen one day. This had been an ecstatic, loving, wonderful relationship, but she had always known the choice he would make if it came to it.

* * *

His life had turned in another direction at that point, he reflected, but further twists and turns were to follow. As if to mirror his story, the lone walker turned sharply south-west and followed the shoreline back out to sea. But unlike the adventures in his life, this was a planned move, a sure and safe route that Walter knew well.

Chapter Twenty-Four

His new track followed the firmer sands towards the headland; then he could turn again to find landfall. Through the ages travellers across the bay would have done what he did, from Romans and Norsemen through to the coach service that ran between Lancaster and Barrow before the railways came. None dared head further north towards the mudflats of the estuary. Like the choice he had to make in life, this was the only choice he could make at this point on his journey.

* * *

And Walter reflected on the pain he'd suffered in making that choice. On their return to Bradford he had given up that beautiful, wonderful girl and returned to his wife and family. Annie had no inkling of what had happened, and Nancy was true to her word. She stayed on for a further fortnight with the Blackpool Seaside Gospel Mission, and Walter realised she had not written to her sister about the dreadful confrontation. On her return Nancy saw that things had settled down between Annie and Walter, so she said no more, much to Walter's relief.

Walter was devastated by the separation from Eliza, but further problems soon followed. Lem casually invited him to his office one afternoon for a chat about business. 'Sales went well, Walt,' he began. 'Those three days in Preston and Blackpool.'

'Yes,' agreed Walter, 'I told you I could do good business there this time of year.'

'You must have been very busy.'

'Oh yes, Lem, those three days were hectic, what with both towns to cover and a lot of new shops opening in the resort.'

Lem nodded as if in agreement. 'There's just one small problem I'd like you to help us sort out. It concerns the order with Latham's of Preston. You remember it, Walt?'

'Oh yes,' Walter replied, settling himself down in the chair. 'It wasn't one of the big ones, like those I got in Blackpool, but it was good enough.'

'There's no problem with that,' his boss went on, a strange mixture of frown and smile crossing his face. 'It's just that Ledger's prides itself in making sure that our customers get their orders delivered in less than a fortnight. Latham's expected that, and as they were running short of the lines they ordered, they wrote in last week to ask why the goods hadn't arrived. They say the order was placed over three weeks ago. What have you got to say to that?' The smiles and bonhomie had disappeared from his face. He stared hard at Walter, enjoying seeing him squirm.

'They must have made a mistake,' suggested the flustered victim. 'They'll have had other salesmen visiting and must have confused the orders.'

'But it isn't the only shop that's complained,' replied his tormentor. 'And when I wrote to check with the other Preston firms, they all said you visited the week before, usually late in the day and on your way back from other places.'

'But what's the point?' asked Walter, panic spreading across his face. 'I did the business, didn't I?'

'Yes, and claimed two nights at that Blackpool hotel,' Lem snarled. 'Don't tell me you worked three days in Blackpool, you lying cheat, 'cos that won't wash. You made good sales, it's true, but those firms were close together near the front. Took a leaf out of your book, I did: I got a map of Blackpool and checked them. You didn't bother with any on the edge of town or up in Fleetwood or Lytham. Easy pickings they were, to hide the fact you spent a couple of days on t'firm's time on holiday, no doubt with some little tart!'

199

Walter stayed silent. He hoped he might get away with a severe reprimand and deductions from his salary.

'The trouble is, you forgot that I spent over twenty years on the road,' Lem continued. 'And I know all the tricks you can pull. I may have pulled a few myself in my time, but never as many as you. I've been looking back over your sales returns and expenses over the last few months, and I'm telling you now that they don't tally.' He stood up and looked down at Walter, cowering in his seat. 'You've been pulling one or two fast ones. You might have got away with it, but I'm too fly for thee, Walter Clough.' His words were met with a stunned silence. 'Now when I had a few words with young Mr Ledger about this he told me summat else. Our cotton buyer reckons he saw you in Liverpool about three months back, and that's definitely not on your patch. Well, my lad, what have you got to say to that?'

'I'll admit to that,' answered Walter sullenly. 'I'd finished my sales assignments and went to see my cousin, who was very ill in hospital. He died the next day, and I didn't make any claims for accommodation or travel.'

'No, but you didn't ask permission, did you? And it were on t'firm's time. We have procedures over things like that and you, you clever bugger, you thought you could ignore them. You've gone too far, my cocky lad, and I've only one more thing to say to you. You're sacked.'

Walter was too stunned to argue, storm out or slam the door. He rose politely and in a dignified manner made his way to the outer office, leaving his case where it lay by Lem's desk. He walked out into the street and strolled as far as the Mason's Arms.

'What's eating you?' asked Sam Lodge. 'You've got a face like a wet Sunday.'

'I've lost my job. Ledger's have sacked me. I'll have a double whisky, Sam, if you don't mind.'

'You can have one on the house, and no more. I don't want you turning up to that niece of mine broke and blind drunk. That's no way to face your family and our Annie. Mind you, you'll need a little bit o' Dutch courage to tell her, 'cos she can be a fiery little madam at times.'

'Thanks,' mumbled Walter. 'You're a good friend.'

'Now, Walt,' Sam began, pouring a generous measure.

'Drink this slowly and tell me all about it. It helps to talk about it before you have to face a problem, you know.'

Walter told his story, but was careful to leave out any details regarding Eliza.

At the end Sam put a hand on his shoulder. 'Look, Walter, I'm short-handed here next week. It's not much pay but I'll show you the ropes. You know, I've been meaning to take our Vera on holiday for a while, but I can't leave the place in the hands of the staff: they'd rob me blind. But I trust you to look after the place for a couple of weeks. You never know, you might like the pub trade and find a place of your own. Though heaven knows what that wife of yours would say, and I doubt if Nancy would speak to you again. Mind you, I don't think you'd miss all that preaching much!' He roared with laughter and Walter joined in. A small chink of light had opened in a dark tunnel.

Warmed and fortified by the whisky, Walter set off down the street with renewed hope. He bought a *Bradford Argus* on the corner and began looking through the situations vacant. By the time he reached the tram stop one job had already caught his eye. He braced himself and walked into the house. Hannah greeted him at the door, flinging her arms around his neck. He sank into the armchair and Rosie joined her sister, hugging and kissing him.

'You're early today, love,' Annie remarked, pleasant and amiable until she caught the smell of whisky on his breath. He looked at her, trying to fend off the attention of his daughters, and she saw in his eye that all was not well – but this was not the time to ask. She retreated to the kitchen looking worried, and busied herself with preparing the evening meal.

Later that evening, when they were alone together, he told her of the day's events. To his great surprise she took it calmly and philosophically.

'Well, I suppose you warned me of this,' she sighed. 'You always said you didn't spend enough time on the road. You know, I'm not really sad at it turning out this way, though heaven knows how we'll cope.'

'Sam's got me some temporary work at the pub, and he says I can manage it for a couple of weeks while he takes a holiday.'

Annie didn't comment. The relief that there would be money coming in fought against her disgust that her husband would be working as a pub landlord.

'I'm already looking for jobs,' Walter added. 'What do you think of this one, Annie?' He passed over the advertisement that had attracted his interest:

Field Brothers of Liverpool, leading British manufacturers in soaps, detergents and other household products, require a sales representative for West Yorkshire. The position will commence in September this year. The successful applicant will have to show a proven record in sales, a good level of general education and a scientific aptitude to explain the processes and advantages of an exciting range of products. He will have to undergo training in the product range before commencing duties. Apply in writing to: Mr D. Fortune. Sales Manager, Field Brothers, Freshfields, Liverpool.

Her face dropped. She looked up at him, her eyes clouded with tears. 'It's another travelling job. You'll be on the road again.'

'Yes, that's true, but it's only for West Yorkshire. And they're different; I've heard all about them. They're not like Ledger's or hundreds of other twopenny-ha'penny firms, scrabbling and fighting for every penny of profit they can wring from their workers and customers. They're a far-sighted company, doing all kinds of scientific research, who've built their workers a beautiful village to live in, a bit like Salt's over at Saltaire. They're the leading national firm in their field. That's the kind of company I'd like to work for, one that looks forward to the future, to a better world.'

Annie saw the dreamer and visionary in him again, reminding her of the old days when the future was bright and welcoming. She came over to the armchair, settled herself in his lap, wrapped her arms around him and kissed him. 'You're right. It sounds perfect for you. But if you're successful, what will you do in the meantime?'

'I'll find something to keep body and soul together, my love,' Walter replied. 'Sam says there are always short-term leases in the licensing trade. Don't worry, that's not the sum of my ambitions; but if I do well for your uncle it'll be something that might see us through for now.'

She smiled, the first real smile he had seen from her for a long time. 'I'll hold you to that – though what Nancy will say I dread to think. You're right, Walt, we've got to face these difficulties together, and take whatever blessings fall our way.'

Despite the worry and uncertainty, it seemed to Walter that he had, in a strange way, got his life back on track. The love and commitment in his marriage had been reawakened and he was starting to think clearly for the first time in years. This was confirmed when he received a letter from Field Brothers inviting him for an interview at their headquarters in Liverpool a fortnight hence.

In the meantime he enjoyed his turn at the Mason's Arms and effectively deputised for Sam. He did not waste the spare time that presented itself, borrowing books about the science of soap manufacture from the library and buying papers and periodicals to learn about his potential employers.

It was on a bright summer's day that Walter arrived at the offices at Freshfields. The place could not have been more appropriately named. Neat rows of whitewashed modern houses were set in green open spaces, bright and gleaming under the cloudless sky. Looking around, he saw a church, public buildings and work in progress on a temple-like structure, which he guessed was the new art gallery. Even the offices, set in attractive gardens, were a delight to the eye. It was like entering a new world where industry had joined with beauty, culture and Christian compassion to create a small heaven on earth. If this was the future for his children and others, Walter felt it would be worth working and struggling for, far better than the mill-bound hovels of his native Bradford and even better than the visionary community of the renowned Titus Salt.

Further surprises were to come. The first was to find he was among a group of thirty or so young men, not the half-dozen or so he'd expected. It soon became clear, however, that the company was recruiting a new sales force, not just for West Yorkshire but for the whole of the country, and these interviews were just one of a series. There was whispered talk among some of the applicants of a new product that might revolutionise the industry.

Walter knew from his researches that Field's had already turned the business on its head, with the introduction of Greenfield Soap some years earlier. This had contained copra to make it lather better than all its rivals, and had been energetically marketed nationwide. With its imaginative name and distinctive pack it had quickly become the market leader, and the firm had become a worldwide exporter. He knew that the company would never rest on its laurels and was looking for the brightest and best in all its departments. Far from being nervous or apprehensive, Walter caught the feeling of enthusiasm and enterprise. He was utterly determined to join such a firm; any other job would be second-best.

The way in which the best applicants were chosen was totally different to anything he had heard of before, but he could see it was based on sound principles. The applicants faced, first of all, a series of written questions to assess their scientific aptitude. Walter's natural intelligence and genuine interests in all things scientific ensured that he, with a few others, outshone the rest. Six of them faced a further interview to assess their abilities and personalities with regard to salesmanship. Walter was grateful that the firm did not subscribe to the hard sell, quick profit routine that most others demanded. His knowledge of psychology and more subtle techniques to achieve sales growth, based on the quality and marketing of the product, impressed his interviewers.

It was to Walter's great relief that after a short and tense wait the sales manager announced, 'Congratulations, Mr Clough. We're happy to offer you the post of sales representative for the West Yorkshire region.'

Walter was delighted, not just because his despair at losing one job had been so soon cancelled out by obtaining another, but because he genuinely believed that Field's was the best firm he could ever work for. He asked his new boss why the post was not available immediately, and Mr Fortune hesitated before replying.

'I suppose I can let you in on the secret. This autumn we're launching the first of a range of new and revolutionary products, and we need a new team of salesmen.' He hesitated, still unsure whether to divulge his secrets to the new recruit. 'The first is a personal soap,' he continued in a quiet, almost inaudible voice. 'It's called "Fresh" and it foams better than any you've seen. And,' he added after a dramatic pause, 'it's scented. The ladies will love it, and Wright's, Hudson's and others would give their right hand to know, so not a word. Breaching confidence can cost you your job in this business, remember that! You'll start training in September before the launch so that it ties in with the advertising campaign. By the way, the next surprise will be our range of laundry products. It'll turn the industry upside down.'

'A new kind of washing soap?' suggested Walter.

'Not exactly a bar of soap,' whispered his boss. 'More a soluble soap flake that with agitation will clean the whole garment. It'll eliminate the need for a lot of scrubbing and will take most of the effort out of washday. Imagine that! You'll learn about it when you start in September. Remember, not a word to anybody. You're a Field's man now!'

'You have my word,' answered Walter, more impressed than ever.

'I know we won't have to do much with you to get you into shape. You seem to have all the qualities we've been looking for. Oh, and another thing. We've changed the boundaries of your sales area. All of Lancashire is too much for one man so we've added Lancaster and Westmorland to your region.'

'That's no problem,' assured Walter. 'I know that area well, and I love the Lakes and Morecambe Bay. They're the most beautiful part of the north.'

They shook hands, and Walter departed a very happy man. The journey back to Bradford flew by, and he was in a state of near ecstasy when he announced to Annie that he would be starting in September as Field Brothers' representative in West Yorkshire. He did not tell her of the adjustment in his area: it would only involve a small amount of extra travelling, and he did not want to spoil the moment.

'What are you going to do in the meantime?' asked Annie, as practical and down to earth as ever, as they sat in the parlour that evening.

'Sam said there may be one or two short-term tenancies around. He promised me he'd put in a good word with the breweries. He thought I did a good job over this last fortnight.'

'Oh, Walt,' Annie begged, 'don't get into one of those rough public houses in the city, where Nancy works. I'd hate you to do that.'

'I promise I won't touch anything like that, my love,' her

husband joked. 'After all, I don't want to turn up for my new job with a broken nose or black eyes.'

Sam was as good as his word. He enquired on Walter's behalf, and presented him with a list of four establishments. As he feared, though, they were premises in the worst parts of the city, which even Sam himself would have baulked at managing.

'I'll tell thee what, Walt,' he suggested. 'Have a look in the *Northern Publican*. It's our trade journal. Mind you, most of the pubs advertised are in small, out-of-the-way places that don't do much trade – but they might just tide thee over. You could take a position, then give them a week's notice when the new job starts. A lot o' that goes on.'

Walter searched the paper. Although there were few advertised around Bradford and the Aire Valley, he was intrigued by one advert, for the Crown Hotel at Arnside on the shores of Morecambe Bay, which offered accommodation for the landlord and his family. He put it to Annie more in hope than expectation, and to his surprise she reluctantly agreed.

'I'm not too happy at living over an inn,' she remarked, 'but it seems a quiet, respectable place. Rosie's had a bad chest these past few months, probably because we live so near to this filthy smoky city, and some time in the warm seaside air should do her good.'

'Sam says that trade might not be too bad over the summer, so perhaps it'll be all right for us financially as well.'

'What about Hannah and Rosie's schooling?' Annie asked. 'They'll miss a few weeks and we don't know what the schools are like round there.'

'I'll buy some school books. They're above their standard already and I'll have the time to keep them up to scratch. They won't need to catch up much.'

So it was decided, and Walter immediately wrote enclosing a reference from Sam Lodge and the brewery. He received an immediate reply confirming his tenancy at the Crown. For Walter a disastrous year had turned the corner, and life was as promising as it had ever been. To Annie it was embarrassing to live over a public house, but amid the chaos and excitement as they packed for their journey to the seaside she comforted herself that none of her friends or the churchgoers of St John's would ever know. To Hannah it was the adventure of a lifetime. She bubbled and chattered like an excited cauldron coming to the boil. Even young Rosie was infected by the excitement, and packed and repacked her dolls and toys. Only young Thomas treated the affair with total indifference: he had no idea what living at the seaside was like.

Chapter Twenty-Five

When Hannah awoke that morning the room was filled with a strange, pale light. She rushed to the window and drew back the curtains. The sight almost took her breath away. The tide had filled the estuary and was an immense lake of shimmering blue and silver, a heady mixture of colours and shades that she had never seen before: greens and browns along the margin of the beach, the turquoise and silver of the water, the dark greys, slate blues and whites of the fells, and an azure sky that seemed to go on for ever.

The thin coastal strip across the bay was bathed in morning sunshine, which picked out white cottages and golden sandstone hotels in a village some two miles away. The thin strip of beach below it, although no doubt as muddy as the Arnside edge, seemed to gleam as yellow as any tropical shore.

Hannah's eyes alighted upon a large building set amid the trees a short distance from the beach. It had a wide frontage of ornate windows, with countless chimneys above. She could not guess whether it was the home of rich local gentry or a grand hotel, nor did she want to: it just made the scene that little bit more special and mysterious.

The family had arrived at the Crown Hotel the previous afternoon. It had been cloudy and damp, and they had been too tired to appreciate their surroundings. By the time they had unpacked a few essentials and eaten a hurriedly prepared supper they had been fit only to tumble exhausted into bed.

Rosie joined her sister at the small bay window under the eaves and stared out, lost in the same wonder. After a few moments Hannah rushed across the landing. For once forgetting all good manners and decorum, she burst into her parents' bedroom. 'Daddy! Mummy! Come and look. Isn't it wonderful?'

Annie, too tired to care, muttered, 'Go and see what's the matter, Walter.'

He slowly climbed out of bed, and was dragged across the landing and to the window by his eager, impatient daughters. Looking out on the awe-inspiring scene, Walter knew instantly why he had brought his family to this wonderful place. He thanked God that he had passed on to his children the ability to regard beauty with awe and wonder.

'Isn't it wonderful?' Hannah gasped. 'It's the most beautiful place on earth.'

'Can we play on the sands?' piped up Rosie. 'I wish I had a bucket and spade.'

Walter immediately sounded a note of caution. 'To start with, this isn't exactly the seaside. It's what's called an inlet or river estuary. The sands can be very muddy and not nice for digging. They can also be dangerous if you wander too far, as they can be very soft, so you sink into them – and then you can't come out. Then there are the fast-flowing tides: it's all too easy to drown. You're *never* to go on the beach without me or your mother. Do you understand?'

Thomas, who had just come into the room, caught his father's tone and joined his sisters in a solemn chorus of 'Yes, Daddy.'

'May we explore the village?' asked Hannah.

'I think I'd better go with you the first time. I'm going to be very busy this morning, getting the place ready for opening, so I'm afraid you'll have to play quietly or even lend a hand with the dusting and cleaning. This afternoon I'll try to snatch an hour off and we can explore the village then. All right?'

For an answer Walter was swamped by hugs and kisses from his enthusiastic family.

After breakfast the children explored every nook and cranny of the quaint building, including the old stables around the yard.

They made instant friends with the brother and sister who worked at the inn: Jack Bibby was barman, drayman and general handyman, and his sister Florence was the cook and general domestic servant. Although they were a pleasant and welcoming couple, they were difficult for the children to understand because of their strange local accent.

During the morning Jack, a well-built, red-faced young man, called the children together in the bar. 'I bet tha a brand piece,' he declared, 'ye dun't know what's under this floor.' He pointed to the boards beneath their feet.

'It seems hollow,' said Hannah.

'Aye, but do you ken why?'

The children shook their heads. Jack carefully removed a mat in front of the fireplace to reveal a trap door. He lifted it back and they could see a flight of stone steps cut into the solid, limestone rock, leading down to a cellar filled with old barrels and furniture.

'What's that for?' asked Rosie.

'It's just a cellar,' remarked Hannah, disappointed.

Jack shook his head. 'Tha may well ask. Maybe one day I'll tell of its secret, if tha doesn't find out thaselves.'

'We'll try to find out,' said Hannah.

Jack let them peer down into the gloomy and dank room, before quickly lowering the trap door, pulling the rug back and disappearing about his business.

It took a day of cleaning, dusting, polishing, tidying, taking deliveries of ale and drinks and ordering victuals and groceries, before the establishment was even half ready to receive its first customer. Annie had vowed she would never help in the bar, but as there were some rooms to let she busied herself cleaning them, changing and washing bed linen, and preparing a small room where guests could eat and relax away from the noise and bustle of the inn. Hannah and Rosie helped their mother by dusting and tidying. Their father was true to his word when he announced midway through the afternoon that they could stop working and explore the village.

Annie resolved to stay and finish a second guest room, so Walter and the children stepped out onto the road in front of the inn. Their first surprise was that, without their noticing, the tide had swept out, leaving acres of sandbanks, pale sea grass and estuarine mud through which three or four channels of the Kent ran on its way to the bay. The inn itself was on a headland, so from over the road they could see up the inlet across the salt marshes and out to the fells and mountains of the Lake District, and to the left Arnside and the villages across the estuary.

They turned left and made their way slowly into the centre of the small town. Hannah's first impression was of a strange mixture of old cottages and elegant newer houses cheek by jowl, all the way to the centre of the village opposite the stone pier. On the sunny summer's day it was busy, with holidaymakers strolling along the newly built promenade and crowding round the shops that huddled together along a short stretch from the pier to The Albion inn.

Further along the promenade they could see a row of brand-new double-fronted houses, some of which were still being built. The impression Hannah had gleaned from her father that Arnside was a small fishing village inhabited by only a few local folk quickly vanished. In high summer the locals blended in with the majority of holidaymakers and trippers, who had turned the once sleepy village into a thriving resort. Walter guessed that many of the fashionable houses with wonderful views of the bay were being built for business and professional men who worked in Lancaster and Barrow. The place had changed dramatically since his brief visit with Annie, on their honeymoon ten years before, thanks to the arrival of the railway.

A large boathouse had recently been erected beside the pier, and three men were visible inside, busy hammering and sawing. The children hovered in the open doorway, curious to see what they were doing.

'May I ask what you're making?' Hannah asked a brawny young man wielding a saw, as charming as she could be.

'Ah, my dear, this is a Lancashire nobby,' he replied. Hannah was bemused. ''Tis for shrimping, for some fishermen from Morecambe. It'll be finished this week. It only takes us three or four week to make. If tha comes down on Thursday or Friday, just before high tide, happen tha'll see it launched.'

'And what's that one?' enquired Rosie, keen to get in on the conversation.

'Why, little miss, yon's a fine private yacht. It's taken a lot longer than t'nobby to finish. It'll be a fine boat indeed, but a bit too expensive for tha pocket.'

'Who's it for?' interrupted Hannah.

'It's for Master Henry Rodgers, over at Ashmeadow House by the point,' replied the patient young man. ''Tis to be called the *Wild Duck*. His father had such a boat but she were wrecked some years ago. I hope they has better luck with this one.'

The girls thanked him and waved goodbye. As they walked back up the beach with their father, a wrinkled old man whom they took to be a fisherman called out, 'Hears tha. Is't tha t'new publican o' t'Fightin Cocks?'

Walter was surprised at the greeting. 'Good morning! You wish to know if I'm the new publican? Yes, I am, but I'm at The Crown at the end of the promenade.'

The old man approached and shook Walter's hand warmly. 'Tha means t'Fighting Cocks,' he insisted. 'Eee, bless ma, I'm na with these new names. T'old Fighting Cocks it was, an' for us t'will always be so. Tha'll see me in t'bar tonight, landlord. Tha kens me as Reuben.' He wandered away down the beach and turned to doff his scruffy grey cap to the girls, who replied with an enthusiastic wave. Hannah's face lit up: she had guessed the answer to the riddle Jack Bibby had set.

They walked further along towards a small promontory. At the end of the promenade was a large barred gate, with the name Ashmeadow House proudly displayed on the stone gatepost. Beyond they could see fine wooded gardens and a magnificent two-storey house; Hannah counted over eight chimneys rising from the sharply pitched roof. The lower storey was surrounded on its two seaward sides by a long veranda fenced by patterned wrought-iron. Along its length wicker chairs and small tables abounded.

'Wouldn't it be lovely if we had a house like that,' said Hannah dreamily. 'We could have breakfast on the veranda being waited on by maids while we gazed out over the bay.'

'Yes, madam,' joked Walter in an unctuous, subservient manner. 'What would madam desire for breakfast?'

'Two eggs,' Hannah replied haughtily. 'Soft boiled, no more than two minutes mind, and soldiers to dip in them, and coffee, not tea. Can't you get anything right?'

'And I want marmalade with my toast!' said Rosie, not wanting to be left out of the joke.

They laughed all the way to Blackstone Point. By then Rosie and Thomas had wandered ahead to explore some rock pools.

Hannah squeezed her father's hand. 'Oh, isn't it wonderful!' she exclaimed. 'I could spend my whole life here, and write and paint and never get bored of it.'

Walter smiled. So could he; but he knew it was not to last. They gazed for a minute at the wide expanse of Morecambe Bay that had come into view, then turned and followed the narrow rocky path back to the village. From the sands they could see the cottages, taller houses and shops jammed higgledy-piggledy along a cramped seafront and rising up the steep hill behind. There was no rhyme or reason to its plan, but this added to its charm and quaintness.

That night, as Walter served behind the bar, he met Reuben again, who engaged him in conversation for most of the evening. Walter's enthusiasm for the beauty of the bay and his genuine interest in the local people and their lives struck a chord with the grizzled old fisherman, and they quickly became firm friends.

'Maybe tha'll come with me out on t'sands next Sunday, when t'missus and t'childer go to church,' he suggested. 'I'll take tha out cockling by Silverdale. But don't ever go out by thaself,' he warned, looking Walter straight in the eye. 'Yon crooked sea, she's a dangerous and unforgiving place if tha don't know her secrets.'

Walter accepted the invitation, but wisely delayed telling Annie of his expedition until the morning arrived. Reuben picked him up in front of the inn in his cart and once they had climbed the hill they jogged along at a good pace. The cart carried nets and a few wooden implements, but was light work for the pony. Reuben pointed out the hills, from the imposing Arnside Knott, which rose over five hundred feet on their right, to the smaller Castlebarrow and Pepperpot. Walter was intrigued by a giant ruined tower, which sat in a col between two hills.

'Tha kens about the invading Scots and pirates?' asked his guide. Walter nodded. 'Aye, well, that tower were refuge for folk whan they came a-visiting. They called all in from t'fields and locked beasts in t'barn and folks in yon tower. 'Twere four floors high and they could live in there for days. But it's been fired and stripped for over two hundred years now, and these ten years past it were part blown down in a storm. Reckon them stones could tell many a tale.'

On the edge of the village they took a right fork down to a cove. Here they met seven or eight folk who followed the cart across the salt marsh and on to the sands. They moved further and further away from the shore. 'Best enjoy the ride,' joked Reuben, 'fer there'll be nay room on t'way back.'

They alighted on a muddy plain and Reuben handed out the tools and wicker baskets to the cocklers. They were as poor and wretched a crowd of people as Walter had ever seen, and all dressed in the same thick ragged clothes. One young girl, aged no more than thirteen, was heavily pregnant, yet took her basket and set to work with the rest.

'I was going to tell tha,' Reuben remarked, 'these folk is a law to themselves. Lads and lasses, way out on t'sand with no one to see. They get egged on by t'others to all kinds o' tricks. She'll not be t'first and not t'last, I'll be bound.'

He handed Walter a jumbo, a large board with two rough handles, one at each end. The men and youths in the party had spread out far and wide, each with a child or woman for company. Pounding the wet sand with their jumbos energetically and rhythmically, the men brought the cockles to the surface, while the women and children scooped up the precious shellfish with the short rakes they called craams, transferring them to their baskets. After ten minutes Walter's back and shoulders ached. The woman who had followed him laughed as he paused to catch his breath.

'Eee, tha kens this lang-legged fella, he's na better than a babby,' she announced to those in earshot. 'Tha take t'craam and basket an I'll get 'em up.'

The others laughed heartily at Walter's feeble attempts. She took the heavy instrument from him and handed him her basket and rake, much to the amusement of the others. She then proceeded to pound the mud with a violence and speed he would not have thought possible from such a small and slight figure. He duly followed, picking out the cockles, but could scarcely keep up with her and drew more censure, providing further amusement for the rest of the group.

Reuben took pity on him, and as the baskets filled up gave him charge of emptying them into fine netting bags, which he then loaded on the cart. It was mid-afternoon when they stopped. Reuben paid the workers a few shillings and they followed the bulging cart back over the sands towards the shore. The old fisherman led the pony as carefully as he could, his eyes continually on the watch for a softer patch of sand or a hidden gulley. One slip and they might have to unload the whole cart. To Walter's relief they made the shore safely. There was no room for either of them on the fully laden and creaking cart, so it was a long walk back to Arnside. He left Reuben to take the cart to the station, so the precious cargo could be transported to restaurants and shops for affluent city-dwellers.

Walter ached from top to toe, and despite the warm summer day was cold from continual exposure to the breezes out in the bay. His hands were sore and raw and bleeding in places. Annie observed him with some satisfaction. 'I hope, Walter Clough,' she said triumphantly, 'this will teach you a lesson about missing church on a Sunday and gallivanting over the sands instead. Anyway, I've run you a hot bath in the hope that at least you'll be fit for work tomorrow.'

Walter smiled and kissed his wife on the cheek. Despite the aches and pains he had enjoyed his commune with nature, but as ever he preferred to watch rather than perform back-breaking work.

Chapter Twenty-Six

The solitary traveller turned back sharply to the right, as he guessed he had now skirted the more dangerous mudflats and quicksands. Walter looked to the other side, but Arnside had vanished behind a headland. Its ruined tower was still visible, nestling between the hills and silhouetted against the afternoon sky. It brought to mind the conversation he had had with his family on the first Monday of that incredible summer.

* * *

'You'll never guess what we saw on the way to the church, Daddy,' Hannah said at the breakfast table.

'It's a tower, a magic tower!' broke in Rosie, much to her elder sister's annoyance.

Thomas was not to be outdone. 'It's the princess's tower where Rapuncle let down her hair,' he blurted out. His sisters burst into fits of laughter.

'No, Tom,' corrected Rosie, in a voice like a governess, 'it's Rapunzel!'

'It was quite strange,' continued Hannah. 'It was in the garden of a large house. It's built in rough white stone and has little windows in it. I asked the vicar, Mr Stevens, and he didn't know what it was. I said it reminded me of Rapunzel's tower.'

'You'll never guess what the vicar said,' broke in Rosie. 'He said Hannah should sit at the top and let her hair grow longer and one day a handsome prince would come for her.'

They all burst into fits of uncontrollable giggling. Annie brought in the toast, and was not amused.

'Really, Walter,' she snapped, 'how do you expect the children to gain any manners at table if you let them laugh at mealtimes? It's a wonder they don't choke on their food.'

'I saw a tower yesterday as well,' Walter said, ignoring his wife's reproof. 'Mine was much bigger, four storeys high. It was built to keep out pirates and invaders, but it's only a ruin now.'

'Can we see it?' begged Hannah.

She was joined in chorus by Rosie and Thomas. Annie's patience had almost gone, but she kept her silence. Walter agreed to take the children, but warned them they would have to wait until he had the time.

'We've got a secret as well,' boasted Hannah, 'and it's here in the inn.'

'Whatever do you mean?' asked her mother.

'It's the cellar where you store things,' said Rosie. 'It's not a cellar at all.'

Hannah was getting more impatient with her younger sister, who was determined to steal her thunder. 'Excuse me!' she barked, 'but I was the one who solved the riddle, so I think I should be the one to tell everybody.'

'Well?' asked Walter, 'what's the secret? Ghosts or smugglers or what?'

'It's not a cellar at all but a cockpit,' she informed the breakfast table. 'Jack told us. It was used for cockfights, where the birds clawed and pecked each other to death. They even put spikes on their legs to stab and wound each other.'

'Enough!' burst in Annie. 'I don't know what's happened to you children. You've become like wild animals, with no manners at all and your heads full of the wildest and most horrible things imaginable. I blame you for encouraging them, Walter!' With that she stormed out of the room; but she knew that her husband's adventurous and free-thinking regime would reign supreme while they were at Arnside, despite all her efforts to exert stricter control.

A week later Walter went out on to the bay with Reuben again, but this time they took Hannah with them. She had pleaded with her father and his friend and, like her father, Reuben found it hard to resist her charm and persistence. This time they went to the fishing bauk that Reuben had set out on the last tide. This was a net some two hundred yards in length attached to stakes that were firmly planted into the sand. It was laid out in a vee, with the open end facing the shore. Fish came in to feed on the incoming tide and became trapped at the apex of the net when they tried to swim out again. The net was visible from half a mile away, as the gulls were swooping over it, screeching and screaming at the treasure that lay trapped below, and diving in to gorge themselves.

A few swift blows from Reuben's craam deterred all but the bravest from coming back to enjoy the feast again. Hannah was scared as the gulls wheeled and shrieked above their heads, but cautiously helped to put the fish into the baskets. She kept away from the few crabs that had got themselves into the trap.

Reuben observed her fear and chuckled. 'Mister crab won't nip, if tha's quick with him. He's mighty easy to catch hold.' He held one by the back leg and dropped it into a basket. Hannah gingerly did the same, choosing the smallest and most inoffensive creature she could find. 'Eee, bless ma,' he laughed, 'tha's not thinking we want a babby like that! He's no fit fer a midget ta eat. Let him free to grow for next season.'

They wandered back across the sands, leading the pony and cart. Reuben had given Hannah her own basket, which she had filled with a few fish as a present for her mother. As they crossed one of the many streams pouring out into the bay, Hannah gave a sharp scream and almost lost her balance. 'I've stepped on something,' she cried, 'and it's live and it moved!'

''Tis only a flounder,' Reuben laughed. 'Why didn't tha catch it, missy? 'Tis a good fish fer eating. Fluke padding be easy. Watch and tha'll see!'

He stepped back into the stream and shuffled along, leaning forwards with his hands cupped. After a minute a flurry of water splashed beneath his feet and he scooped his hands suddenly upwards. A flat fish flew into the air and landed on the bank. The expert triumphantly dropped it into a basket.

'Can I have a try?' his pupil begged.

'Aye, but tha'll try all morning afore tha gets one,' warned Reuben. 'Tha's got to be very slow and quiet. He can hear tha coming and is right quick.'

Hannah was not to be deterred and waded knee deep into the water, proceeding to tiptoe slowly and gently upstream in exact imitation of her instructor. She had not gone five yards when there was a flurry and splashing. Walter and Reuben were about to laugh at Hannah's plight as she tumbled into the water, until they saw the desperate, flapping creature on the edge of the bank. Hannah rose like Neptune from the deep, grabbed the fish before it could make its escape and held it triumphantly aloft. Her audience applauded.

Her next audience was not so appreciative. Annie was astounded at the sight of her daughter, caked in sand and mud and, although almost dried by the warm sun, still with the appearance of a drowned rat. Annie said nothing, but one look to her husband told all. Smiling sweetly, Hannah presented her mother with a basket of fresh fish, which she proudly claimed she had chosen herself for the evening meal for the family and the hotel's guests. On top of the pile was the prize flounder, which appeared to be sharing her triumph; in death it had the same smug smile as its bedraggled captor.

Annie was somewhat averse to filleting the catch, but this proved to be no problem for Florence Bibby, who like most local folk was adept at killing, plucking and gutting.

Reuben took Walter out a few times in his boat, to the skears around the bay where he scraped mussels from the rocky outcrops. This was much more lucrative than cockling but was hard work for the fishermen, who had to stand up to their thighs in water, wielding the craams that they always used with great skill. Walter became more used to the hard physical work, but was always given the job of washing out the precious catch. In return he was able to offer his guests mussels as fine as you would find in the best London restaurants. Reuben often dropped off some of his catch, either fish or shellfish, at the hotel and in return received free beer. The bargain suited them both: Walter received the best local produce, while Reuben's healthy capacity for beer was satisfied.

The children became a frequent sight in the village. Hannah was never without her notepad, and filled book after book with writing and sketches.

'I don't know what tha fills yon with, young lassie,' remarked the postmistress, as Hannah bought yet another notebook from her. 'I'm going to have to send off an order for some more,' she joked. 'I've already sold my normal summer's quota.'

As promised, Walter took the children on a walk to the ruined tower. Close up they could see that it was crudely constructed of unprepared stones, cemented together with lime mortar and infilled with rubble and pebbles.

'What was it for?' enquired Rosie. 'It's not a real castle.'

'But its past is just as bloody and exciting,' explained her father. 'In days long ago bands of pirates, Vikings or warriors from Scotland used to sail into the bay and rob and kill the villagers. They built the tower to protect themselves.'

'But the bay's too shallow for big ships,' Hannah pointed out.

'Not in those days,' explained Walter. 'Before the railway bridge was built the channel was much deeper, and this village was a busy port.'

Walter and the children played Vikings and villagers for a time, until he and Thomas were soundly defeated by an invading army of wild and violent valkyries. Exhausted, they scrambled up the track to the top of Arnside Knott and were rewarded by as fine a view as you ever could see. The day was clear, with just a few wisps of clouds clinging to the top of the dark mountains far to the north. The white cottages of the village peeked from the trees below them, while to the left they could see the piers of Morecambe, and further inland the churches and factories of Lancaster. The sailing boats and shrimpers were tiny white and black dots sprinkled across the bay. They suddenly reminded Walter of the surprise he had withheld.

'I suppose I'd better tell you about Arnside Sports and Regatta next week,' he announced, as they sprawled at the top of the hill.

'What's a regatta, Daddy?' asked Rosie. 'Is it some kind of foreign food?'

'Don't be so silly,' said her elder sister. 'It's a day of boat races. There'll be sailing races, rowing races, wrestling, fell running, stalls, a small fair and most of it will be organised from our own inn, The Crown. I'm right, aren't I?'

'Clever girl,' said Walter. 'I suppose you've seen it on posters and handbills.'

'Yes,' Hannah replied, 'and I've read about it in the newspaper.'

When they eventually wandered back down the hill into the village the tide was in. Resting at the edge of the beach was a sailing boat, new and pristine, its white hull topped by a blue sail.

'Oh!' shouted Rosie. 'The *Wild Duck*. They've finished her. Let's look.'

They wandered down to the water's edge, where a smart middle-aged man dressed in a blazer and straw boater was attending to the sail, helped by the burly carpenter they had seen in the boat shed. He waved to the children.

'Oh, she's beautiful,' Hannah said to the young man. 'You've done a wonderful job. She's the loveliest sailing boat I've ever seen.'

'And who are you to lavish such praise on my new boat?' asked the immaculate sailor.

Walter made a formal introduction. 'Good afternoon. I'm Walter Clough, landlord of The Crown, and these are my children, Hannah, Rosie and Thomas.'

The two men shook hands and the sailor doffed his boater to the children. 'I'm Henry Rodgers,' he announced. 'I was intending to come over and see you, Mr Clough, regarding arrangements for the day. You know, rooms for stewards, refreshments and the like.'

'You're the gentleman from that fine house at the end of the promenade,' said Hannah. 'The house with the lovely veranda and all those chimneys.'

'I am indeed,' Rodgers replied.

'Will you be sailing your boat in the *regatta*?' asked Rosie. She was pleased with the new word and was determined to use it as often as she could.

'I certainly will,' answered the proud owner.

'We'll all be cheering you, Mr Rodgers,' Rosie continued.

'We want the *Wild Duck* to win at the regatta. We saw her being built when we first came to this lovely place, and she's the most beautiful boat we've ever seen. I'm sure she's the fastest.'

'I suppose you'd like a little trip in her while the tide's in,' he suggested. 'It's the least I can offer my team of enthusiastic supporters.'

Hannah, for once, was speechless. Rosie's eyes were open wide and Thomas could hardly contain his excitement. The gallant owner helped them on board and they spent some twenty minutes on a turn down the channel and a circle towards the far shore by Humphrey Head. On alighting they got their feet wet, but none of the children cared a jot. What was the discomfort of wet socks and feet compared with such a treat?

The Arnside Sports and Regatta was also a treat, not missed by anyone in the district. They came from all the nearby villages, Silverdale, Flookborough, Grange and Carnforth, to compete. The fishermen showed their prowess in the four oared boats that raced up and down the channel in a series of races, and a team of sturdy men from over the estuary in Flookborough comfortably beat all comers. Burly farmers and their sons competed in wrestling matches, where the object was to lift one's opponent off the ground rather than pin him down. Thin, wiry men, some from as far away as Workington and Preston, raced each other on the steep fells, and finished exhausted at the finishing line outside the inn. Local folk, children and holidaymakers thronged the stalls set up on the promenade and the amusements run by churches and local organisations.

The Crown was at the hub of it all. As was their custom, the stewards settled themselves down in the bar and, apart from when there was an occasional dispute or organisational problem, seemed reluctant to move. Walter had never worked so hard pulling pints, even in the Mason's Arms on a Friday night. Annie and Florence, with additional help recruited for the day, were on their feet the whole time, serving a never-ending stream of customers with refreshments. And what of the three children? They had the time of their lives among the stalls, cheering the wrestlers and runners and trying every activity and competition there was.

At four o'clock the final event took place, the regatta race for First Class Sail Boats. A flagpole was raised opposite the inn and a small cannon mysteriously appeared on the edge of the promenade. After a deafening bang, which shook the windows of the inn and its neighbouring houses, the gaily coloured yachts and sailing boats made their way down the deep and out into the bay as far as Jenny Brown's Point, where they turned round a buoy and headed back for the channel. A large white yacht from Grange-over-Sands led the way to Blackstone Point, but Henry Rodgers's local knowledge of the Kent currents worked to his advantage. The *Wild Duck* raced neck and neck and took the prize on the line. Hannah, Rosie and Thomas were hoarse with shouting and cheering.

A large crowd gathered outside the inn as the stewards announced the prize winners, and the trophies were presented by the Reverend William Riddell Stevens, Vicar of Arnside. A special cheer went up for the owner of the *Wild Duck*, as he had regained the yachting trophy for the village. He had collected his prize and thanked the stewards when Hannah stepped forward from the crowd, curtseyed and presented him with a picture, an exquisite pencil sketch of the winning boat in full sail, mounted in a beautiful wooden frame. It was difficult to say who was the more astonished, the recipient or Walter.

'That was a lovely thing to do,' whispered Hannah's father in her ear. 'But where did you get it framed and how could you afford it?'

'I showed the drawing to Mr Crossfield at the boat yard, and he thought it was so good that he made a frame for me.'

'But how did you know the boat would win?'

'I had a feeling it would. Everything was so right that I knew it would end this way.'

She was interrupted by the triumphant yachtsman, resplendent in his striped blazer and usual straw boater. 'This picture will take pride of place on my study wall. You must all come along to view it, and I'm sure you wouldn't mind if we offered you tea on that veranda you so admire.'

Hannah did not know what to say. It was the perfect end to a perfect day.

Unhappily it was not so for her mother. Drinking and revelry went on in the bar until late. Just as Annie finally got to bed she heard yet more commotion and shouting in the yard behind the inn, which did not diminish but seemed to increase as midnight approached. She quickly dressed and went down to discover the source of the noise.

When she reached the yard she could scarcely believe her eyes. One of the outbuildings had been cleared and an arena of crates and straw bales had been constructed in the centre. Around it a noisy and excited group of men was drinking, shouting and wagering, but this was nothing compared with what was going on in the middle. Amid a flurry of feathers, screeching and bloody mayhem, two cockerels were fighting to the death, clawing and pecking each other. Finally one of them fell lifeless and bleeding on the stone floor. Money was exchanged, and the carnage began again with fresh contestants. Her husband was leaning against the wall, chatting and casually observing the fray. Annie turned away and retraced her steps back to bed, disgusted and sickened.

When she confronted Walter in the morning he was indifferent. 'It's the life of these folk, Annie. It's how they've lived for centuries,' he explained.

His wife's patience had run out. 'But it's illegal! You could have had your licence revoked and been thrown in jail for allowing it.'

'Hardly, when two of the organisers are local magistrates. Anyway, it only happens once or twice a year. It won't be regular.'

'I know *you* like this life . . .' Annie shook her head and sighed. 'It's your communing with nature and the simple life you're always on about. But I *hate* it, and the moment we're back in Bradford and you're in a regular job won't be a moment too soon for me.'

Chapter Twenty-Seven

There are those nagging doubts that cloud your mind when you have set your mind on a course of action, which make you think of opting for the safer alternative. Walter was now on the last stretch of his journey, so why did he suddenly have such misgivings? Why had he suddenly started to think about abandoning his scheme and returning to the bosom of his family? He turned to look back the way he had come. A flight of geese flew low over the silvery sand, keeping perfect formation on their way to the feeding grounds on the eastern shore. Here they would stay until dusk, gorging themselves on the lush marsh grass before their short flight home to roost.

* * *

After those glorious summer months at Arnside the family arrived back home on a Saturday afternoon, and found a mountain of post waiting for them behind the door. To Walter, Bradford seemed ugly and humdrum after two months away, but at least he had his new job to look forward to.

Annie had hardly spoken a word to him during the whole journey. She seemed relieved to be back home. Yes, there was cleaning and cooking to do, children to care for and, of course, her work for the church – but these activities defined her horizons now. It saddened Walter to realise that she had made

225

no effort in the last two months to share his enjoyment of the simple, exquisite existence they had in the village by the sea. She had seen no beauty in the awesome landscape, no virtue in the simple fishing folk, and had no interest in village life. Even her visits to church were only out of duty and habit, and she had made no effort to make any friends or join in the activities. Walter thought her sullen manner might be down to her condition. Annie was pregnant again; the baby was due the following May.

Hannah was her usual bubbly self, keen to tell her friends about her wonderful holiday and looking forward to her return to school. She had promised everyone she was going to write a book about the last few months, so they could all share her experiences and adventures.

Walter settled down in the front room to sort through the pile of mail. There were accounts, family letters and handbills. Two envelopes caught his eye. The first was from his mother. She had written to them throughout their stay at Arnside, of course, but had anticipated their arrival home and had put a note through the letterbox. Enos had taken a turn for the worse and was now confined to his bed, and she begged Walter to go and see him, hinting that he needed to hurry before it was too late. This he promised himself he would do, not through any affection for his old tormentor, but for his mother's sake and out of a sense of duty.

The other letter that took Walter's interest was one he was anticipating. It had the Field Brothers' crest on the back of the envelope and summoned him to the headquarters in Liverpool in a week's time, for training and preparation for his new employment a fortnight hence. It stated terms, conditions and salary, all of which were satisfactory. He noted that it required his attendance at head office on the last Friday of each month, which he guessed might be for sales analysis, training and collecting his salary – and might often require an overnight stay. It was the kind of thing that a forward-looking company with a scattered national sales force demanded. He didn't mind, but knew that Annie would baulk at the inconvenience. It would be difficult for her, pregnant again and for the moment without Harriet's welcome help, but she would have to manage; many wives did in far worse circumstances and without the help of the comfortable salary they would enjoy. One thing surprised him about the letter. It was addressed to Mr Walter Adams. By some error the company had missed his surname off the envelope and from the body of the letter.

Still, Walter thought, these things happen. I'll sort it out with Mr Fortune next week. He thought no more of it and put the letter in his pocket.

The following morning Walter called at the draper's shop, foregoing attendance at church with his family. The shop looked scruffy and uncared-for. Paint was peeling from the window frames and the signs and advertisements looked faded and tatty. The shop window, which for a time had looked smart and professional under the care of Mrs Booth, was now drab; clothing and linens were piled haphazardly on the stands, with no thought as to position or appearance.

His mother greeted him at the door. She was pale and her eyes were dark and tired; the effort of nursing her husband through the long nights had taken its toll. Walter followed her up the narrow stairs to the bedroom. Enos lay there wheezing and breathing heavily.

'Walter's come to see you. Annie will come round when she can.'

His stepfather's face and form were shrunken. Enos had hardly the energy to speak, never mind argue, as had been his custom. His eyes stared fixedly at the ceiling. Then he gasped, 'Good of you to come, Walter! Good of you to come.' He slumped back on his pillow, exhausted by the effort. For once Walter felt embarrassed. A lot of the hatred he'd had for his stepfather drained away. He tried to make polite conversation, and to pass on family news, but it seemed empty and pointless. For the sake of Harriet he persisted.

'I enjoyed running The Crown,' he said. 'I bet you would have liked to run a pub, Father,' persisting in calling Enos 'Father' for convention's and for his mother's sake. For once Enos smiled.

'Aye,' he whispered. The thought of running a pub appealed to him; he liked the joke. After twenty minutes or so of gentle, one-sided conversation, Walter gave up, said his goodbyes and wandered downstairs.

'The doctor said it's only a few days now,' his mother informed him.

The doctor was wrong. Enos died that afternoon. Walter felt happy that in a strange way he had made his peace with his stepfather, at least outwardly. He was also relieved that by so quickly and unexpectedly departing this life Enos had given Walter the time he needed to help his mother make the funeral arrangements, sort out the business and attend the ceremony, without having to ask for time off work from his new employer. All in all, it was the one thing his stepfather had managed to do to Walter's satisfaction.

Walter even managed to find the time to help his mother move to her new home. He worked hard all day, and when he was satisfied that everything was in its place he kissed his mother and turned to go.

'Thank you for all you've done,' she whispered. 'I know you and Enos never got on, but this week you've shown him real consideration and respect, even though he little deserved it.' Walter was shocked by his mother's words, and wanted for once to be honest with her – but his love for her and consideration for her feelings forbade it. 'It's even more commendable because you knew he wasn't your father.'

For a moment Walter was struck dumb, then he bade her sit down. He looked her straight in the eye and asked, 'How long have you known that I knew, Mother?'

'A long time,' she replied. 'Oh, I don't know exactly when. You're a clever lad and I reckon you worked it out long, long ago. But you were kind and didn't want to hurt my feelings or bring back painful memories. Perhaps now's the time for us to be honest with each other.'

'Who is my father?' Walter asked quietly. 'Why didn't you marry him?'

The clock ticked slowly. Harriet wiped a tear from her eye. She stared ahead at the picture above the mantelpiece, at all costs avoiding her son's gaze.

He looked at her imploringly, then said, 'You couldn't marry him.'

She nodded. 'He was already married, but unhappy in his marriage. He was a wonderful man, talented, exciting, the only man I ever loved. He's passed a lot of that on to you,

Walter, and to your children – especially your eldest.'

'But why did you marry Enos?'

'He offered security, and perhaps if we'd had children it might have brought us closer together. Or he might have treated you even worse: who can tell? Perhaps it worked out for the best in the end. But I'm not going to tell you your father's name. I know you, Walter. You'd try to track him down, and you're clever and persistent enough to do it.'

He turned, kissed his mother goodbye and made his way slowly to the door. Harriet's eyes did not follow him. She walked to the mantelpiece and stared ahead.

'Be content that another man, not Enos, was your father,' she said. 'And a wonderful man he was. In a strange way he's watched over you through the years, as you've played in the parlour, done your homework, had your rows with Enos and brought round Annie and then your children. I suppose you could say that.'

Walter closed the door behind him, puzzled and disturbed. Who was his father? What did his mother mean? He was haunted by the scene that had taken place, and couldn't get her words out of his mind.

* * *

And still he couldn't forget, two years later, as he made his solitary way towards the shore. Was that mystery the seed of doubt that made him hesitant in going through with his plan?

The shoreline between Kents Bank and Humphrey Head was now visible in detail. Walter could pick out the cottages and farms and the winding road that skirted the coast. Behind, the telegraph poles showed the line of the railway. His journey was nearly done. Or was it? Uncertainty still clouded his mind, and he only had a mile or so to go.

* * *

Walter arrived at Liverpool on a misty autumn morning. The fog hung over the Mersey, masking ships, cranes and warehouses, which seemed to loom suddenly like giants peering from the murky shroud. By the time he reached Freshfields the sun was

229

breaking through, and the prim, white, workers' cottages were bathed in a gentle rosy light. The gardens, trees and avenues weren't quite their usual immaculate selves: no one could stop autumn depositing its russet and gold leaves all over the lawns and streets, not even an army of company gardeners. It gave the area a slightly wanton, untidy look which appealed to him.

He got his first shock when he introduced himself to the receptionist. He showed her his letter, and she looked at him over her spectacles and smiled. 'Ah, Mr Adams, you're the first to arrive. I'm afraid Mr Fortune and Mr Dawson will not be running the training, nor will they be your managers. Both have moved to London to our export office. Mr Fieldhouse is your new sales manager, and will be ready to see you in twenty minutes.'

She smiled again and resumed her work. Walter's first reaction was to point out the mistake in his name, but for some strange reason he stopped mid-sentence.

'Yes, what is it please?' the secretary asked.

'Oh, nothing,' he replied. 'I'm sure Mr Fieldhouse can sort it out.'

He sat down, deep in thought. The thoughts slowly turned to daydreams. If this was to be his new life, then why not a new name? No, it wasn't a new name, it was more his name than Clough had ever been. Enos was gone, and all association with his name and his shop. He might even persuade Annie to change the family name. It could be done. All it would require was a declaration by deed poll with the help of a solicitor. Perhaps he should remain silent for the present and see how things worked out. If the firm quickly realised, he would claim it was an administrative mistake and nothing would be lost. But what if? What if the mistake had been made early on and no-one was aware of it? He could assume the mantle of . . . No, no, it would soon be sorted out. But if, just if . . . if a mistake had been made and nobody knew. If a bank account were opened here in his new name and the salary drawn in cash, no-one would ever know.

He dreamed on, imagining a double life: Walter Clough in Bradford, Walter Adams, a new man, here in Liverpool and out on the road. His dreams were broken by the arrival of other young men, as smart and eager as he was. The meeting started. Mr Fieldhouse was in the same mould as his predecessor, an astute and professional manager.

Walter's secret hopes were realised. Throughout his training he was addressed as Mr Adams. His cards had been printed in that name; it seemed as if the mistake had been perpetrated from the very beginning, and in all documentation. The die was cast. Walter Adams he was going to be!

Walter was more careful than before. No more train tickets or any other incriminating evidence were to be found in his pockets, and all papers, cards and references to Walter Adams were left in his other case in the left luggage office at Bradford station. Why he did this he did not know. Half of him wanted to broach the change with Annie; the other half wanted the romance and mystery of his secret personality and the thrill of deception. When a stray letter came to his home he added the name 'Clough' – but he wasn't worried: if any got away he could claim they were the fault of a careless typist at the office.

Walter began to enjoy his double life. Annie grumbled about his monthly visit to the company offices in Port Sunlight, but generally he was able to be home at night and had time for the children. This was particularly welcomed by his older daughter, who was displaying all the traits of her father, with a keen, enquiring brain and a dreamy imagination. As promised, she had begun a journal about Arnside and their holiday, and the many characters she had met there. Walter could see his creative talents in her, but more so, as she was still some months younger than when he had written that fateful essay about his stay in Morecambe, and this was a far more mature work.

Hannah showed her deep and perceptive intelligence again after a surprise meeting in Bowling Park one warm afternoon in early spring the following year. It was shortly after the birth of their youngest, Agnes. While Annie rested on a bench, Walter busied himself with the children. They went to see the celebrated fossilised tree, but Rosie and Tom were easily bored and wanted to play, while Hannah, who had brought her sketchbook, wanted to stay and capture every detail. They were on their way back to the park entrance when they met Eliza on the arm of a young man.

'How do you do, Mr Clough,' she began. 'Fancy meeting you here! I remember you from Ledger's. I hear you've left them.'

The chance meeting shook Walter for a moment, but he was quickly able to gain his composure. He smiled and raised his hat. 'Why, Miss Smith! How nice to meet you again! May I introduce my wife Annie; and these are my children, Hannah, Rosie and Tom and our new baby Agnes. Miss Smith once worked in the office at Ledger's.'

Annie nodded, and the older girls smiled and performed a neat curtsey.

'Oh, she's lovely!' said Eliza, looking longingly at the young infant asleep in the pram. 'May I introduce Mr Webster?' she continued. 'Percy Webster, a good friend of mine.' The young man nodded and beamed.

'I understand you've been doing well since you left Ledger's,' Walter remarked.

'How kind of you to say so,' she replied. 'It's true, things *are* going well. I'm a bookkeeper and an auditor as well as a lecturer now. And I hope things go well for you, Walter. I've heard you're working for a soap company.'

'Indeed I am,' he replied. 'But now I'm afraid we must be on our way. We can't keep our baby out too long in the cool air. It was nice meeting you again, and Mr Webster.'

'She seemed a very charming young lady,' Annie commented as the family made their way homewards. 'So nice and well-mannered. Don't you think so, Hannah?'

Her daughter nodded, but remained silent. Later that evening, while her father read to her, she asked him. 'Why were you so sad to meet that lady in the park?'

'Sad? Why do you say that, love? We laughed and chatted. You saw how pleasant and polite we were.'

'You may have smiled,' she observed, 'and said nice things with your lips, but your eyes were sad and so were hers. I could tell.'

Chapter Twenty-Eight

Those sad eyes still haunted him, just as they had after their sudden encounter. They made Eliza look more alluring than ever, and he could see them wherever he looked, into the sky or down into the sand. They strengthened his resolve to stick to his plan whenever he started to weaken.

* * *

If meeting Eliza in the park had been a shock to Walter, then their meeting on the station platform two days later came as a pleasant surprise. He'd arrived early for his train to Leeds and had taken his case from the luggage lockers when he was aware of someone behind him.

'Why, Walter, it's you again,' she exclaimed. 'Fancy, meeting you again so soon!'

'If you're going to bump into me anywhere, it'll be on Exchange Station this time of a morning, when I'm setting off for the shops of Yorkshire.'

'It can't be better than working for Ledger's.'

'It is,' Walter insisted. 'It's a much better job. They're a good company to work for and trade's steady. After all, people always need to keep themselves and their clothes clean, and if you've got the best products it's not too difficult to achieve good sales figures.'

'You've persuaded me,' she smiled. 'I'll have a box of that new scented soap.'

They laughed just as they always did. It seemed like old times to Walter, as if nothing had really changed between them.

'And why are you here?' he asked. 'Some urgent business? Or are you meeting your Mr Webster for a secret holiday?'

Her face clouded. 'He doesn't mean much to me, Walter, you've got to know that,' she insisted. 'Oh, he's a nice, handsome man, one of many who've shown an interest, but . . .'

'Have you ever . . . ?'

'Oh no, Walt!' she interrupted, stepping a pace nearer so that no one could overhear. 'You're the only man I've ever made love to, and the only one I ever wanted. You must know that.'

'Why *are* you here?'

'I'm on my way to Huddersfield to see some new clients, but my train doesn't leave for half an hour and I've already been waiting forty minutes in the hope that I'd see you, Walt. Nothing's changed. I realised that when we met in the park.'

Walter wanted to take her in his arms and kiss her, but there might have been Nancy spying on him from behind the information board or half a dozen people he knew crossing the concourse or waiting on the platforms. But Eliza did not need a show of love and affection: she could see everything in his face.

So their affair began again, but it was different now. Before it had been a careless fling; now it was something more intense, with a woman who believed in what he cherished and would not so readily give up those dreams and ambitions again. Their liaisons were easier this time, not as frequent but not as furtive and hurried. They met once a month when he stayed overnight in Liverpool: she had clients in Manchester for whom she audited and advised on bookkeeping, so she too could slip away without suspicion. They realised that their meeting with Nancy had been sheer bad luck, and that if they were discreet and managed their affair far away from Bradford their romance might never be discovered. The plan went well, until one of those chance happenings that can never be predicted took place.

They had been careful to use several hotels in Liverpool, sometimes the North West Railway Hotel, at other times the Feathers or Lord Nelson. As a special surprise Walter sometimes treated Eliza to the city's grandest hotel, the Adelphi, as he had done on this occasion. She had come down on the afternoon train from Manchester as usual. He had already let her into the secret of his alter ego, and had booked the room in the name of Walter Adams.

The exquisite foyer was busy. Elaborate chandeliers lit by electric bulbs cast their light over the elegant reception area. The buzz of refined chatter filled the air as well-dressed gentlemen and ladies crowded around the desk and lifts, or swept up and down the magnificent staircases.

Walter and Eliza were standing by the hotel desk waiting to register and collect their key while the couple in front booked their room. When they turned to collect their luggage Walter found himself staring into the round, flustered face of Lem Metcalf. He glanced at Walter, then at Eliza and immediately realised the situation. But there was no word, no gloating triumph nor sarcastic comment from Walter's erstwhile manager, just a look of horror as he turned a deep red.

His companion picked up her small valise. She was as shocked as the other three. Her auburn hair was no longer in a tight bun but flowed down to her shoulders, while the spectacles that were usually balanced on her nose were nowhere to be seen and her plain, dark dress had been replaced by something a good deal more fashionable. But there was no mistake: it was the very prim and proper Miss Dobson from Ledger's office.

Eliza bit her lip to stop herself from laughing out loud at the ridiculous, comical scene that was unrolling before their eyes. Walter caught her mood. It was as good as any playwright could conceive and as funny as any music hall act. Madge Dobson stared at Eliza, as if hypnotised by her sparkling, laughing eyes.

'Miss Smith, how, how nice to see you . . .' Her voice trailed away to a whisper.

'And you, Miss Dobson, and with Mr Metcalf of all people.'

Madge's face changed to a look of sheer horror. She turned and pulled at Lem's sleeve, and they made a hurried departure from the desk, taking the stairs to their room without waiting for a porter to help with their luggage.

'Are you all right, sir?' the hotel clerk asked Walter.

'Oh yes, thank you,' he replied. 'Mr and Mrs Adams. I booked this morning.'

'Ah yes,' the clerk confirmed. 'The room is on the second

floor where the other couple, Mr and Mrs Metcalf, are. They're from Bradford too. I assumed you were travelling as a party, so I put you in adjoining rooms.'

By now Eliza had lost all control and burst into fits of laughter. After what seemed an age she regained her composure. Walter had visions of the French farce becoming even more hilarious and embarrassing. Discretion took the better part of valour.

'Have you a room on a higher floor?' he asked.

'Certainly, sir,' responded the smiling clerk, who had caught an inkling of the true situation. 'I have one on the fifth floor, number five hundred and twenty.'

When Walter and Eliza reached their room they flung themselves on the bed, and for five minutes were convulsed with helpless laughter. Eliza had the same vision as Walter of the portly Lem conjoined with the strait-laced Miss Dobson. 'You're a coward, Walt,' she giggled. 'We should have taken that room!'

'And knowing you,' he roared, 'you'd have spent the night with a glass against the wall and your ear pressed to it!' They fell into each others' arms, still hysterical with laughter.

When they went down for breakfast the following morning there was no sign of Lem and Miss Dobson, who had obviously made a hurried departure to avoid any contact with them across the breakfast room. Walter guessed that his erstwhile boss might have accompanied his unlikely mistress on a buying expedition to the warehouses in Liverpool. Neither Walter nor Eliza regarded the chance meeting as a risk and, if it was not forgotten about, it was soon put to the back of their minds.

Relations between Annie and Walter had descended to that loveless but tolerant state that had characterised the latter years of their marriage. She was occupied for the most part with baby Agnes, who seemed to have taken a leaf out of Hannah's book. After two passive, compliant infants, it was a shock to have a demanding baby again, who took up more and more of her time. When Walter suggested a holiday Annie was more than pleased.

'That's the best suggestion you've made this year. I've no doubt you'll want it to be Morecambe again.'

'Wherever you want,' Walter replied.

'Let's make it Morecambe,' insisted Hannah. 'There's so much to see and do there.'

On clear days the previous summer, Hannah had seen the towers and piers of the resort from Arnside Point. She had wanted to know what they were and had begged her father to take her. He had refused, saying they did not have the time or the money, and she had spent the next two days in a sulk. But this year a week in Morecambe in a comfortable private hotel was a different matter. Annie could see Hannah's point of view, and could also see that her husband would take the older children off her hands for a while, giving her some welcome respite. They even asked Harriet if she wanted to accompany them, but she was happy running her market stall, with the company of her friend Charlie Hargreaves.

Morecambe had changed a great deal since Walter's childhood. Now a busy and thriving resort, the biggest in northern England, it had extended a further two miles to the south-west along the West End, the Battery and on to the low cliffs called Sandylands. Dominating the hotels, shops and boarding houses in this part of the resort was Warwick's Revolving Tower, which was set back in gardens behind the front. It proved an immediate magnet to the family, but Annie was not impressed. 'You're not taking me up on that contraption,' she complained. 'It's not safe.'

Hannah was not to be thwarted. 'Yes, yes, Daddy, let's go on it,' she shouted.

'It looks very high, Walter,' Annie said. 'I think I might be sick if I got up there, and it's not cheap for a whole family.'

'Just Daddy and I can go, then,' interrupted Hannah, never one to miss taking her father's side.

'If you go then Rosie and Tom can as well,' insisted Walter.

'So I've got to wait down here for half an hour with Agnes while you all go up that thing,' Annie complained; but she knew in her heart that it was no use arguing if her husband and Hannah had joined forces.

Walter smiled. 'Half an hour, love? It goes up and down in less than ten minutes. We'll be back before you realise we've gone.'

Hannah squeezed his arm. It was another victory for the forces of imagination and adventure!

Walter gave Annie a peck on the cheek and the four were gone, marching to the base of the black spindle, which was totally encircled by a slim, elegant platform, rather like a giant geometric nut wound on to an amazingly tall bolt. The sound of sweet music reached their ears: inside the pavilion a small orchestra, composed entirely of young women, played popular tunes for those who were patiently queuing to pay their sixpences. They were smartly dressed in navy blue uniforms and a sign announced them to be 'The Grand Ladies Navy Orchestra'. As if to emphasise this they struck up with a medley of sea shanties, followed by 'All the Nice Girls Love a Sailor'. The happy queue joined in the chorus.

With a grinding and clanking of metal the circular viewing platform slowly corkscrewed down and came to rest by the turnstile. A wire mesh gate swung open and excited, chattering holidaymakers emerged; some stopped to view the cinematograph which was projecting moving pictures at the back, while others crowded round the display board that showed views and sketches and facts and figures about Warwick's Amazing Revolving Tower. The queue inched forward. Walter feared they were too far back and would have to wait for the next turn, but to his relief they were among the last to be squeezed on.

The gate clanged shut and was securely bolted. A bell rang and the contraption started to move in a clockwise direction, gradually gaining height. As it cleared the pavilion they caught sight of Annie and Agnes and waved frantically. Annie gave a tentative wave back, as if in fear for the safety of her precious family. The scene changed to the rooftops of Morecambe, then the sea, and then the whole shoreline came into view. The platform reached the top of its twisting climb with more grinding and squeaking, and the children chattered, waved and pointed.

Walter remained silent and gazed out. There was the bay as he had never seen it before, laid out before his eyes like a giant map. He was lost in thought for five minutes as he noted the sands, the pebbly skears, the tracks and channels that lay before him. He borrowed a small telescope from an obliging gentleman next to him and picked out the groups of cocklers, some no more than specks in the distance. Far away was the silvery ribbon of the Kent winding its way southwards, widening as it went until, far out to the left, it joined the sea. He returned the telescope to its owner and thanked him. The grinding and clanking began as the platform spiralled down again, and Walter tried to keep that fascinating picture firmly in his mind all the way down.

Besides the revolving tower and numerous fairground rides and exhibitions, Morecambe had a reputation for entertainment of all kinds. The Winter Gardens, Victoria Pavilion, West End Pier and Regent Pavilion hosted a wide variety of attractions, including orchestras, soloists, acrobats, jugglers, clowns, comedians, magicians and even performing elephants. As one of the highlights of the week the family opted for a matinée performance on the West End Pier. Agnes, for once, slept through the whole proceedings and Tom was bored by most turns apart from some clowns, but the rest of the family was captivated. Annie particularly enjoyed the orchestra and Mr De Jongh, alleged to be 'the World's Greatest Flautist'. But it was the acrobats and dancers who enthralled and amazed Hannah and Rosie, especially the Sisters Onjar who whizzed above their heads on the flying trapeze.

When Walter asked Hannah which had been her favourite act, she replied without hesitation that it was Mademoiselle Mills, billed as 'the Greatest Fire Dancer of the Age'. 'Oh, how I'd love to dance on a stage!' she swooned, 'especially in a costume like that!'

Annie was not amused. 'I hope you'll never disport yourself in such a fashion!' she snapped.

The brief and too-revealing costume had also attracted the attention of many gentlemen in the audience, who paid less attention to Mlle Mills's daring tricks with flaming torches than her gyrations round the stage. Walter laughed, and his daughter joined him in uncontrolled merriment, much to Annie's chagrin.

The weather was fine for most of the week, and the family mixed busy days with lazy days. The children found the sands as enjoyable and frustrating as children had always done at Morecambe: Walter had ensured that they were well armed with buckets and spades. Rosie was a good elder sister to young Tom, and he played and dug with her until his arms ached. Hannah purchased a sketchpad, notebook and pencil, and spent much of the time drawing ships, boats, piers and people, and writing short stories about them. Even Walter found he had time to relax with a book or a newspaper. It was one warm, lazy afternoon that he opened the *Morecambe Visitor* and read the headline, 'Holidaymaker Vanishes out on the Bay: Disappearance of Young Man who took a Walk out onto the Sands.'

For a man who took little note of newspapers while he was on holiday, the story seemed to fascinate him. Walter read on with interest.

Chapter Twenty-Nine

The sand was soft as Walter began the last stage of his journey towards the low shoreline around Humphrey Head. Someone had recently been on the path before: they had stuck a line of twigs and small branches into the silt at intervals of four hundred yards or so. Brobbing was often used by fishermen who ventured out into the trickier parts of the bay, so they knew they had a safe passage back should they need to hurry in the face of the oncoming tide. To the weary Walter Clough the line of twigs was a beacon guiding him home. It seemed to signal that his plan would succeed, and that the whole harrowing venture would end in triumph.

* * *

After the enjoyable holiday in Morecambe with his family, Walter's life resumed its settled pattern, even if it seemed to be an uneasy time. Annie was still rather cold and indifferent, fearful of the chance of yet another pregnancy, but the holiday had settled her down, and she was coping better with the lively and often difficult Agnes.

Walter swore his youngest would become an explorer, for no sooner had she learned to crawl than she was off, under tables and chairs, through doorways and into every room of the house. This was particularly annoying to the other children, who were

241

now prone to be interrupted constantly in their play and when engaged upon more gentle activities. When Walter arrived home one evening he was met with the excited voices of his children, all clamouring to speak to him at the same time.

'Daddy, look at this,' shouted Rosie, while her elder sister proceeded to place baby Agnes on the floor in the middle of the room. She was no sooner down than she was off, making a beeline for the table and hiding under the forest of chair legs.

'Naughty Aggie,' said Thomas, in a voice that sounded like his disapproving older sister as he tried to pull her out. But the escapee thought it was wonderful and shrieked with delight.

A few days later a game developed. When her older siblings tried to imprison her, using a variety of furniture and household equipment, the determined prisoner knocked down piles of books, pushed aside chairs and wriggled through the narrowest of holes to effect her escape – much too clever for her jailers. This was typical of the household: it was a happy, boisterous place, particularly when it was under Walter's supervision.

Rosie, in particular, was beginning to take on a more confident role, and was not always under the shadow of the more dominant Hannah. She was more compliant than her elder sister, but was starting to show the creative streak that Walter had wanted to foster in all his children. Always quiet and studious, she was starting to excel at school and show hidden depths. Thomas was still a little boy, very much under the influence of his older sisters. He was especially attached to Rosie, who mothered him and guided him in all he did, but he was not without his own boyish charm and individuality.

On occasion Walter took the older children out on some expedition, often with an air of impulsiveness. This did not always deceive Hannah, who knew he sometimes carefully planned the next surprise. Annie was always grateful for an afternoon with just Agnes for company, or, if the infant decided for once to sleep, for a lie-down with a book.

The four went into Bradford, and after calling at Kirkgate Market to see Harriet and the effusive but kindly Charlie Hargreaves, they wandered down the hill to Forster Square and waited by the tram stop.

'Where are we going?' asked Rosie. 'Is it a treat?'

'I want to go to the park and play on the swings,' Thomas said.

Hannah remained silent, and smiled in a knowing way at her father. She was not averse to reading bits of the *Bradford Telegraph* and for a child her age was remarkably aware of all the local news and issues, even questioning him the previous week about the headline 'Bowling Ironworks goes into liquidation' and asking what it meant for all the poor souls who worked there. She had a shrewd idea that this adventure was to do with an article she had read three days before.

In a few minutes the children got their answer. A tall double-decker tram clanged and banged its way into the square far faster than any they had seen before. To their amazement there were no horses to be seen or a steaming, smoking engine grinding along at walking pace. It glided along the rails under its own power.

'On top! On top!' shouted Thomas, pointing to the upper deck.

'All right,' said Walter, 'top deck it is. Be careful as you climb the stairs.' He paid the conductor a few coppers while the small invading army climbed the spiral stairs and made the upper deck their own. What joy! They were the first there, and like all children they made a bee-line for the front seat in a chatter of excitement and laughter. Rosie and Thomas had decided to be driver and conductor.

'Ding, ding!' they shouted, as the tall vehicle lurched forward and they pretended to move the hand controller. They then proceeded to shout 'ding! ding!' at every pedestrian and wave at them furiously.

The tram lumbered on through the streets of Bradford, with its happy band of passengers.

Hannah remained thoughtful. 'I guessed you were taking us on the electric tram,' she remarked. 'Where are we going?'

'I thought we might end up at Lister Park,' Walter replied.

'I suppose that's the thing that picks up the electricity from the wires,' she said, pointing at the pantograph that rose from a large, buzzing box in the middle of the deck.

'Quite right!' he answered. 'You seem to know all about it.'

'Well, our teacher said that some day electric motors will do more than run trams and lifts. We'll have them in our homes to do lots of things and make our lives easier.'

'Clever teacher,' Walter observed. 'I've heard that in

America they've even patented an electric machine to do the washing. I'm sure your mother would like one of them, particularly with all the mess and mud you children bring in on your clothes.'

These outings provided one of the two highlights in Walter's ordinary existence, making life more bearable.

The other highlight was without any doubt the brief hours of delight he enjoyed with his beautiful mistress. Sometimes their monthly assignations were spent in Birkenhead or in Southport, but when they returned to the Adelphi there was never any sign of Lemuel Metcalf or the surprising Miss Dobson, so they assumed that the unlikely paramours had decided to continue their affair in other towns, far away from Liverpool.

The love between Eliza and Walter had deepened further. They seemed to understand each other instinctively, always felt delight in each other's company and found such joy in their consummation that nothing else in the world mattered. Walter sensed, however, a growing frustration on the part of Eliza, that she could not have him to herself. Their partings became more fraught, and she began to show more resentment whenever he mentioned his family and his home life.

Walter's job had become a job, but more than tolerable and infinitely better than selling items of drapery. The firm was not driven by commission: it trusted its salesmen, once trained, to get on with selling. This meant that most of Walter's income was in the form of a steady salary, not subject to the whim of sales targets and bonuses, which suited both him and Annie.

Life became more interesting in October when Field Brothers finally launched their new Soap Flakes, more hectic too. After trials in various parts of the country the secret was out, and Walter was besieged by all his customers for samples and presentations. He became adept at demonstrating the product, using a small bucket and wooden spoon to simulate the action of a wash tub and dolly peg. He took along a number of heavily soiled small squares of material in a paper bag, and sometimes, when the shop had told a few customers, he was met by an audience that was keen to watch his demonstration.

He soaked a square of dirty material in the bucket of hot water and explained at length the advantage of his wonderful product. Then he agitated the material for some time and lifted it clean from the water. Inevitably there was the question, 'When do you soap and scrub it?'

'You don't have to soap it or scrub it, madam, that's the beauty of Field's Soap Flakes. They can take the work out of washday.'

Walter enjoyed the drama of his little act and welcomed the odd bout of banter and jokes; it helped to break the tedium and monotony of his daily round. The only thing he didn't like was that his hands became sore.

'Daddy, why have your hands become so rough?' asked an inquisitive Rosie one day.

'It's because, as your mother tells us,' he laughed, 'a woman's work is never done.'

* * *

Walter's long chuckle at the memory of that joke was cut short. The line of twigs had come to an abrupt end and he felt that the sand beneath his feet was no longer firm and stable. If not quicksand, it was the next worse thing, a deep cloying mud that made every step a slow and tricky venture. And he was so near to the welcoming shingle, no more than half a mile. He had wandered on, oblivious to danger, thinking his path was secure. He was getting tired or careless, not noticing whence it led. And a month ago his secure life had changed, just as his path over the sands had, and just as suddenly.

* * *

It was the last Friday in the month, and Walter was at the station early for the first Manchester train. As usual Eliza did not travel with him to Liverpool. She took a later train, then met him during the afternoon at their appointed hotel or a regular meeting spot. He was about to climb into the carriage when he felt a hand upon his shoulder.

'Not so fast, Walter,' came a familiar voice. 'I've a word or two for you.'

He spun round to face an angry Lem Metcalf, who certainly meant business. 'What's the matter?' asked Walter, angered by the abrupt, hostile manner of his former boss.

'Well may you ask, smart arse!' replied Lem. 'Think it funny, do you, to spread stories of my misdeeds, when you're dipping your bread around in other people's gravy yerself?'

'I don't know what you're on about,' protested Walter. 'I know we met at the Adelphi a few months back, and I'm aware of the circumstances we both were in. But I'm not daft enough to talk about it. I haven't mentioned it to anyone.'

'Nice try, Walt, but that doesn't wash, not even in your bloody soap flakes,' Lem snarled. 'I knew you wanted your own back after I sacked you, and as luck would have it I gave you a perfect opportunity. I must admit that meeting came as a surprise, even to me.' For once Walter was lost for words. He decided not to argue or shout; better to let the storm subside and then try to reason with his accuser. 'I knew you'd got a little tart on the side,' Lem said with a smirk on his face, 'but even I didn't guess it was the high and mighty Miss Eliza Smith, who every bloke in Ledger's wanted a piece of . . . But you played it cool, I'll give you that. That was always you, crafty to the last. But you tried to pull one too many again. You made me the laughing stock of Ledger's, and poor Madge Dobson too.'

'I'm sorry, but that's none of my doing. If I'd have been staying at that hotel on my own it would have been an opportunity to sort you out, too tempting to miss. But do you think I'd risk telling anyone when I'm in the same boat? You're mad!'

'Rubbish! Who else could it be? Madge and I have kept our friendship secret for years and been very careful about meeting. No one else has had an inkling about it. You must think I'm daft but I'm not. What's sauce for the goose, Walter bloody Clough, is sauce for the gander. Let's see how your sordid little affair lasts when Ackroyd's folk and your wife find out what you've been up to these last few years.'

With that Lem turned, and was off down the platform and out of the station before Walter could utter a word of protest. He climbed into the compartment and slumped on the seat. The train chugged out of Bradford Exchange, through a few gloomy tunnels and even gloomier stations in the dull morning light. It rattled along the Calder valley, the grey hills closed in and the rain beat on the carriage windows. The scene was miserable, and so was Walter.

The weather brightened as the next train steamed across Chat Moss on its way to Liverpool, but nothing brightened Walter's spirits. The day dragged on with its interminable meetings and demonstrations. He collected his wages cheque and made his way back to the centre of Liverpool. After depositing the cheque in Lloyd's Bank, he drew cash and slowly made his way to the park behind St George's Hall, where they always met. Eliza was waiting for him as usual, but her face was pale and tearful.

He was reluctant to reveal his news to her immediately, so he kissed her gently. 'What's the matter, my love? You've been crying.' He took hold of her hand tenderly, and stroked the back of her fingers.

For a few minutes she said nothing. Then she turned to face him. 'Oh, Walt, it's happened. What we always feared . . . I'm carrying your baby. I've guessed it for some time now, but I've known for two weeks. I don't know what to think. I was worried I'd never see you again.'

If Walter had been made punch drunk by the news he had received earlier that day, then this was the knock-out blow. He was stunned, saying nothing for a full five minutes. They wandered over to a bench and sat down, from time to time comforting each other, crying or putting an arm round a drooping shoulder, sometimes staring blankly in front of them. 'In a way,' he finally whispered, 'it makes the news I received this morning all the more terrible.'

'What do you mean, Walt? What news? Who's spoken to you?'

'Lem confronted me on the platform at the station. Someone must have seen him, Miss Dobson as well, and it's common knowledge. It may even have reached his wife.'

'And he thinks . . .'

'Yes. He thinks I let the cat out of the bag to get my revenge on him. But it's worse. He's threatened, and I've no doubt he means it, to let Annie and her family know.'

'I suppose this means it's over,' she sobbed. 'Oh, I know you'll see me right with the child. But that's not it, Walt. You're the only man I love or ever will, you know that.'

'But I don't *want* to lose you.'

'You've got to make a choice,' Eliza said gently, tears

running down her cheeks. 'We can't go on now as we always have done. We both knew one day it would come to this. You've got to decide, Annie or me.'

'You offer me an impossible choice,' he answered. 'How *can* I give you up? You're my reason for living, but so are my family, my children.'

'You're a coward sometimes,' she sobbed. 'What's the matter? Can't you face the shame and criticism if you go back to them? It'll be much worse for me, an unmarried woman. And I'll have a child to bring up. It'll always remind me of you, for the rest of my life.'

'But what will we do? Where will we live? What will we live on?'

'I'm sure you're clever enough to work something out, Walt. After all, you've managed to deceive your family for so long . . . and your employers. Field Brothers needn't even know you've left them all behind. I could be Mrs Adams. We could move away, you could keep your job, and no-one would even know. If that's the way you want to do it.'

Walter stared at her, tears welling up in his eyes. But he was thinking too much to cry . . . 'If I've got to make a choice, this time it's you, Eliza,' he declared. 'I don't know how, but I'll do it, whatever the cost.'

Standing on the sands he remembered those words, and he knew the cost. He was to give up Annie, his children and a life of ordered respectability for a leap in the dark, a leap of faith, for the only woman he wanted to share his life with.

The details of the momentous change had proved far easier than Walter had thought possible. He got wind of a vacancy in the firm for the Cheshire area, applied and got the transfer with no difficulty, and explained that he and his wife liked the Wirral and wished to settle down there with their new family. This suited Field Brothers, and Walter made arrangements for the move the next month. With the baby due in November this would give them time to settle in a new home. They would live there in perfect respectability as Mr and Mrs Adams, unknown as any other to neighbours, tradesmen and his employers. He would always be able to prove his identity through the firm's paperwork and from his original birth certificate, a copy of which he had obtained through a solicitor. If they decided to emigrate one day, he would have the proof for a passport. His plan was perfectly simple, and he knew it could work.

It was the final details of his disappearance that bothered him. He didn't want enquiries to be made at his employers, even if he was working there under another name. He needed to draw a line that would end his life in Bradford completely. The idea came to him one night during their next stay at the Adelphi. He could see that headline from the Morecambe paper, 'Holidaymaker Vanishes out on the Bay'. It was the perfect scenario, one that would not expose his wife and family to enduring poverty, and would kill Walter Clough for ever.

Chapter Thirty

The sand became even more unstable as Walter approached Kent's Bank. Thick, cloying silt stuck to his shoes and trousers and made every step take an age. He was very tired now; the walk had taken far more out of him than he had expected. A terrible thought crossed his mind. Initially he had been faced with two choices, maybe three. One was to go back to Annie, admit all and face the opprobrium of her family, and perhaps even his own mother. Life would never be the same, and he would never see Eliza again nor the child they had conceived. The second had been to continue with his plan, to flee with the adorable, the perfect Eliza to the Wirral, to live in a sham marriage in the name of Walter Adams and to welcome a new family. Eventually there might be adventure and a new life far away, but he would never see his family again. They would be helped by the life insurances he had taken out, but life would still be hard for them. Then, of course, there was the alternative he had always discounted, the choice that was no choice at all: to end his life out there on the sand of Morecambe Bay. But he had always dismissed that from his mind, whether through cowardice or because he recognised the futility of such an action he could not decide. It did not matter anyway.

But now there was the distinct possibility of a fourth outcome, one that Walter had never contemplated. Had he miscalculated the time and distance needed? So close to safety, might he founder and die on the incoming tide? His pace increased. He tried not to plunge too hard or too deeply into the enveloping ooze. An accident was something he had never considered; he thought he knew the bay too well. He had not heeded Reuben's warning.

Walter could feel his heart pounding within him, and began to regret his arrogance. He had shown scant respect for the crooked sea. Now he feared it would wreak its own terrible revenge.

He walked briskly with as light a step as possible, but even this was too great an effort: he had to stop and draw breath. Turning round to look behind him to the south, Walter could see the bay was filling. He could clearly make out the silver line in the distance that marked the division between sand and sea; and for the first time since he had begun his journey he began to doubt his course of action. He turned back to the shore. Having regained his breath, he moved on, slower this time. Every step towards Kent's Bank was a struggle. The wet, unstable silt was deeper: cloying mud. It sucked at Walter's feet, weighed down his clothes, made him scrabble for a firm grip. Once or twice he nearly lost his footing when the ooze beneath him gave way and he almost overbalanced into the deep mud. Walter was panicking now. If he stumbled and fell there was no way he would get up. His brain was racing. He thought of his family, his mother, of Eliza, of the child to be, of Emily, of Albert, of his own agonising death.

He thought of Reuben. What would he have done? What would his advice have been? What actions might save him? Surely this had happened to cocklers and fishermen out on the bay. Many had survived – although a few he knew had died, despite a lifetime out on the sands. This filled him with dread. What chance had he got?

Walter stopped again, utterly exhausted, and turned towards the south-west. The wind that always whipped across the wild sands of Morecambe Bay had died down to a whisper. The clouds in the west had obligingly parted, to reveal a firework show of red and orange shafts of light mixed with pink and purple clouds. Even the celebrated artist Turner, who Walter knew had visited long ago to capture the bay's morning and evening glory, could never paint so wonderful a sunset as the one that nature had painted that evening. On cue, shrimpers coming out on the rising tide appeared like perfect, black triangles on the horizon. Calmness spread over him. Whether it was the inevitability of accepting his fate, he could not tell.

Walter could hear a faint sound in the distance, a continuous whoosh or roar just within the point of audibility, gradually, oh so gradually, becoming louder. It was the surf on the incoming tide. Occasionally it rattled over the shingle beds or slapped against the rocky outcrops where mussels clung so doggedly to their tenuous existence. A plaintive bell joined the faint chorus, warning any soul still on the sands that now was the time to hurry to the safety of the shore. He walked slowly and deliberately towards the incoming tide. It was coming towards him faster than a galloping horse. His hope was to reach a bank of higher and possibly firmer sand that reached out from the shore a couple of hundred yards away.

The watery surge had been so slow as to be imperceptible, then so swift as to be unbelievable. The water was strangely warm and welcoming against his ankles, then his knees. The banks and dykes had vanished into a perfectly flat and shimmering plain. Walter looked out on the incredible scene. He had never seen the crooked sea look so straight.

The sequel to *The Crooked Sea, The Answer (Return to the Crooked Sea)*, is due to be published in 2010. See www.bankhousebooks.com or the author's website www.thecrookedsea.com for further information.

If you are interested in the beautiful area that comprises the coast and sands of Morecambe Bay, Cedric Robinson's publications, *Between the Tides* and *Forty Years on Morecambe Bay* (Great Northern Books), are highly recommended.

About the Author

Trevor Raistrick was born in 1944 in Pudsey, West Yorkshire. He spent over thirty-five years as teacher and headteacher in Staffordshire where he now lives. *The Crooked Sea* is his first novel and was inspired by his interest in genealogy. It is based on a strange event in his own family history.